P9-EEK-868

WOMEN OF MYSTERY

WOMEN OF MYSTERY

CYNTHIA MANSON

Carroll & Graf Publishers, Inc.
New York

First Carroll & Graf edition 1992

Carroll & Graf Publishers, Inc.
260 Fifth Avenue
New York, NY 10001

Library of Congress Cataloging-in-Publication Data

Women of mystery / edited by Cynthia Manson. — 1st Carroll & Graf ed.
p. cm.
ISBN 0-88184-806-9 : $18.95
1. Detective and mystery stories, American. 2. Detective and mystery stories, English. 3. American fiction—Women authors. 4. English fiction—Women authors. 5. Women detectives—Fiction. I. Manson, Cynthia.
PS648.D4W59 1992
813'.0872089287—dc20 92-8825
CIP

Manufactured in the United States of America

Grateful acknowledgment is made to the following for permission to reprint their copyrighted material:

A LITTLE MORE RESEARCH by Joan Hess, copyright © 1990 by Davis Publications, Inc., reprinted by permission of the author; **THE TAKAMOKU JOSEKI** by Sara Paretsky, copyright © 1983 by Davis Publications, Inc., reprinted by permission of the Dominick Abel Literary Agency, Inc.; **DIGBY'S FIRST CASE** by Anne Perry, copyright © 1988 by Davis Publications, Inc., reprinted by permission of the author; **NIGHT VISION** by Bonnie K. Stevens, copyright © 1991 by Davis Publications, Inc., reprinted by permission of the author; **CONSTITUTION STREET** by Janet Stockey, copyright © 1989 by Davis Publications, Inc., reprinted by permission of the author; **A CASE FOR CLARA CATES** by Carolyn Jensen Watts, copyright © 1989 by Davis Publications, Inc., reprinted by permission of the author; all stories previously appeared in **ALFRED HITCHCOCK'S MYSTERY MAGAZINE**, published by Davis Publications, Inc.

STOWAWAY by Mary Higgins Clark, copyright © 1958 by Mary Higgins Clark, first published in EXTENSION magazine under the title "Last Flight from Denubia," reprinted by permission of McIntosh & Otis, Inc.; **TANIA'S NO WHERE** by Amanda Cross, copyright © 1987 by Davis Publications, Inc., reprinted by permission of the Ellen Levine Literary Agency, Inc.; **THE UPSTAIRS FLAT** by Elizabeth A. Dalton, copyright © 1989 by Davis Publications, Inc., reprinted by permission of the author; **OLD FRIENDS** by Dorothy Salisbury Davis, copyright © 1975 by Dorothy Salisbury Davis, reprinted by permission of McIntosh & Otis, Inc.; **THE GIRL WHO WANTED TO SEE VENICE** by Antonia Fraser, copyright © 1985 by Antonia Fraser, reprinted by permission of Curtis Brown, Ltd.; **GUILT FEELINGS** by Celia Fremlin, copyright © 1987 by Davis Publications, Inc., reprinted by permission of the author; **DISCARDS** by Faye Kellerman, copyright © 1990 by Faye Kellerman, reprinted by permission of the Karpfinger Agency; **CHAIN OF TERROR** by Patricia McGerr, copyright © 1979 by Davis Publications, Inc., reprinted by permission of Curtis Brown, Ltd.; **A PAIR OF YELLOW LILIES** by Ruth Rendell, copyright © 1988 by Kingsmarkham Enterprises, Ltd., reprinted by permission of Sterling Lord Literistic, Inc.; all stories previously appeared in **ELLERY QUEEN'S MYSTERY MAGAZINE**, published by Davis Publications, Inc.

ACKNOWLEDGMENTS

I want to thank Cathleen Jordan for her invaluable assistance with this project and for her editorial acumen as reflected in *Alfred Hitchcock's Mystery Magazine*, where many of the stories in this book were first published. Thanks are also due to Charles Ardai for his editorial suggestions and to Herman Graf, whose belief in this project has brought it to fruition.

Contents

Introduction

The world's two leading mystery magazines, *Ellery Queen's Mystery Magazine* and *Alfred Hitchcock's Mystery Magazine*, have published a wide variety of short stories, including hundreds of stories that feature strong female characters. *Women of Mystery* presents a selection of the latter. Moreover, all the stories in this collection were written by women, to some extent a reflection of the current popularity of female sleuths created by women writers. Women writing about women bring their own distinct perceptions, values, and sensitivity to the characters. The reader, therefore, whether male or female, should find each female protagonist's voice authentic.

In each story, the main character faces a problem that needs resolution. The way she accomplishes this is what makes the story so compelling and suspenseful.

Some of the series characters represented here may be familiar to the reader: Amanda Cross's Kate Fansler, looking into the disappearance of a fellow professor; Antonia Fraser's Jemima Shore, tv journalist and investigator, hired by a newlywed to find his missing bride; Patricia McGerr's Selena Mead, government agent, who plays the dual role of victim and level-headed operative in an exciting thriller; and, of course, the widely renowned Sara Paretsky's V.I. Warshawski, who gets involved in a complicated game, in the literal sense of the word.

In addition to this impressive lineup are authors whose stories provide insights into how women view themselves in their relationships with others. Ruth Rendell penetrates the psyche of a woman undergoing a liberation from her former self in "A Pair of Yellow Lilies." Celia Fremlin's "Guilt Feelings" probes family loyalty as seen through the eyes of a dying woman's daughter-in-law. Dorothy Salisbury Davis perceptively examines the complicated relationship between "Old Friends."

Stories that highlight the heroic side of womankind include Mary Higgins Clark's story of a stewardess whose strength of character and clarity of mind under duress enable her to protect a "Stowaway"; Elizabeth Dalton's "The Upstairs Flat," in which a battered wife finds the courage to fight back; and Janet Stockey's "Constitution Street," in which a female cop's conscience leads her to expose the corruption in her precinct.

On a lighter note we present Anne Perry's Digby, an amateur sleuth and lady's maid who solves a noblewoman's murder in "Digby's First Case"; B.K. Stevens's amusing mother/daughter detective agency in "Night Vision"; and Carolyn Jensen Watts's middle-American housewife Clara Cates, investigating a murder from long ago in "A Case For Clara Cates."

I hope these brief descriptions whet your appetite for the skillfully crafted mysteries by women and about women that follow. Enjoy!

—Cynthia Manson

STOWAWAY

by MARY HIGGINS CLARK

Carol shivered inside her smoke-blue uniform coat and tried to ignore her growing uneasiness. As she glanced around the waiting room of the air terminal she thought that the gaily dressed peasant dolls in the showcases made an incongruous background for the grim-faced policemen who passed in front of them. The handful of boarding passengers, watching the policemen, were standing together, their eyes full of hatred.

As she walked toward them, one of the passengers was saying: "The chase is taking too long. The hunters are not pleased." He turned to Carol. "How long have you been flying, stewardess?"

"Three years," Carol answered.

"You look too young for even that length of time. But if you could have seen my country before it was occupied. This room was always full of gaiety. When I returned to America from my last visit, twenty relatives came to see me off. This time no one dared come. It isn't wise to make a public display of one's American connections."

Carol lowered her voice. "There are so many more policemen today than usual. Do you know why?"

"A member of the underground has escaped," he whispered. "He was spotted near here an hour ago. They'll surely catch him, but I hope I don't see it."

"We'll be boarding the plane in fifteen minutes," Carol answered reassuringly. "Excuse me. I must see the Captain."

Tom had just come in from the Operations Office. He nodded when his eyes met hers. Carol wondered how much longer it would be before her heart stopped racing painfully at every glimpse of him, before she stopped being so aware of his splendid tallness in the dark uniform. She reminded herself sternly that it was time she regarded him as just another pilot and not as the man she had loved so dearly.

She spoke to him, her gray eyes veiled, noncommittal. "You wanted me, Captain?"

Tom's tone was as businesslike as her own. "I was wondering if you've checked Paul."

Carol was ashamed to answer that she'd not thought of the purser on the flight since they'd landed in Danubia an hour before. Sick from the effect of booster shots, Paul had stayed in the crew bunk while the plane was refueled for the return flight to Frankfurt.

"I haven't, Captain. I've been too interested in the hide-and-seek our friends are playing." She inclined her head in the direction of the police.

Tom nodded. "I'd hate to be that poor guy when they catch him. They're positive he's on the field somewhere."

For a moment Tom's voice was familiar, confidential, and Carol looked at him eagerly. But then he became the Captain speaking to the stewardess again. "Please go aboard and see if Paul needs anything. I'll have the ground rep bring the passengers out."

"Right, Skipper." And she walked toward the entrance to the field.

The cold airport seemed desolate in the half darkness of the October evening. Three policemen were entering the plane next to hers. The sight of them made her shiver as she boarded her plane and went forward to find Paul.

He was asleep, so she gently placed another blanket over him and came back to the cabin. Ten minutes more and they'll all be aboard, she thought, checking her watch. She pulled out her hand mirror and ran a comb through the short blonde hair that curled from under her overseas cap.

Just then she realized with a drenching fear that the mirror was reflecting a thin hand grasping the pole of the small open closet behind her seat. *Someone was trying to hide in the tiny recess there!* She glanced frantically out the seat window for help. The police detachment had left the next plane and was heading in her direction.

"Put away the mirror, mademoiselle." The words were quiet, the English clear, the accent a heavy undertone. She heard the hangers being pushed aside. She whirled and faced a thin boy of about seventeen with heavy blonde hair and intelligent blue eyes.

"Please—do not have fear. I will not harm you." The boy glanced out the window at the rapidly approaching police. "Is there another way off this plane?"

Carol's fear changed swiftly. It was for him now that the feeling of disaster swept her. His eyes were frightened and he backed away from the window like a trapped animal, beseeching, urgent, his hand stretched toward Carol, his voice imploring: "If they find me, they will kill me. Where can I hide?"

"I can't hide you," Carol protested. "They'll find you when they search the plane, and I can't involve the airline." She had a clear picture of Tom's face if the police discovered a stowaway on board, especially if she were concealing him.

Feet were ascending the ramp now, heavy shoes clanging on the metal. A loud series of bangs crashed against the closed door.

Carol stared in fascination at the boy's eyes, at the black hopelessness in them. Frantically, she glanced around the cabin. Paul's uniform jacket was hanging in the clothes closet. She pulled it out and snatched his hat off the shelf. "Put these on, quick."

Hope brightened the boy's face. His fingers raced at the buttons and he stuffed his hair under the cap. The banging at the door was repeated.

Carol's hands were wet, her fingers numb. She shoved the boy into the rear seat, fumbled at the catch of the ship's portfolio, and scattered baggage declarations in his lap.

"Don't open your mouth. If they ask me your name, I'll say Joe Reynolds and pray they don't check the passports."

Her legs seemed too weak to carry her to the cabin door. As she pulled at the handle, the realization of what she was doing swept over her and she thought how pitifully transparent the boy's disguise was. She wondered if she could possibly keep the police from searching the plane. The handle turned and the door swung open. She blocked the entrance and forced an annoyed tone as she faced the policemen. "The steward and I are checking our papers. What's the reason for this?"

"Surely you are aware that a search is being made for an escaped traitor. You have no right to hinder the police in its work."

"*My* work is being hindered. I'll report this to the Captain. You have no right to enter an American plane."

"We are searching every plane on the field," the leader snapped. "Will you step aside? It would be unpleasant to have to force our way in."

Realizing it was no use to argue, Carol quickly sat on the seat next to the boy, her body shifted toward him, her back shielding him from the direct view of the police. His head was bowed over the papers. In the dim light, his uniform was passable, and the absence of a tie was not noticeable in his hunched position.

Carol pulled some declarations off his lap and said: "All right, Joe, let's get this finished. 'Kralik, Walter, six bottles cognac, value thirty dollars. One clock, value—' "

"Who else is aboard?" the leader asked.

"The purser, who's asleep in the crew bunk," Carol said nervously. "He's been very ill."

The inquisitor's gaze passed over "Joe" without interest. "No one else? This is the only American plane here. It is the logical one for the traitor to head for."

The second policeman had checked the lounges, the clothes closet, and the floor under the seats. The third member of the party came back from the flight deck. "There is only one man there, asleep. He is too old to be our prisoner."

"He was spotted near here fifteen minutes ago," the leader snapped. "He must be somewhere."

Carol glanced at her watch. One minute of eight. The passengers must be starting across the field. She had to get rid of the police, hide the boy—in one minute.

She stood up, careful to keep her body directly in front of Joe. By glancing out the opposite window, she could see the waiting-room door opening. She said to the leader: "You've searched the plane. My passengers are about to board. Will you please leave?"

"You seem strangely anxious to be rid of us, stewardess."

"My paperwork isn't finished. It's difficult to do it while I'm tending the passengers."

Steps were hurrying up the ramp. A messenger came in and said to the leader, "Sir, the Commissioner wants an immediate report on the search."

To Carol's relief, all three policemen scurried out.

The ground representative and passengers were at the foot of the ramp as the policemen descended. The crew were entering the plane through the forward entrance.

"Joe!" Carol called. The boy was out of the seat, crouching in the aisle. Carol pulled him into the tail and pointed to the men's lounge. "In there. Take off the uniform and don't open the door for anyone except me."

She stood at the cabin door and forced a smile at the ground rep and passengers. The ground rep handed her the manifest and waited while she greeted the passengers and showed them their seats.

There were six names on the manifest. Five were typed, and the last one, "Vladimir Karlov," had been written in. Next to it were four letters, "exco."

"Extreme courtesy—who's the VIP?" Carol asked the ground rep softly.

"A real big-shot, the Commissioner of Police in Danubia. He's one of their worst butchers, so handle him with kid gloves. He stopped to talk to the searching party about the escaped prisoner."

The Commissioner—on her flight! Carol felt sick, but as he

climbed the ramp she extended her hand, smiling. He was a tall man of about fifty with thin nostrils, tight lips.

"I have been assigned to seat forty-two."

Carol knew she couldn't let him sit in the rear of the plane. He'd be sure to see "Joe" when she brought him out of the lounge. "It's a beautiful flight to Frankfurt," she said, her smile easy. "It would be foolish not to sit in front of the wing—"

"I prefer a rear seat," he said. "It gives a considerably smoother flight."

"This hop is one of our smoothest runs. The front seats won't be bumpy and will give you a better view."

The Commissioner shrugged and followed her down the aisle. She glanced at the manifest and debated whether to seat him with another passenger. If she did, they might start a conversation and he'd be less likely to be looking around when she brought Joe out of the lounge. But then, remembering the passengers' bitter comments about the search, she decided against it, led him to seat three, placed his bag on the overhead rack, and told him to fasten his seatbelt.

The passenger in seat seven got up and started to walk to the rear. Carol caught up to him at the door of the men's lounge. "Sir, please take your seat. The plane is starting to move."

The man's face was white. "Please, stewardess. I may be ill. I get a little frightened at takeoff."

Carol took his hand and forced him to let go of the doorknob before he realized it was locked. "I have some pills that will help. Everyone must be in his seat until we're aloft."

After she'd seen him seated, she snapped on the mike. "Good evening, I am your stewardess, Carol Dowling. Please fasten your seatbelts and don't smoke until the sign over the forward door goes off. Our destination is Frankfurt, our anticipated flight time two hours and five minutes. A light supper will be served shortly. Please don't hesitate to ask for anything you want. A pleasant trip, everyone."

When she went to the flight deck, the plane had stopped taxiing and the engines were thundering. She bent over Tom. "Cabin secure, Captain."

Tom turned so quickly that his hand brushed against her hair. She felt a warm glow from the touch and unconsciously raised her hand to her hair.

"Okay, Carol."

The engines were racing—it was hard to catch his words. A year ago he would have looked up at her and his lips would have formed, "Love you, Carol," but that was over now. She had an instant of fierce regret that they hadn't somehow made up their quarrel. On sleepless nights, she'd admitted to herself that Tom had tried: he'd made overtures, but she hadn't given an inch. So his attempts at making up had only ended in worse quarrels, and then he'd been stationed in London for six months so they hadn't seen each other. And now they were on a flight together, two polite co-workers giving no hint that things had ever been different.

She started to turn back to the cabin, but Tom motioned her to wait. He nodded to the first officer and the engines became subdued. She felt an immense loneliness when he turned away from her. There had been a few moments on this flight when he'd seemed friendly, warm—moments when it looked as though they might be able to talk things through. But this will finish it, she thought. Even if I can get Joe to Frankfurt, Tom will never forgive me.

"Carol, did you speak to the Commissioner yet?"

"Just when I showed him his seat. He's not very chatty."

"Take good care of him. He's important. They're talking about closing Danubia to American planes. If he likes the service, it might help a little. I'll send Dick back to give you a hand with dinner once we're aloft."

"Don't! I mean, it's just a cold supper. With only six passengers, I can manage."

Back in the cabin, she smiled reassuringly at the man afraid of takeoffs as she passed him. The plane had reached the runway and the crescendo of engines was deafening. All the passengers, including the Commissioner, were staring out the windows. She went back, tapped on the door of the men's lounge, and softly called to Joe.

Noiselessly, he slipped out. In the dim light, his thin body seemed more like a shadow than a human creature. She put her lips to his ear. "The last seat on the right. Get on the floor. I'll throw a blanket over you."

He moved warily and disappeared into the seat recess. He walks like a cat, Carol thought. Or like a kitten, she amended, remembering the boyish fuzz that had brushed her face.

It was hard to balance in the ascending plane and, steadying herself by one hand on the lounge bulkhead, she took the aisle seat by Joe, flipped a blanket from the overhead rack, and threw it over him, shaking it wide. To a casual glance, the blanket might not seem unusual; to a searching glance, it would be odd that anything so shapeless could make such a thick mound.

She glued her eyes to the sign over the cabin door. FASTEN YOUR SEATBELTS—NO SMOKING. *Attachez vos ceintures—ne fumer pas.* While the sign was on, she had a reprieve, a safe island. But when it flashed off she'd have to turn on the bright cabin lights that would make a farce out of Joe's hiding place and let the passengers leave their seats.

For the first time she seriously considered what would happen to her for concealing Joe. She thought about what Tom would say and remembered unhappily his reaction last year when she'd caused trouble on his ship.

"But, Tom," she'd protested, "what if I did let that poor kid take her dog out of the crate? She was traveling alone, to be adopted by strangers. It was night and the cabin was dark. No one would have known if that woman hadn't gone over to her and got nipped for her trouble."

And Tom had retorted: "Carol, maybe someday you'll learn to obey basic rules. That woman was a stockholder and raised Cain in the front office. I took the blame for letting the dog loose because I knew it wouldn't cost me my job. But after seven years with a clean record, I don't like having a reprimand in my brief now."

She recalled uneasily how she'd flared at him, telling him she was delighted he didn't have a perfect record to live up to anymore—that now, maybe, he'd relax and act human—maybe he'd stop treating the company manual like the Bible.

It wasn't hard to remember everything they'd said, she'd relived that quarrel so often.

She tried to picture what Charlie Wright, Northern's station manager at Frankfurt, would do. Charlie was a "company man," too. He liked the planes to arrive and depart on schedule, the passengers to be satisfied. Charlie would definitely be upset at having to report a stowaway to the front office and would undoubtedly suspend her immediately or fire her outright.

Joe's blanket moved slightly and her mind jolted back to the problem of finding a safe hiding place for him. The plane leveled off. As the seatbelt sign died, she rose slowly. Hating to do it, she reached for the switch on the bulkhead and turned the cabin lights from dim to bright.

She started to pass out magazines and newspapers. The man who'd been nervous about takeoff was no longer strained-looking. "That pill helped a lot, stewardess." He accepted a newspaper and fumbled for his glasses. "They must be in my coat." He got up and started toward the rear.

Carol said numbly, "Let me get them for you."

"Not at all." He was passing Joe's hiding place—Carol following, scarcely breathing. The blanket was glaringly out of place in the tidy cabin. The passenger got his eyeglasses, started back down the aisle, and stopped. Carol swiftly reflected that this man was the *neat* type—hadn't he straightened his coat on the hanger, smoothed the edges of his newspaper? In just one second he'd pick up that blanket. He was bending, saying, "This must have fallen—"

"Oh, please!" Carol's hand was on his arm, her grip firm. "Please don't bother. I'll get it in a minute." She eased him forward, scolding lightly: "You're our guest. If the Captain saw me letting you tidy up, he'd drop me out the window."

The man smiled, but went amiably to his seat.

Carol's eyes searched the cabin hopelessly. The blanket *was* too obvious. Anytime someone went to the rear of the plane Joe could be discovered.

"Magazine, stewardess."

"Of course." Carol brought a selection to the passenger

seated behind the Commissioner, then walked forward. "Would you care to see a magazine, Commissioner Karlov?"

The Commissioner's thin fingers were tapping the armrest, his lips pursed in concentration. "Some piece of information eludes me, stewardess. Something I have been told does not fit in. However—" he smiled coldly "—it will come back to me. It always does." He waved away the magazine. "Where is the water fountain?"

"I'll get you a glass of water—" Carol said.

He started to rise. "Don't bother, please. I detest sitting so long. I'll get it myself."

The water fountain was opposite the seat where Joe was hiding. The Commissioner was not a naive observer. He'd be sure to investigate the blanket.

"No!" She blocked the way into the aisle. "The flight's getting bumpy. The Captain doesn't want the passengers moving."

The Commissioner looked significantly at the unlighted seatbelt sign. "If you will let me pass—"

The plane tilted slightly. Carol swayed against the Commissioner, deliberately dropping the magazines. It *was* getting rough.

If she could just stall him, Tom was sure to flash the sign on. The Commissioner, looking exasperated, picked up a few of the magazines.

Still blocking his way, she slowly picked up the others, carefully sorting them by size. Finally, unable to delay any longer, she straightened up. And the seatbelt sign was flashing!

The Commissioner leaned back and studied Carol intently as she went to the tank, drew him a glass of water, and brought it to him. He didn't thank her but instead observed, "That sign seemed like a direct answer to a plea of yours, stewardess. It must have been important to you that I did not leave my seat."

Carol felt panic, then anger. He knew something was up and it amused him to watch her squirm. She took his barely touched glass. "Sir, I'm going to let you in on a trade secret. When we have a very important passenger on board, a mark is made next to his name on the manifest. That symbol means we're to show every courtesy to that person. You're that passenger on this flight and I'm trying to make your trip as pleasant as possible. I'm afraid I'm not succeeding."

The flight-deck door opened and Tom stepped down. The passengers were all seated near the front half of the cabin. Carol stood by the last one. The odds were that Tom merely wanted to say hello to them. He wouldn't bother going all the way through with no one seated in back.

Tom welcomed the Commissioner, shook hands with the man behind him, pointed out a cloud bank to the two friends playing checkers. Carol studied his movements with vast aching. Every time she saw him a different memory flashed back. This time it was Memorial Day in Gander and their flight was canceled because of a freak snowstorm. Late that night, she and Tom had had a snowball fight. Tom had looked at his watch and said: "Do you realize in two minutes it will be June first? I've never kissed a girl in a snowstorm on June first before." His lips brushed her cheek and were cold, found her mouth and were warm. "I love you, Carol." It was the first time he had said it.

Carol swallowed against the hurt and came back to reality. She was standing in the aisle and Tom was before her and Joe was in danger and there was no way out.

"Sure you don't want help with dinner, Carol?" His tone was impersonal but his eyes searched hers. She wondered if he had flashes of remembering, too.

"No need," she said. "I'll start on it immediately." It would mean going up to the galley and leaving Joe for anyone to discover, but—

Tom cleared his throat and seemed to search for words: "How does it feel to be the only woman on board, Carol—"

The words hung in Carol's mind for seconds before their full import sank in. She gazed from passenger to passenger: the Commissioner, the man afraid of takeoffs, the mild fortyish one, the elderly man sleeping, the two friends at checkers. Men, all men. She'd prayed for a hiding place for Joe, and

Tom of all people had pointed it out! The ladies' lounge! Perfect. And so simple.

Now, as Tom studied her, she said casually: "I love being the only woman here, Captain. No competition."

Tom started to go forward and hesitated. "Carol, have coffee with me when we get to Frankfurt. We've got to talk."

It had come. He missed her, too. If she said to him now, "I've discovered a stowaway on board," it would be so easy. Tom could take the credit and Danubia would be grateful. It might mean Northern's charter being extended and make up to him for last year's trouble. But she couldn't murder Joe even for Tom's love. "Ask me in Frankfurt if you still want to," she said.

After Tom had gone back to the flight deck, she returned to the seat beside Joe and studied the passengers swiftly. The checker game was absorbing the two players. The elderly man dozed. The fortyish man watched clouds. The neat one was bent over his newspaper. The Commissioner's head was leaning against the back of the seat. It was too much to hope he was napping. At best he was in deep thought and might not turn around.

She leaned over the blanketed form. "Joe, you've got to get to the rear of the plane. The ladies' lounge is on the left. Go in and lock the door."

Just then she met the Commissioner's glance as he turned in his seat. "Joe, I've got to turn the lights off. When I do, get out of there fast! Do you understand?"

Joe slipped the blanket from his head. His hair was tousled and his eyes blinked in the strong light. He looked like a twelve-year-old roused from a sound sleep. But when his eyes got used to the light, they were the eyes of a man—weary, strained.

His faint nod was all Carol needed to assure her that he understood. She got up. The Commissioner had left his seat and was hurrying toward her.

It took her a second to cross to the light switch and plunge the cabin into darkness. Cries of alarm came from the passengers. Carol made her cries louder than the rest. "I'm sorry! How stupid of me! I can't seem to find the right switch—"

The click of a door closing—had she heard it or merely wanted to hear it?

"Turn on that light, stewardess." An icy voice, a rough hand on her arm.

Carol threw the switch and stared into the face of the Commissioner—a face distorted with rage.

"Why?" His voice was furious.

"Why what, sir? I merely intended to turn the microphone on to announce dinner. See—the mike switch is next to the lights."

The Commissioner studied the panel, uncertainty crossing his face. Carol turned the mike on. "I hope you're hungry, everybody. I'll serve dinner in minutes, and while you're waiting we'll have a cocktail. Manhattans, martinis, or daiquiris. I'll be right there to get your orders." She turned to the Commissioner and said respectfully, "Cocktail, sir?"

"Will you have one with me, stewardess?"

"I can't drink while I'm working."

"Neither can I."

What did he mean by that, Carol wondered, passing the cocktail tray. More cat-and-mouse stuff, she decided as she yanked prepared food from the cubbyhole refrigerator in the galley and made up trays. She took special pains with the Commissioner's dinner, folding the linen napkin in creases and pouring the coffee at the last minute to keep it steaming hot.

"Aren't there usually two attendants?" the Commissioner asked as she placed the tray in front of him.

"Yes, but the purser's ill. He's lying down."

She served the others, poured second coffees, brought trays to the crew. Tom turned over the controls to the first officer and sat at the navigator's table. "I'll be glad when we get to Frankfurt," he said uneasily. "With this tail wind, we should be in in half an hour. I've been edgy this whole flight. Something seems wrong, but I can't put my finger on it." He grinned. "Maybe I'm just tired and need some of your good coffee, Carol."

Carol pulled the curtain from the crew bunk up slightly. "Paul certainly has been asleep a long time."

"He just woke up and asked me to get his jacket. He wanted to give you a hand. But I made him stay put. He feels rotten."

Joe's fate was hanging in such delicate balance. If Paul had come back, he'd have seen Joe. If Paul's jacket hadn't been hanging in the cabin, the police would have found Joe. If Tom hadn't said she was the only woman aboard—

"I'll pick up the trays since we've only a half hour to go," she said.

She started collecting trays from the passengers, working her way forward. The Commissioner's tray was untouched. He was staring down at it. A premonition warned Carol not to disturb him. She cleared and stacked the other trays. But then her wristwatch told her they'd land in ten minutes. The seatbelt sign came on. She went for the Commissioner's tray. "Shall I take it, sir? I'm afraid you didn't eat much."

But the Commissioner stood up. "You *almost* got away with it, Miss, but I finally realized what's been eluding me. At Danubia the search party said the purser was ill and the stewardess was checking baggage declarations with the steward." His face turned cruel. "Why didn't a steward help you with dinner? Because there isn't any." His fingers dug into Carol's shoulder. "Our prisoner *did* get on this plane and you've hidden him."

Carol fought rising panic. "Let me go."

"He *is* on board, isn't he? Well, it's not too late. The Captain must take us back to Danubia. A thorough search will be made."

He pushed her aside and lunged for the door to the flight deck. Carol grasped at his arm but he flung her hand away. The other passengers were on their feet, staring.

Her last hope was these men who with bitterness had watched the search. Would they help?

"Yes, there's an escaped prisoner on board!" she shouted. "He's a kid you'd love to shoot, but I won't let you do it!"

For a moment, the passengers seemed frozen as they

clutched seat backs for support in the sloping plane. Carol, in utter despair, thought they wouldn't help. But then, as though they finally understood what was going on, they lunged forward together. The mild one threw himself against the Commissioner and knocked his hand from the doorknob. A checker-player pinned his arms behind his back. The plane was circling the field, the airport lights level with the window. A faint bump—Frankfurt!

The passengers released the Commissioner as the flight-deck door opened. Tom stood there, angrily taking in the scene. "Carol, what the devil is going on?"

She went to him, shutting her eyes against the Commissioner's hatred, and against the impact of her words on Tom. She felt sick, drained. "Captain—" her tongue was thick, she could barely form the words "—Captain, I wish to report a stowaway . . ."

She gratefully sipped steaming coffee in the station manager's office. The past hour was a blur of airport officials, police, photographers. Only vivid was the Commissioner's demand: "This man is a citizen of my country. He must be returned immediately." And the station manager's reply: "This is regrettable, but we must turn the stowaway over to the Bonn government. If his story checks, he'll be granted asylum."

She stared at her hand where Joe had kissed it before being taken into custody.

He'd said, "You have given me my life, my future."

The door opened and Charlie Wright, the station manager, walked in, followed by Tom. "Well, that's that."

He looked squarely at Carol. "Proud of yourself? Feeling real heroic and dying to see the morning headlines? 'Stewardess hides stowaway in thrilling flight from Danubia.' The papers won't print that Northern won't be welcome in Danubia any more and will lose a few million in revenue because of you. As for you, Carol, you can deadhead home and there'll be a hearing in New York, but—you're fired."

"I expected it. But you've got to understand Tom knew nothing about the stowaway."

"It's a Captain's business to know what goes on in his

plane," Charlie shot back. "Tom will probably get away with a stiff calldown unless he gets heroic and tries to take the blame for you. I hear from the grapevine he did that once before."

"That's right," Carol said. "He took the blame for me last year and I didn't have the decency to thank him for it." She looked into Tom's strangely inscrutable face. "Tom, last year you were furious with me, and rightly so. I was completely wrong. This time, I'm truly sorry for the trouble you'll have over this but I couldn't have done otherwise."

She turned to Charlie, fighting tears. "If you're finished, I'm going to the hotel. I'm dead."

He looked at her with some sympathy. "Carol, unofficially I can understand what you did. Officially—"

She tried to smile. "Good night." She went out and started to walk down the stairs.

Tom caught up with her at the landing. "Look, Carol, let's put the record straight—I'm *glad* the boy got through! You wouldn't be the girl I love if you'd handed him over to those butchers."

The girl I love . . .

"But thank God you won't be flying on my plane any more. I'd be afraid to sit at the stick wondering what was going on in the cabin." His arms slipped around her.

"But if you're not on my plane, I wish you'd be there to pick me up at the airport. You can hide spies and dogs and anything you darn please in the back seat. Carol, I'm trying to ask you to marry me."

Carol looked at him, the splendid tallness of him and the tenderness in his eyes. Then his lips were warm against hers and he was saying again the words she'd wanted so long to hear, "Love you, Carol."

The waiting room of the terminal was dim and quiet. After a moment, they started down the stairs toward it, their footsteps echoing ahead.

CONSTITUTION STREET

by JANET STOCKEY

The subject was Washington. Given name: Morris. He was arrested by Thomas (given name: Jeff) and Madison (given name: Martin). They read him his rights, handcuffed him, and put him into the squad car with some rudeness, but no roughness.

At the Constitution Street precinct, Washington waived his right to a lawyer and made a statement. This statement was taken down by Jamie Fitzgeorge.

Fitzgeorge typed as Washington spoke. Washington's statement horrified her. It was a full confession.

He had, he said, robbed seven gas stations and murdered four persons in eleven days. Three of his victims had been gas station employees; one had been a cop. He was, he said, the man they had been looking for; he had no accomplices. He described the robberies and murders, neatly filling in the blanks for the police.

Jamie typed.

Washington spoke of words he had exchanged with his victims, amounts of cash he had obtained in the robberies, where the cash was now, his girlfriend cooking him spaghetti before he went out "to work" and how she never asked what he did. And the dead policeman's blood in his nappy gray hair. He spoke coldly, tiredly, without pause or inflection, without fear, blood lust, or sorrow. He had a remarkable memory and an organized mind.

Jamie's fingers were cold. She wanted to stop typing and sit on her hands. She had known the dead cop. They all had known him, for he had worked in the Constitution Street precinct with them. His name had been Quentin Bixby. He had been a cop for forty years, and would have retired in five months.

The thought of anyone's having been a cop for forty years intrigued Jamie, who was thirty years old. She always had felt two ways about her job and she did not know how long she would want to keep it. She was afraid of dying young—for herself and for her baby and her husband. She hated to see criminal after criminal go free through plea copping, or through a jury's doubt, or through probation that he would violate within a month.

But she liked being part of the system that slowly, painstakingly, brought just punishment (or help) to a few. She loved returning lost children to their mothers. The mothers would always, always bend over, hug the child, and cry into its hair. They then would say the hair was dirty.

Jamie had made one hundred and twenty-two narcotics arrests. She knew that at least two of those she had arrested had quit taking drugs; this thrilled her.

And she loved arrest.

She had confided this to only three people. One was her husband. One was Jeff Thomas, her best friend at the precinct. And the other was Quentin Bixby.

A lot of people had disliked Bixby; they had called him "that crazy old nigger" because he'd been dry and sharp and cynical. He'd been round and short, with eyes red and a voice whispery from cigarettes. His grim, settled ways had scared Jamie a little at first. She thought he considered her bigoted because she talked so little.

But one day she had talked to Bixby, and ever afterward they had grinned at each other several times a day. He'd been the only person Jamie ever knew who saw arrest as she did.

"It's a ceremony," Bixby had said.

That was how Jamie thought of it. A ceremony. A rite. You

met your suspect; you identified yourself, you handcuffed him and read him his rights, you escorted him to the car. It was like a wedding, complete with ritual words that everyone knows. Complete with simple jewelry to seal the pact. And it was so right, decent, and civilized.

Her friend Jeff Thomas understood every word she said on most subjects, but Bixby had been her special companion in justice. He'd helped her to like her job.

She hated Morris Washington, who had murdered him. She jabbed the typewriter keys. She smelled the ribbon. Morris Washington. Why had he been born? What was it for? Presumably he had killed Bixby to avoid arrest, but why had he killed all those gas station attendants?

"I just got sick and tired" was all he said.

When Washington's statement was ready, Jamie gave it to him to read and to sign. Washington swallowed and his Adam's apple bobbed. He looked at the first page almost pleadingly. Then Jamie knew he couldn't read.

She felt a stab of pity until she remembered who he was. She took the statement and snappishly read it to him. She wasn't thinking of the words on the page, though; she was thinking of the cake she had baked early that morning. *Three eggs,* the cookbook had said, *one-half cup of butter*. Thanks to her first grade teacher, she had been able to make her son a birthday cake.

Jamie got up to leave the room then, touching the bridge of her nose. Jeff Thomas and Martin Madison would handle Washington.

Madison was telling Washington what he thought of him. Jamie despised Madison. She thought him the worst cop she knew. He had been named after Martin Luther King. That, and his skin color, were his only points of resemblance to Dr. King. He was shallow and selfish and cruel in an adolescent way. Jamie was sure he took bribes, but he dared not let even a hint about it drop in Commander Benedict's precinct. Madison discouraged citizens from filing missing-persons reports until they were frantic. If a man were found frozen to death, Madison accused him of being homeless. If a girl were raped, Madison accused her of being pretty, or just of being female.

If a wife were battered, Madison accused her of being married.

He accused criminals, too. He met hundreds of thugs, pushers, pimps, robbers, burglars, loan sharks, arsonists, and murderers. He accused them of being fat, bald, dirty, short, arthritic, homosexual, and badly dressed.

He was accusing Morris Washington of being illiterate. Washington began to show signs of shame and embarrassment. He looked down at his cuffed hands and moved his head from side to side.

Commander Benedict followed Jamie out of the room.

"Some statement," he said.

"Yes," said Jamie.

"Do you have a headache, Jamie?" Benedict asked her.

"Yes, sir, I do."

"Well, take an aspirin. Betsey has some, I think. Isn't Matt's party tonight?"

"Yes, sir."

"Time flies. Well, why don't you go home?"

"Well, I get off in forty minutes anyway, sir."

"So go home. Forty minutes is forty minutes. Don't you have a lot to do?"

"Yes, sir, I do. Thank you, sir."

Benedict actually patted her shoulder. She looked at him. He was a square-built man with smooth white hair and a child's innocent blue eyes. The look she gave him was to tell him that she was a grown woman, that he didn't have to be so condescending. But he could have been worse. She might have worked for somebody downright obnoxious. Benedict was straight and well-respected. His only quirk seemed to be a nostalgia for "the old days." Jamie gathered that the old days were when the mayor and the chief both were square-built and blue-eyed. In his behavior, though, Benedict had moved with the times.

Jamie found Betsey (who was a splendid typist) hammering away at her own machine at eighty words per minute. Betsey had shown no curiosity about the Gas Station Killer, who had been famous for the past week and a half. Her bleached hair stood nearly on end, and she cracked gum as she typed.

"Yeah?" she said.

"Do you have any aspirin?" asked Jamie.

"I've got these," said Betsey. She opened a drawer, gave Jamie a bottle from it, and started typing again without a word.

It was ibuprofen, not aspirin. Jamie never had taken ibuprofen before, so she read the instructions.

When Jamie got home, she found Bob watching television in their bedroom. Matt was sitting up by his side, trying to eat a plastic monkey-wrench. Jamie kissed both of them—Matt on his hair.

"When's your show?" she asked Bob. He was a stand-up comedian.

"Not till eleven," said Bob. "The cake needs frosting."

Matt was one year old that day. Jamie's parents and Bob's were coming over for a birthday dinner. Matt was everyone's favorite baby because he was extraordinarily cheerful and attractive. Jamie wondered if he'd grow to be a good man, but she already was proud of him.

"So," said Bob, "I see they caught him."

"Yep. As a matter of fact, Jeff and Madison caught him. I took down the statement. He just admitted everything."

"God. So it looks good?"

"He'll probably get the chair." Their state was one of the few that actually had executions, though never as originally scheduled.

"Well, that's what you wanted, wasn't it?"

"Yes," said Jamie.

Matt never touched the ground after his grandparents arrived. He was passed from lap to lap during dinner.

Jamie's mother held her napkin up to her face and turned to Matt, who was on his other grandmother's lap.

"Peek-a-boo. Peek-a-boo," she said, lowering and raising the napkin. Matt laughed hilariously. Jamie loved him so much in that second that she wanted to snatch him away from her mother-in-law and put him on her own lap. She smiled.

Bob said, "I should put him in the audience." Everybody laughed. Bob reminded Jamie a little of Curly Howard. He was funny in his sleep. He was the only person she loved more than Matt. It was right, she thought, to feel this way.

Jamie was made to tell the story of Washington's booking. She had only taken his statement, but her father looked as pleased as if Jamie had caught him herself. She felt tired. She had risked her life hundreds of times, but her father was proud because she had taken the statement of someone passingly famous.

When their folks had gone home and Matt had gone to sleep, Bob went into the bathroom to get ready for work. He took a radio with him.

Jamie lay on the couch and closed her eyes. She thought of getting up to wash the dishes.

"Hey," said Bob. Jamie woke from a light sleep. "What did you people do?"

"What are you talking about?" said Jamie.

"Your Mr. Washington's lawyer was on the radio saying the police beat a confession out of his client."

"What! He didn't want a lawyer. He didn't have one. And of course nobody beat him."

"Well, he must have changed his mind about the lawyer because I heard the guy myself in a live interview. He says the Constitution Street precinct police beat a confession out of his client because they can't find the real killer."

"Well, he has to say something, you know. He's playing with no cards," said Jamie. "But I was there for the whole statement, and nobody laid a finger on Washington. In the first place, it never happens with our group because Benedict wouldn't hold with it. In the second place, Washington might be able to get out of it that way, and they all know it. In the third place, if we had the wrong guy, it wouldn't be any use trying to make him confess because the real one would go right on knocking off gas station attendants. In the—"

"The lawyer's name is Glenn Rubin," said Bob. "Do you know him?"

"Yes," said Jamie, a little uneasily. "I do."

"What about him?"

"Seems okay. For a lawyer."

"Well, Jamie, I wouldn't be surprised if they beat him up after you left. You came home early."

"Benedict sent me home. For the birthday party," said Jamie. It sounded ridiculous.

"For the birthday party. Yes. Well, I'd like to know how the lawyer could say all this if Washington isn't even injured. You should ask your friend about it tomorrow." Bob always called Jeff Thomas "your friend."

"It's a court day for me tomorrow," said Jamie.

"Doesn't your friend have to bring Mr. Washington in for arraignment or something?" asked Bob.

Jamie said, "It's his court day anyway. We're having lunch. I'll ask. But it's impossible. Benedict—"

"Never bagged a cop-killer before," said Bob. "You said so."

That night Jamie dreamed of bells. Not of bells ringing, just of bells.

The morning paper had two competing headlines. One read GAS STATION KILLER SEIZED (with a mug shot of Washington) and the other read RACE BAITING HEATS UP IN MAYOR'S RACE. Jamie read the story about Washington. To her dismay, the story had moved quickly to its second page. Glenn Rubin's charge was almost the first thing mentioned.

According to Rubin, the police had beaten Washington with their fists, with a monkey wrench, and with a metal wastebasket. They also had tortured him with an electric cattle prod.

A cattle prod? Jamie knew that no such object was in the precinct. Nobody would have dared to anger Benedict by having it around.

She would talk to Jeff. But she wanted to see Morris Washington first. She got to the courthouse as soon as possible and waited.

She had to wait less than a minute. Morris Washington was

hustled in rather early. She looked at him. It seemed that Bob had guessed right.

Jeff Thomas already was in a booth when Jamie got to the restaurant. Jeff slumped as he always did, frowning down at his napkin.

"What's been going on?" asked Jamie immediately. She sat down.

"Don't you know yet?" asked Jeff sullenly. He was sullen by nature. His marriage was miserable. He flushed easily, especially around Jamie. He reminded her of a sensitive little boy who stays indoors. They were friends because Jamie was much the same type of person herself. But Jamie's husband kept her laughing.

"What does Benedict say?" asked Jamie.

"To the press? He just denies it. I think he's already scared, though."

"I mean what did he say to the guys?"

"He didn't say anything. We just knew."

Jamie considered this remark.

"I only gave him one punch," said Jeff. "Just to get in, or whatever. Then I left. I didn't want to see that. I didn't want to understand." Jeff was shredding his napkin.

"Understand what?"

"The prod."

"Where the hell did that come from?" asked Jamie.

"What are you talking about? It's the same one."

"What same one?"

"Benedict's—trophy."

"Trophy! What are *you* talking about?"

"It's been in his desk drawer for years. My God, you were there before me and you don't even know? I thought everybody knew. It's from the 'old days.' "

Jamie gawked at him.

"I hated it," said Jeff. "I feel sick as a dog. Everybody hated it, I think, except Benedict and McManigle. But we couldn't get out of it, you know? It was kind of like shooting a sick dog. You hate it, but you—"

"Jeff, you're crazy," said Jamie.

"You don't know. You've had it easy all your life."

Jamie didn't ask what he meant by that.

"McManigle ran off to his wife when he was through," said Jeff. "That's how it was. I don't think anybody could have stopped it. All of us—except Benedict and McManigle—hated it."

"Even Madison?" asked Jamie.

"Of course Madison hated it," said Jeff.

Jamie gawked again. She said, "But he's such a bastard."

"Well, maybe he's not the broad-minded bastard you think he is," said Jeff. "What will you do?"

"I don't know," said Jamie. "Do you realize that this might wreck the case?"

"Of course I realize it. And we're all scared, you know."

Jamie liked Jeff no less, but she thought of turning them all in. To whom?

"There's a chance nobody will believe Washington," said Jeff. "The public, I mean."

Jamie thought of "taking her case to the public." It seemed risky, unofficial, indecent.

"What will you do?" Jeff asked again. "I just want to get ready for it."

"I don't know," said Jamie. "And I'd be interested to know if you feel you understand Washington any better now."

"What do you mean, understand him?"

"Why he does the things he does."

"Not exactly," said Jeff. He was very red.

"I've got some advice for you," said Jamie. "Next time, tell them all to go out back and see who can pee the farthest."

That night in bed, she fought with Bob.

"If you do *anything,* you'll get fired," Bob said.

"I'm sick of this job. I don't know why I ever wanted it. I'm going to quit," said Jamie, sitting up.

"Why do you want to quit all of a sudden?"

"I just don't like it."

"If you just wait a little while, you won't be so worried about it."

"That would be terrible," Jamie said.

"There's nothing you can do about it." Bob punched his pillow into shape.

"I don't have to put up with it," Jamie said.

"I'd like to know how old you're going to be when you snap out of it," said Bob.

This went on for forty-five minutes. Jamie went to sleep in tears. It might be a month before her marriage got back to normal.

In the morning she felt hung over, although she was not. She decided to take the day off to think, and possibly to act.

She called Betsey at the station and said she was sick. She paused, then asked Betsey, "Did you ever get to see the suspect?"

"Listen to you," said Betsey. *"Suspect."*

"Did you see him?"

"No, I didn't see him," said Betsey, "because I left right after you did."

"Why?"

"Benedict sent me home."

"What excuse did he have?"

"No excuse," said Betsey. "He just said, 'I think you should leave, Betsey.' And I left."

"Didn't you wonder what was going on?" asked Jamie.

"Oh, come off it." Betsey gave her an untroubled, disagreeable laugh.

Jamie looked through the paper for any new story about Washington. There was a tiny one, and a large picture, a picture of two women. They were identified as Washington's sister and girlfriend.

The sister was a tall, thin woman who looked straight into the camera and had her hands on her hips. She seemed much older than her brother. No doubt she had played peek-a-boo with little Morris, and he had laughed uncontrollably.

The girlfriend had very red eyes. Jamie could see this even from the black and white photograph.

What could she do? She folded the paper and thrust it onto the kitchen table. She could tell the chief of police. And she could tell the press. Then the chief of police probably would tell the press that Jamie Fitzgeorge was a bribe-taker and a drug addict.

Even if she managed to take action against Benedict and the others, how would she feel? *No worse than I feel now,* she thought. It would ruin their careers. True, but if they were arrested, no one would beat them up. And they were very unlikely to serve any time in prison.

Maybe Jeff and Martin Madison, the most reluctant ones, could cut a deal. But Jeff's marriage would become worse, if that were possible. If his marriage ended, it might be a blessing. And Jamie felt that Jeff was too sensitive to be a cop. As she was. He'd go crazy.

As for Madison, the force would be well rid of him. And Benedict—

Commander Benedict was the most responsible, she thought. They all had swooped down on Washington like buzzards, but a word from Benedict could have stopped them. Instead, he had led them. *A cattle prod.* Had she ever known the man? She had thought his worst sin was that of condescending to his female subordinates.

What would *his* wife say?

Well, what difference did it make? *If people will do such things,* thought Jamie, *they must pay the consequences.* It was how she thought of Washington's legal plight, too.

Oh, must they? Whom could she tell? Washington's attorney hadn't been able to raise anyone's interest, really. Of course everyone thought he was lying. A doctor would testify at Washington's trial, no doubt, to prove that Washington had been beaten. But so what? That wouldn't be an action against Benedict and Company. It might get Washington off. Two wrongs, not one.

Jamie picked up the newspaper again. The headline read KIRBY'S LEAD NARROWS.

Then she knew what to do.

It might not work, but it was her best hope. Better than all the red tape. To go to Benedict's superior, or straight to the chief of police, would be a bad gamble. They'd find it in their best interests to discredit her. Benedict had a good reputation.

Jamie went downtown to the county building. Here she and Bob had come for their marriage license. It was a big old building, decorated inside with green malachite. New road dust streaked the shiny marble floor. The commuters had brought it in—the thousands of people who worked here. They were "at work" now, in the stories above her head. They were drinking coffee, eating rolls, looking into mirrors, and worrying about their marriages.

Jamie wanted only one of them, the state's attorney, who was the county's chief prosecutor. His name was John Kirby, he was thirty-seven years old, and he was squeaky-clean in a sanctimonious, self-conscious way. Jamie thought no less of him for it; sanctimony was one of her own shortcomings.

She found the area easily, but she knew it wouldn't be easy to get an interview with the man. He'd very likely be out. And all his workers would do their best to stop her.

She was wearing her uniform; they'd be less likely to think her a random lunatic that way. They'd be afraid of her gun, although she wouldn't touch it.

Jamie opened one glass door. She saw a receptionist. On impulse, she nodded at the receptionist and passed. By some miracle, the receptionist did not stop her.

The next glass door brought her to a row of secretaries in front of a row of wooden doors. She looked toward the corner office. Its door read JOHN J. KIRBY in brass letters. The door was half open. Her heart leaped as she saw a man's shiny wingtip shoe. A man sat on the sofa in Kirby's office reading a newspaper.

"Can I help you?" asked two of the secretaries at once.

One of the secretaries who had spoken was Kirby's own secretary. Jamie looked at her, then looked at the wingtip shoe.

"I want to see Mr. Kirby immediately," she said to the shoe. "I have no appointment, but it's very urgent."

"Mr. Kirby is busy now," said the secretary.

"He is not," said Jamie.

"Of course I am," said a voice. It came from behind her.

She turned around. There was John Kirby.

The man sitting on the sofa in Kirby's office gave in to his curiosity and put down the paper. Jamie thought he looked familiar, but she couldn't place him.

Jamie turned to John Kirby. He looked at her from behind black-framed glasses, younger and plumper than she had thought him.

"How can I help you, officer?" he asked.

Jamie wondered why he was being so polite.

"I have something to tell you," said Jamie. "It concerns a civil rights violation. A—a horrible and blatant civil rights violation, and nobody is doing anything about it."

The man in the office stood up and walked to the door. He looked at Kirby. Kirby looked at him, and then back at Jamie.

"Violent?" Kirby asked.

"Yes—violent. A violent crime that nobody will do anything about." Then she added, "Against a black man."

She realized suddenly that the man in the office was a famous journalist. Kirby turned to him. "Will you wait out here, please?" he said. Then to Jamie he said, "Come into my office."

The state's attorney was running for mayor.

Washington's blackness wasn't the issue; some of his tormentors and all of his victims had been black. It wasn't a race discrimination case. But it had helped Jamie into Kirby's office.

He was not offended when he learned this. He said nothing about it. After Jamie had spoken for a few minutes, he called in his secretary to take notes, and asked Jamie to start again.

She told him about Washington's being brought in for booking; about his cold, straightforward confession; about how he couldn't read, and Madison's sarcastic comments; about her headache and Matt's birthday cake; about Bob and what he had heard on the radio; about seeing Washington in the courthouse; about her lunch with Jeff and her fight with Bob and her phone call to Betsey.

Kirby took off his glasses and asked his secretary to leave.

He held his face in his hands for so long that Jamie thought he had fallen asleep.

"Do you want to make the arrests yourself?" he asked finally.

Jamie's lips were dry. "I never thought of that."

"You *can* do it, I think," said Kirby. "I'll have to check. I'll have to get you some backup, too, naturally. Just a minute." He got up and left the room, closing the door behind him.

Jamie relaxed. Her hands were slippery on the leather arms of the chair.

She wondered how she might like being a waitress. (She had an irrational desire for a job in which she could wear her own clothes, but if she could get past that, she'd try being a waitress.) She was young; she had tact and a phenomenal memory. She thought she'd be a good waitress, and she wouldn't be a hash-slinger for long. She could see herself storming a male bastion in a few years. Standing by a table in a black wool dress with her hands behind her back, leaning forward a little, describing the crayfish sauce with the best French accent in the place. Then she'd drop the accent after a few years.

Her parents would look down on it at first, but so what? She remembered how they had scoffed at *her* becoming a police officer. Quiet, shy Jamie. And now they were so proud of her. Her father would be exasperated at her quitting. And she'd never explain. It would take her about two hundred years to explain. But what of it?

Bob understood already, although he pretended he did not. Bob would calm down when she was back in a routine.

She hoped that Morris Washington would die in the electric chair. (He was likely to be phobic about electricity; this bothered her.) She hoped he'd learn to read and write before he died. She hoped his confession wouldn't be thrown out.

She hoped Kirby would say she could arrest Benedict and the others. She imagined herself walking into Benedict's office on Constitution, followed by strangers. Benedict might have Jeff Thomas sitting with him. Benedict, who always had been kind to her. Jeff, who loved her and whose love she did not return. Jeff would flush and remain silent. He would understand. Benedict would start talking.

But Jamie would cut him off. In the ritual way, she would remind him that he had rights.

A PAIR OF YELLOW LILIES

by RUTH RENDELL

A famous designer, young still, who first became well known when she made a princess's wedding dress, was coming to speak to the women's group of which Bridget Thomas was secretary. She would be the second speaker in the autumn program, which was devoted to success and how women had achieved it. Repeated requests on Bridget's part for a biography from Annie Carter so that she could provide her members with interesting background information had met with no response. Bridget had even begun to wonder if she would remember to come and give her talk in three weeks' time. Meanwhile, obliged to do her own research, she had gone into the public library to look Annie Carter up in *Who's Who*.

Bridget had a precarious job in a small and not very prosperous bookshop. In her mid-thirties, with a rather pretty face that often looked worried and worn, she thought that she might learn something from this current series of talks. Secrets of success might be imparted, blueprints for achievement, even shortcuts to prosperity. She never had enough money, never knew security, could not have dreamed of aspiring to an Annie Carter ready-to-wear even when such a garment had been twice marked down in a sale. Clothes, anyway, were hardly a priority, coming a long way down the list of essentials which was headed by rent, fares, and food, in that order.

In the library she was not noticeable. She was not, in any case and anywhere, the kind of woman on whom second glances were bestowed. On this Wednesday evening, when the shop closed at its normal time and the library later than usual, she could be seen by those few who cared to look wearing a long black skirt with a dusty appearance, a T-shirt of a slightly different shade of black—it had been washed fifty times at least—and a waistcoat in dark striped cotton. Her shoes were black-velvet Chinese slippers with instep straps and there was a hole she didn't know about in her turquoise-blue tights, low down on the left calf. Bridget's hair was wispy, long and fair, worn in loops. She was carrying an enormous black-leather bag, capacious and heavy, and full of unnecessary things. Herself the first to admit this, she often said she meant to make changes in the matter of this bag but she never got around to it.

This evening the bag contained a number of crumpled tissues, some pink, some white, a spray bottle of Wild Musk cologne, three ballpoint pens, a pair of nail scissors, a pair of nail clippers, a London tube pass, a British Telecom phonecard, an address book, a mascara wand in a shade called After-Midnight Blue, a checkbook, a notebook, a postcard from a friend on holiday in Brittany, a calculator, a paperback of Vasari's *Lives of the Artists,* which Bridget had always meant to read but was not getting on very fast with, a container of nasal spray, a bunch of keys, a book of matches, a silver ring with a green stone, probably onyx, a pheasant's feather picked up while staying for the weekend in someone's cottage in Somerset, three quarters of a bar of milk chocolate, a pair of sunglasses, and her wallet—which contained the single credit card she possessed, her bank-check card, her library card, her never-needed driving license, and seventy pounds, give or take a little, in five- and ten-pound notes. There was also about four pounds in change.

On the previous evening, Bridget had been to see her aunt. This was the reason for her carrying so much money. Bridget's Aunt Monica was an old woman who had never married and whom her brother, Bridget's father, referred to with brazen insensitivity as "a maiden lady." Bridget thought this outrageous and remonstrated with her father but was unable to bring him to see anything offensive in this expression. Though Monica had never had a husband, she had been successful in other areas of life, and might indeed almost have qualified to join Bridget's list of female achievers fit to speak to her women's group. Inherited-money wisely invested brought her in a substantial income, and this added to the pension derived from having been quite high up the ladder in the Civil Service made her nearly rich.

Bridget did not like taking Monica Thomas's money. Or she told herself she didn't—actually meaning that she liked the money very much but felt humiliated, as a young healthy woman who ought to have been able to keep herself adequately, taking money from an old one who had done so and still did. Monica, not invariably during these visits but often enough, would ask her how she was managing.

"Making ends meet, are you?" was the form this inquiry usually took.

Bridget felt a little tide of excitement rising in her at these words because she knew they signified a coming munificence. She simultaneously felt ashamed at being excited by such a thing. This was the way, she believed, other women might feel at the prospect of lovemaking or discovering themselves pregnant or getting promotion. She felt excited because her old aunt, her maiden aunt tucked away in a gloomy flat in Fulham, was about to give her fifty pounds.

Characteristically, Monica prepared the ground. "You may as well have it now instead of waiting till I'm gone."

And Bridget would smile and look away—or, if she felt brave, tell her aunt not to talk about dying. Once she had gone so far as to say, "I don't come here for the sake of what you give me, you know," but as she put this into words she knew she did. And Monica, replying tartly, "And I don't see my little gifts as paying you for your visits," must have known that she did and they did, and that the two of them were involved in a commercial transaction, calculated enough, but imbrued with guilt and shame.

Bridget always felt that at her age, thirty-six, and her aunt's, seventy-two, it should be she who gave alms and her aunt who received them. That was the usual way of things. Here the order was reversed, and with a hand that she had to restrain forcibly from trembling with greed and need and excitement she had reached out on the previous evening for the notes that were presented as a sequel to another of Monica's favorite remarks, that she would like to see Bridget better dressed. With only a vague grasp of changes in the cost of living, Monica nevertheless knew that for any major changes in her niece's wardrobe to take place a larger than usual sum would be required and another twenty-five had been added to the customary fifty.

Five pounds or so had been spent during the course of the day. Bridget had plenty to do with the rest, which did not include buying the simple dark coat and skirt and pink twinset Monica had suggested. There was the gas bill, for instance, and the chance at last of settling the credit-card account, on which interest was being paid at twenty-one percent. Not that Bridget had no wistful thoughts of beautiful things she would like to possess and most likely never would. A chair in a shop window in Bond Street, for instance, a chair which stood alone in slender, almost arrogant elegance, with its high-stepping legs and sweetly curved back, she imagined gracing her room as a bringer of daily renewed happiness and pride. Only today a woman had come into the shop to order the new Salman Rushdie and she had been wearing a dress that was unmistakably Annie Carter. Bridget had gazed at that dress as at some unattainable glory, at its bizarreries of zips round the sleeves and triangles excised from armpits, uneven hemline and slashed back, for if the truth were told it was the fantastic she admired in such matters and would not have been seen dead in a pink twinset.

She had gazed and longed, just as now, fetching *Who's Who* back to her seat at the table, she had stared in passing at the back of a glorious jacket. Afterward, she could not have said if it was a man or woman wearing it, a person in jeans was all she could have guessed at. The person in jeans was pressed fairly close up against the science-fiction shelves, so that the back of the jacket, its most beautiful and striking area, was displayed to the best advantage. The jacket was made of blue denim with a design appliqued on it. Bridget knew the work was applique because she had learned something of this technique herself at a handicrafts class, all part of the horizon-widening, life-enhancing program with which she combated loneliness. Patches of satin and silk and brocade had been used in the work, and beads and sequins and gold thread as well. The design was of a flock of brilliant butterflies, purple and turquoise and vermilion and royal blue and fuchsia pink, tumbling and fluttering from the open mouths of a pair of yellow lilies. Bridget had gazed at this fantastic picture in silks and jewels and then looked quickly away, resolving to look no more, she desired so much to possess it herself.

Annie Carter's *Who's Who* entry mentioned a book she had written on fashion in the early Eighties. Bridget thought it would be sensible to acquaint herself with it. It would provide her with something to talk about when she and the committee entertained the designer to supper after her talk. Leaving *Who's Who* open on the table and her bag wedged between the table legs and the leg of her chair, Bridget went off to consult the library's computer as to whether the book was in stock.

Afterward she recalled, though dimly, some of the people she had seen as she crossed the floor of the library to where the computer was. An old man in gravy-brown clothes reading a newspaper, two old women in fawn raincoats and pudding-basin hats, a child that ran about in defiance of its mother's threats and pleas. The mother was a woman about Bridget's own age, grossly fat, with fuzzy dark hair and swollen legs. There had been other people less memorable. The computer told her the book was in stock but out on loan. Bridget went back to her table and sat down. She read the sparse *Who's Who* entry once more, noting that Annie Carter's interests were bob-sleighing and collecting netsuke, which seemed to make her rather a daunting person, and then she reached down for her bag and the notebook it contained.

The bag was gone.

The feeling Bridget experienced is one everyone has when they lose something important or think they have lost it, the shock of loss. It was a physical sensation, as of something falling through her—turning over in her chest first and then tumbling down inside her body and out through the soles of her feet. She immediately told herself she couldn't have lost the bag, she couldn't have done, it couldn't have been stolen—who would have stolen it among that company?—she must have taken it with her to the computer. Bridget went back to the computer, she ran back, and the bag wasn't there. She told the two assistant librarians and then the librarian herself and they all looked round the library for the bag. It seemed to Bridget that by this time everyone else who had been in the library had swiftly disappeared—everyone, that is, but the old man reading the newspaper.

The librarian was extremely kind. They were about to close and she said she would go to the police with Bridget, it was on her way. Bridget continued to feel the shock of loss, sickening overturnings in her body and sensations of panic and disbelief. Her head seemed too lightly poised on her neck, almost as if it floated.

"It can't have happened," she kept saying to the librarian. "I just don't believe it could have happened in those few seconds I was away."

"I'm afraid it did," said the woman, who was too kind to say anything about Bridget's unwisdom in leaving the bag unattended even for a few seconds. "It's nothing to do with me, but was there much money in it?"

"Quite a lot. Yes, quite a lot." Bridget added humbly, "Well, a lot for me."

The police could offer very little hope of recovering the money. The bag, they said, and some of its contents might turn up. Meanwhile, Bridget had no means of getting into her room, no means even of phoning the credit-card company to notify them of the theft. The librarian, whose name was Elizabeth Derwent, saw to all that. She took Bridget to her own home and led her to the telephone and then took her to a locksmith. It was the beginning of what was to be an enduring friendship. Bridget might have lost so many of the most precious of her worldly goods, but as she said afterward to her Aunt Monica, at least she got Elizabeth's friendship out of it.

"It's an ill wind that blows nobody any good," said Monica, pressing fifty pounds in ten-pound notes into Bridget's hand.

But all this was in the future. That first evening, Bridget had to come to terms with the loss of seventy pounds, her driving license, her credit card, her checkbook, the *Lives of the Artists* (she would never read it now), her address book, and the silver ring with the stone which was probably onyx. She mourned, alone there in her room. She fretted miserably, shock and disbelief having been succeeded by the inescapable certainty that someone had deliberately stolen her bag. Several cups of strong hot tea comforted her a little. Bridget had more in common with her aunt than she would have liked to think possible, being very much a latter-day maiden lady in every respect but maidenhood.

At the end of the week, a parcel came. It contained her wallet (empty but for the library card), the silver ring, her address book, her notebook, the nail scissors and the nail clippers, the mascara wand in the shade called After-Midnight Blue, and most of the things she had lost but for the money and the credit card and the checkbook, the driving license, the paperback Vasari, and the bag itself. A letter accompanied the things. It said: "Dear Miss Thomas, This name and address were in the notebook. I hope they are yours and that this will reach you. I found your things inside a plastic bag on top of a litter bin in Kensington Church Street. It was the wallet which made me think they were not things someone had meant to throw away. I am afraid this is absolutely all there was, though I have the feeling there was money in the wallet and other valuable things. Yours sincerely, Patrick Baker."

His address and phone number headed the sheet of paper. Bridget, who was not usually impulsive, was so immediately brimming with amazed happiness and restored faith in human nature that she lifted the phone at once and dialed the number. He answered. It was a pleasant voice, educated, rather slow and deliberate in its enunciation of words, a young man's voice. She poured out her gratitude. How kind he was! What trouble he had been to! Not only to retrieve her things but to take them home, to parcel them up, pay the postage, stand in a queue no doubt at the post office! What could she do for him? How could she show the gratitude she felt?

Come and have a drink with him, he said. Well, of course she would, of course. She promised to have a drink with him and a place was arranged and a time, though she was already getting cold feet. She consulted Elizabeth.

"Having a drink in a pub in Kensington High Street couldn't do any harm," said Elizabeth, smiling.

"It's not really something I do." It wasn't something she had done for years, at any rate. In fact, it was two years since Bridget had even been out with a man, since her sad affair with the married accountant which had dragged on year after year before it finally came to an end. Drinking in pubs had not been a feature of the relationship. Sometimes they had made swift furtive love in the small office where clients' VAT files were kept. "I suppose," she said, "it might make a pleasant change."

The aspect of Patrick Baker which would have made him particularly attractive to most women, if it did not repel Bridget at least put her off. He was too good-looking for her. He was, in fact, radiantly beautiful, like an angel or a young Swedish tennis player. This, of course, did not specially matter that first time. But his looks registered with her as she walked across the little garden at the back of the pub and he rose from the table at which he was sitting. His looks frightened her and made her shy. It would not have been true, though, to say that she could not keep her eyes off him. Looking at him was altogether too much for her, it was almost an embarrassment, and she tried to keep her eyes turned away.

Nor would she have known what to say to him. Fortunately, he was eager to recount in detail his discovery of her property in the litter bin in Kensington Church Street. Bridget was good at listening and she listened. He told her also how he had once lost a briefcase in a tube train and a friend of his had had his wallet stolen on a train going from New York to Philadelphia. Emboldened by these homely and not at all sophisticated anecdotes, Bridget told him about the time her Aunt Monica had burglars and lost an emerald necklace which fortunately was insured. This prompted him to ask more about her aunt and Bridget found herself being quite amusing, recounting Monica's financial adventures. She didn't see why she shouldn't tell him the origins of the stolen money and he seemed interested when she said it came from Monica, who was in the habit of bestowing like sums on her.

"You see, she says I'm to have it one day—she means when she's dead, poor dear—so why not now?"

"Why not indeed?"

"It was just my luck to have my wallet stolen the day after she'd given me all that money."

He asked her to have dinner with him. Bridget said all right, but it mustn't be anywhere expensive or grand. She asked Elizabeth what she should wear. They were in a clothes mood, for it was the evening of the Annie Carter talk to the women's group which Elizabeth had been persuaded to join.

"He doesn't dress at all formally himself," Bridget said. "Rather the reverse." He and she had been out for another drink in the meantime. "He was wearing this kind of safari suit with a purple shirt. But, oh, Elizabeth, he is amazing to look at. Rather too much so, if you know what I mean."

Elizabeth didn't. She said that surely one couldn't be too good-looking? Bridget said she knew she was being silly, but it embarrassed her a bit—well, being seen with him, if Elizabeth knew what she meant. It made her feel awkward.

"I'll lend you my black lace if you like," Elizabeth said. "It would suit you and it's suitable for absolutely everything."

Bridget wouldn't borrow the black lace. She refused to sail in under anyone else's colors. She wouldn't borrow Aunt Monica's emerald necklace, either—the one she had bought to replace the necklace the burglars took. Her black skirt and the velvet top from the secondhand shop in Hammersmith would be quite good enough. If she couldn't have an Annie Carter, she would rather not compromise. Monica, who naturally had never been told anything about the married accountant or his distant predecessor, the married primary-school teacher, spoke as if Patrick Baker were the first man Bridget had ever been alone with, and spoke, too, as if marriage were a far from remote possibility. Bridget listened to all this while thinking how awful it would be if she were to fall in love with Patrick Baker and become addicted to his beauty and suffer when separated from him.

Even as she thought in this way, so prudently and with irony, she could see his face before her, its hawklike lineaments and its softnesses, the wonderful mouth and the large wide-set eyes, the hair that was fair and thick and the skin that was smooth and brown. She saw, too, his muscular figure, slender and graceful yet strong, his long hands and his tapering fingers, and she felt something long-suppressed, a prickle of desire that plucked very lightly at the inside of her and made her gasp a little.

The restaurant where they had their dinner was not grand or expensive, and this was just as well since at the end of the meal Patrick found that he had left his checkbook at home and Bridget was obliged to pay for their dinner out of the money Monica had given her to buy an evening dress. He was very grateful. He kissed her on the pavement outside the restaurant, or, if not quite outside it, under the archway that was the entrance to the mews. They went back to his place in a taxi.

He had quite a nice flat at the top of a house in Bayswater, not exactly overlooking the park but nearly. It was interesting what was happening to Bridget. Most of the time she was able to stand outside herself and view these deliberate acts of hers with detachment. She would have the pleasure of him, he was so beautiful, she would have it and that would be that. Such men were not for her, not at any rate for more than once or twice. But if she could once in a lifetime have one of them for once or twice, why not? Why not?

The life, too, the lifestyle, was not for her. On the whole, she was better off at home with a pot of strong hot tea and her embroidery or the latest paperback on changing attitudes to women in Western society. Nor had she any intention of sharing Aunt Monica's money when the time came. She had recently had to be stern with herself about a tendency, venal and degrading, to dream of that distant prospect when she would live in a World's End studio with a gallery, fit setting for the arrogant Bond Street chair, and dress in a bold, eccentric manner, in flowing skirts and antique pelisses and fine old lace.

Going home with Patrick, she was rather drunk. Not drunk enough not to know what she was doing, but drunk enough not to care. She was drunk enough to shed her inhibitions while being sufficiently sober to know she had inhibitions, to know that they would be waiting to return to her later and to return quite unchanged. She went into Patrick's arms with delight, with the reckless abandon and determination to enjoy herself of someone embarking on a world cruise that must necessarily take place but once. Being in bed with him was not in the least like being in the VAT records office with the married accountant. She had known it would not be and that was why she was there. During the night the central heating went off, and failed, through some inadequacy of a fragile pilot light, to restart itself. It grew cold, but Bridget, in the arms of Patrick Baker, did not feel it.

She was the first to wake up. Bridget was the kind of person who is always the first to wake up. She lay in bed a little way apart from Patrick Baker and thought about what a lovely time she had had the night before and how that was enough and she would not see him again. Seeing him again might be dangerous and she could not afford, with her unmemorable appearance, her precarious job, and low wage, to put herself in peril. Presently she got up and said to Patrick, who had stirred a little and made an attempt in a kindly way to cuddle her, that she would make him a cup of tea.

Patrick put his nose out of the bedclothes and said it was freezing, the central heating had gone wrong, it was always going wrong. "Don't get cold," he said sleepily. "Find something to put on in the cupboard."

Even if they had been in the tropics, Bridget would not have dreamt of walking about a man's flat with no clothes on. She dressed. While the kettle was boiling, she looked with interest around Patrick's living room. There had been no opportunity to take any of it in on the previous evening. He was an untidy man, she noted, and his taste was not distinguished. You could see he bought his pictures ready-framed at Athena Art. He hadn't many books and most of what he had was science fiction, so it was rather a surprise to come upon Vasari's *Lives of the Artists* in paperback between a volume of fighting fantasy and a John Wyndham classic.

Perhaps she did, after all, feel cold. She was aware of a sudden unpleasant chill. It was comforting to feel the warmth of the kettle against her hands. She made the tea and took him a cup, setting it down on the bedside table, for he was fast asleep again. Shivering now, she opened the closet door and looked inside.

He seemed to possess a great many coats and jackets. She pushed the hangers along the rail, sliding tweed to brush against serge and linen against wild silk. His wardrobe was vast and complicated. He must have a great deal to spend on himself. The jacket with the butterflies slid into sudden brilliant view as if pushed there by some stage manager of fate. Everything conspired to make the sight of it dramatic, even the sun which came out and shed an unexpected ray into the open closet. Bridget gazed at the denim jacket as she had gazed with similar lust and wonder once before. She stared at the cascade of butterflies in purple and vermilion and turquoise, royal blue and fuchsia pink that tumbled and fluttered from the open mouths of a pair of yellow lilies.

She hardly hesitated before taking it off its hanger and putting it on. It was glorious. She remembered that this was the word she had thought of the first time she had seen it. How she had longed to possess it and how she had not dared look for long lest the yearning became painful and ridiculous! With her head a little on one side, she stood over Patrick, wondering whether to kiss him goodbye. Perhaps not, perhaps it would be better not. After all, he would hardly notice.

She let herself out of the flat. They would not meet again. A more than fair exchange had been silently negotiated by her. Feeling happy, feeling very light of heart, she ran down the stairs and out into the morning, insulated from the cold by her coat of many colors, her butterflies, her rightful possession.

DISCARDS

by FAYE KELLERMAN

Because he'd hung around long enough, Malibu Mike wasn't considered a bum but a fixture. All of us locals had known him, had accustomed ourselves to his stale smell, his impromptu orations and wild hand gesticulations. Malibu preaching from his spot—a bus bench next to a garbage bin, perfect for foraging. A man that weatherbeaten, it had been hard to assign him an age, but the police had estimated he'd been between seventy and ninety when he died—a decent stay on the planet.

Originally, they'd thought that Malibu had died from exposure. The winter had been a chilly one, a new Arctic front eating through the god-awful myth that Southern California was bathed in continual sunshine. Winds churned the tides grey-green and charcoal clouds blanketed the shoreline. The night before last had been cruel. But Malibu had been protected under layers and layers of clothing—a barrier that kept his body insulated from the low of forty degrees.

Malibu had dressed in layers even when the mercury grazed the hundred-degree mark. That fact was driven home when the obituary in the *Malibu Crier* announced his weight as one-twenty-six. I'd always thought of him as chunky, but now I realized it had been the clothes.

I put down the newspaper and turned up the knob on my kerosene heater. Rubbing my hands together, I looked out the window of my trailer. Although it was grey, rain wasn't part of the forecast and that was good—my roof was still pocked with leaks that I was planning to fix today. But then the phone rang.

I didn't recognize the woman's voice on the other end, but she must have heard about me from someone I knew a long time ago. She asked for Detective Darling.

"Former Detective," I corrected her. "This is Andrea Darling. Who am I talking to?"

A throat cleared. She sounded in the range of middle-aged to elderly. "Well, you don't know me personally. I'm a friend of Greta Berstat."

She paused, allowing me to acknowledge recognition. She was going to wait a long time. "Greta Berstat," she repeated. "You were the detective on her burglary? You found the men who had taken her sterling flatware and the candlesticks and the tea set?"

The bell went off and I remembered Greta Berstat. When I'd been with LAPD, my primary detail was Grand Theft Auto. Greta's case had come my way during a brief rotation through Burglary.

"Greta gave you my phone number?" I inquired.

"Not exactly," the woman explained. "You see, I'm a local resident and I found your name in the Malibu Directory—the one put out by the Chamber of Commerce. You were listed under Investigation, right between Interior Design and Jewelers."

I laughed to myself. "What can I do for you, Ms.—?"

"Mrs. Pollack," the woman answered. "Deirdre Pollack. Greta was over at my house when I was looking through the phone book. When she saw your name, my-oh-my did she sing your praises, Detective Darling."

I didn't correct her this time. "Glad to have made a fan. How can I help you, Mrs. Pollack?"

"Deirdre, please."

"Deirdre it is. What's up?"

Deirdre hemmed and hawed. Finally she said, "Well, I have a little bit of a problem."

I said, "Does this problem have a story behind it?"

"I'm afraid it does."

"Perhaps it would be best if we met in person."

"Yes, perhaps it would be best."

"Give me your address," I said. "If you're local, I can probably make it down within the hour."

"An hour?" Deirdre said. "Well, that would be simply lovely!"

From Deirdre's living room, I had a one-eighty-degree view of the coastline. The tides ripped relentlessly away at the rocks ninety feet below. You could hear the surf even this far up, the steady whoosh of water advancing and retreating. Deirdre's estate took up three landscaped acres, but the house, instead of being centered on the property, had been perched on the edge of the bluff. She'd furnished the place warmly—plants and overstuffed chairs and lots of maritime knickknacks.

I settled into a chintz wingchair. Deirdre insisted on making me a cup of coffee, and while she did I took a moment to observe her.

She must have been in her late seventies, her face scored with hundreds of wrinkles. She was short, with a loose turkey wattle under her chin. Her cheeks were heavily rouged, her thin lips painted bright red. She had flaming red hair and false eyelashes that hooded blue eyes turned milky from cataracts. She had a tentative manner, yet her voice was firm and pleasant. Her smile seemed genuine even if her teeth weren't. She wore a pink suit, a white blouse, and orthopedic shoes.

"You're a lot younger than I expected," Deirdre said, handing me a china cup.

I smiled. I'm thirty-eight, but to a woman Deirdre's age thirty-eight still could be younger than expected.

"Are you married, Detective?" Deirdre asked, positioning herself opposite me on a loveseat.

"Not at the moment." I smiled.

"I was married for forty-seven years." She sighed. "Mr. Pollack passed away six years ago. I miss him."

"I'm sure you do." I put my cup down. "Do you have children?"

"Two. A boy and a girl. Both are doing well—they visit often."

"That's good," I said. "So you live by yourself."

"Well, yes and no," she answered. "I sleep here alone, but I have daily help—one woman for weekdays, another for weekends."

I looked around the house. We seemed to be alone and it was ten o'clock Tuesday morning. "Your help didn't show up today?"

"That's the problem I wanted to tell you about."

I took out my notebook and pen.

"Well, the story involves my weekday housekeeper, Martina Cruz."

I wrote down the name.

"Martina's worked for me for twelve years," Deirdre said. "I've become quite dependent on her. Not just to give me pills and clean the house. We've become good friends. Twelve years is a long time."

I agreed.

Deirdre went on. "Martina lives far away from Malibu, far away from the house. But she's never missed a day in all these years without calling me first—she's very responsible. I respect her and trust her: that's why I'm puzzled. Even though Greta thinks I'm being naive. Maybe I *am* being naive, but I'd rather think better of people than be cynical."

"Do you think something's happened to her?"

"I'm not sure." Deirdre bit her lip. "I'll tell you what's happened and maybe you can offer a suggestion."

I told her to take her time.

Deirdre said, "Well, like many old women I've acquired things over the years. I tell my children to take whatever they want, but there are all kinds of things they don't want—old flowerpots and cookware, out-of-date clothing. So if I find something I no longer need, I usually give it to Martina.

"Last week I was cleaning out my closets. Martina was helping me." She sighed. "I gave her a pile of old clothes to take home. I remember it because I asked her how in the world she'd be able to carry it all on the bus. She just laughed. And, oh, how she thanked me. Such a sweet girl—twelve years she worked for me."

I nodded, waited.

"I feel so silly about this," Deirdre said. "One of the robes I gave her—it was Mr. Pollack's old robe, actually. I threw out most of his things after he died—it was hard for me to look at them. I couldn't imagine why I'd kept his old robe."

She looked down at her lap. "Not more than fifteen minutes after Martina left, I realized why I hadn't given the robe away. I kept my diamond ring in one of the pockets. I have three different diamond rings—two of which I keep in a vault. But it's ridiculous to have rings and keep them in a vault. So this one—the smallest of the three—I kept at home, in the left pocket of Mr. Pollack's robe. I hadn't worn it in ages and I guess it simply slipped my mind.

"I waited until Martina arrived home and phoned her just as she walked through the door. I told her what I'd done and she looked in the pockets of the robe and announced she had the ring. I was not only relieved that nothing had happened to it but delighted by Martina's honesty. She said she'd return the ring to me on Monday. I realize now that I should have called my son and asked him to pick it up at that moment, but I didn't want to insult her."

"I understand."

"Do you?" Deirdre said, reaching across for my hand. "You don't think I'm foolish for trusting someone who has worked for me for twelve years?"

Wonderfully foolish. "You didn't want to insult her," I reminded her.

"Exactly," Deirdre answered. "Well, it's now Tuesday. I still don't have my diamond and I can't reach Martina."

"Is her phone disconnected?"

"No. It just rings and rings and no one answers it."

"Why don't you send your son down now?"

"Because—" She sighed. "Because I don't want him to think of his mother as an old fool. Would you go there for me? I'll pay you for your time, of course."

I shrugged. "Sure." I told her my rates, which were fine

with her, and she handed me a piece of paper with Martina's name, address, and phone number. I didn't know the exact location of the house but I knew the area. "If it looks like Martina took off with the ring," I said, "would you like me to inform the police for you?"

"No!" she said adamantly.

"Why not?" I asked her.

"Even if she took the ring, I wouldn't want to see her in jail. We have too many years together for me to do that."

"You can be my boss any time," I told her, heading for the door.

"Why?" she said. "Do you do housekeeping, too?"

I informed her that I was a terrible housekeeper, leaving her looking both grateful and confused.

Martina Cruz lived on Highland Avenue south of Washington —a street lined by small houses tattooed with graffiti. The address on the paper was a wood-sided white bungalow with a tarpaper roof. The front lawn, mowed but devoid of shrubs, was bisected by a cracked red-plaster walkway. There was a two-step hop onto a porch, whose decking was wet and rotted. The screen door was closed, but a head-sized hole had been cut through the mesh. I knocked through the hole, but no one answered. I turned the knob and, to my surprise, the door yielded, screen and all.

I called out a hello, and when no one answered walked into the living room—an eight-by-ten rectangle filled with hand-me-down furnishings. The sofa fabric, once gold, had faded to dull mustard. Two mismatched chairs were positioned opposite it. There was a scarred dining table off the living room, its centerpiece a black-and-white TV with rabbit ears. Encircling the table were six folding chairs. The kitchen was tiny, but the counters were clean, the food in the refrigerator still fresh. The trash, brimming over with Corona beer bottles, hadn't been taken out in a while.

I went inside the sole bedroom. A full-sized mattress lay on the floor. There were no closets. Clothing was neatly arranged in boxes—some filled with little-girl garments, others stuffed with adult apparel. I quickly sifted through it, trying to find Mr. Pollack's robe.

I didn't find it—no surprise. Picking up a corner of the mattress, I peered underneath but didn't see anything. I poked around a little longer, then checked out the back yard —a dirt lot with a rusted swing-set and some deflated rubber balls.

Back around to the front I decided to question the neighbors. The house on the immediate left was occupied by a diminutive thick-set Latina matron. She was dressed in a floral print muumuu and her hair was tied into a bun. I asked her if she'd seen Martina lately and she pretended not to understand me. My Spanish, though far from perfect, was understandable, so it seemed as if we had a little communication gap. Nothing that couldn't be overcome by a ten-dollar bill.

After I gave her the money, she informed me her name was Alicia and she hadn't seen Martina, Martina's husband, or their two little girls for a few days. But the lights had been on last night, loud music booming out of the windows.

"Does Martina have any relatives?" I asked Alicia in Spanish.

Martina had a sister, but Alicia didn't know where she lived. Probing further, I found out the sister's name—Yolanda Flores. And I also learned that the little girls went to a parochial school run by the Iglesia Evangelica near Western Avenue. I knew the church she was talking about.

Most people think of Hispanics as always being Catholic. But I knew from past work that Evangelical Christianity had taken a strong foothold in Central and South America. Maybe I could locate Martina or the sister, Yolanda, through the church directory.

The Pentecostal Church of Christ sat on a quiet avenue—an aqua-blue stucco building that looked more like an apartment complex than a house of worship. About twenty-five primary-grade children were playing in an outdoor parking lot, the perimeter defined by a cyclone fence. The kids wore green-and-red uniforms and looked like moving Christmas-tree ornaments.

I went through the gate, dodging the racing children, and walked into the main sanctuary. The chapel wasn't large but the high ceiling made it feel spacious. There were three distinct seating areas—the Pentecostal triad: married women on the right, married men on the left, and mixed young singles in the middle.

The pews faced a stage which held a thronelike chair upholstered in red velvet. In front of the throne was a lectern, sandwiched between two giant urns sprouting plastic flowers. Off to the side were several electric guitars and a drum set, the name *Revelacion* taped onto the bass drum.

I heard footsteps from behind and turned around.

The man looked to be in his early thirties, with thick, dark straight hair and bright-green eyes. His face held a hint of Aztec warrior—broad nose, strong cheekbones and chin. Dressed in casual clothing, he was tall and muscular and I was acutely aware of his male presence. I asked him where I might find the pastor and was surprised when he announced he was the very person.

I stated my business and his eyes never left mine as I spoke. When I finished, he stared at me for a long time before telling me his name—Pastor Alfredo Gomez. His English was unaccented.

"Martina's a good girl," he said. "She would never take anything that didn't belong to her. Some unrelated problem probably came up. I'm sure everything will work out and your *patrona* will get her ring back."

"What kind of unrelated problem?" I asked him.

The pastor shrugged.

"An immigration problem?" I probed.

Another shrug.

"You don't seem very concerned by her disappearance."

He gave me a cryptic smile.

"Can you tell me one thing?" I asked. "Are her children safe?"

"I believe they're in school now," Gomez said.

"Oh." I brightened. "Did Martina bring them in?"

"No." He frowned. "No, she didn't. Her sister brought them in today. But that's not unusual."

"You haven't seen Martina today?"

Gomez shook his head. I thought he was telling me the truth, but maybe he wasn't. Maybe the woman was hiding from the INS. Still, after twelve years you'd think she'd have applied for amnesty. And then there was that alternative—that she had taken the ring and was hiding out somewhere.

"Do you have Martina's husband's work number?" I asked him. "I'd like to talk with him."

"Jose works construction," Gomez said. "I have no idea what crew he's on or where he is."

"What about Martina's sister, Yolanda Flores? Do you have her phone number?"

The pastor hesitated.

"I'm not from the INS." I fished around inside my wallet and came up with my private investigator's license.

He glanced at it. "This doesn't mean anything."

"Yeah, that's true." I put my I.D. back in my purse. "Look, Pastor, my client is really worried about Martina. She doesn't give a hoot about the ring. She specifically told me not to call the police even if Martina did take the ring."

Gomez stiffened and said, "Martina wouldn't do that."

"Okay. Then help us both out. Martina might be in some real trouble. Maybe her sister knows something."

Silently, Gomez weighed the pros and cons of trusting me. After a while he told me to wait a moment, then he came back with Yolanda's work number.

"You won't regret this," I assured him, taking a final gander at those beautiful green eyes before I slipped out the door.

I found a pay booth around the corner, slipped a quarter in the slot, and waited. An accented voice whispered hello.

Using my workable Spanish, I asked for Yolanda Flores. Speaking English, the woman informed me she was Yolanda. In the background, I heard the wail of a baby.

"I'm sorry if this is a bad time," I apologized. "I'm looking for your sister."

There was a long pause at the other end of the line.

Quickly, I said, "I'm not from *Immigracion.* I was hired by Mrs. Deirdre Pollack to find Martina and was given your work number by Pastor Gomez. Martina hasn't shown up for work in two days and Mrs. Pollack is worried about her."

More silence. If I hadn't heard the same baby crying, I would have thought she'd hung up the phone.

"You work for Missy Deirdre?" Yolanda asked.

"Yes," I said. "She's very worried about your sister. Martina hasn't shown up for work. Is your sister okay?"

Yolanda's voice cracked. "Ees no good. Monday *en la tarde,* Martina husband call me. He tell me she don' work for Missy Deirdre and she have new job. He tell me to pick up her girls 'cause Martina work late. So I pick up the girls from the school and take them with me. Later I try to call her she's not home. I call and call but no one answers. I don' talk to Jose, I don' talk to no one. I take the girls to school this morning. Then Jose, he call me again."

"When?"

"About two hour. He ask me to take girls. I say yes, but where is Martina? He tell me she has to sleep in the house where she work. I don' believe him."

It was my turn not to answer right away. Yolanda must have been bouncing the baby or something because the squalling had stopped.

"You took the children yesterday?" I asked.

"I take her children, yes. I no mind takin' the kids but I want to talk to Martina. And Jose—he don' give me the new work number. I call Martina's house, no one answer. I goin' to call Missy Deirdre and ask if Martina don' work there no more. *Ahorita,* you tell me Missy Deirdre call *you.* I—scared."

"Yolanda, where can I find Jose?"

"He works *construcion*—I don' know where. Mebbe he goes home after work and don' answer the phone. You can go to Martina's house tonight?"

"Yes, I'll do that," I said. "I'll give you my phone number, you give me yours. If you find out anything, call me. If I find out something, I'll call you. Okay?"

"Okay."

We exchanged numbers, then said goodbye. My next call

was to Deirdre Pollack. I told her about my conversation with Yolanda. Deirdre was sure that Martina hadn't taken a new job—first of all she would never just leave Deirdre flat and secondly she would never leave her children to work as a sleep-in housekeeper.

I wasn't so sure. Maybe Martina had fled with the ring and was lying low in some private home. But I kept my thoughts private and told Deirdre of my intention to check out Martina's house tonight. She told me to be careful. I thanked her and said I'd watch my step.

At night, Martina's neighborhood was the mean streets, the sidewalks supporting pimps and prostitutes, pushers and buyers. Every half hour or so, the homeboys cruised by in souped-up lowriders, their ghettoblasters pumping out body-rattling bass vibrations. I was glad I had my Colt .38 with me, but I wished it were a Browning pump.

I sat in the truck waiting for some sign of life at Martina's place. My patience was rewarded two hours later. A Ford pickup parked in front of the frame house and out came four dark-complexioned men dressed nearly identically: jeans, dark windbreakers zipped up to the neck, and hats. Three of them wore ratty baseball caps, the biggest and fattest wore a bright white painter's cap. Big-and-Fat was shouting and singing. I couldn't understand his Spanish—his speech was too rapid for my ear—but the words I could pick up seemed slurred. The other three were carrying six-packs of beer. From the way they were acting the six-packs weren't their first of the evening.

They went inside. I slipped my gun into my purse, got out of the truck, walked up to the door, and knocked. My luck: Big-and-Fat answered.

Up close, he was nutmeg brown with fleshy cheeks and thick lips. His teeth were rotten and he smelled of sweat and beer.

"I'm looking for Martina Cruz," I said in Spanish.

He stared at me—at my Anglo face. He told me in English that she wasn't home.

"Can I speak to Jose?"

"He's no home, too."

"I saw him come in." It was an educated guess. Maybe one of the four men was Jose.

Big-and-Fat stared at me, then broke into a contemptuous grin. "I say he no home."

I heard Spanish in the background, a male voice calling out the name Jose. I peered past Big-and-Fat's shoulders, but he stepped forward, making me back up. His expression was hostile and I always make it a point not to provoke drunk men who outweigh me.

"I'm going," I announced with a smile.

"Pasqual." A thinner version of Big-and-Fat stepped out onto the porch and addressed him. "Pasqual, *que pasa?*"

"I'm looking for Jose Cruz," I said. "I've been hired to look for Mart—"

The thinner man blanched.

"Go away!" Pasqual thundered. "Go or I kill you!"

The morning paper stated that Malibu Mike, having expired from natural causes, was still in deep-freeze, waiting for a relative to claim his body. He'd died buried under tiers of clothing, his feet wrapped in three pairs of socks stuffed into mismatched size 12 shoes. Two pairs of gloves had covered his hands and three scarves had been around his neck. A Dodgers cap was perched atop the ski hat that cradled his head. In all those layers, there wasn't one single piece of I.D. to let us know who he really was.

After all these years, I thought he deserved a decent burial and I wasn't the only one who felt that way. The locals were taking up a collection to have him cremated. Maybe a small service, too—a few words of remembrance, then his ashes would be mixed with the tides.

I thought Malibu might have liked that. I took a twenty from my wallet and began to search the trailer for a clean envelope and a stamp. I found both and was addressing the envelope when Yolanda Flores called me.

"Dey find her," she said, choking back sobs. "She *dead*. The police find her in a trash can. She beat to death. Es *horrible!*"

"Yolanda, I'm so sorry." I felt sick. "I wish I could do something for you."

"You wan' do somethin' for me?" Yolanda said. "You find out what happen to my sister."

Generally, I like to be paid for my services, but my mind flashed to little dresses in cardboard boxes. I knew what it was like to live without a mother. Besides, I was still fuming over last night's encounter with Pasqual.

"I'll look into it for you," I promised.

There was a silence across the line.

"Yolanda?"

"I still here," she said. "I—surprise you help me."

"No problem."

"Thank you." She started to cry. "Thank you very much. I pay you."

"Forget it."

"No, I work for you on weekends—"

"Yolanda, I live in a trailer and couldn't find anything if you cleaned up my place. Forget about paying me. Let's get back to your sister. Tell me about Jose. Did Martina and he get along?"

There was another long silence. Yolanda finally said, "Jose no good. He and his brothers."

"Is Pasqual one of Jose's brothers?"

"How you know?"

I told her about my visit with Pasqual the night before, about his threat. "Has he ever killed anyone?"

"I don' know. He drink and fight. I don' know if he kill anyone when he drunk."

"Did you ever see Pasqual beating Martina?"

"No," Yolanda said. "I never see that."

"What about Jose?"

Another moment of silence.

Yolanda said, "He slap her maybe one or two time. I tell her to leave him, but she say no 'cause of the girls."

"Do you think Jose could kill Martina?"

Yolanda said, "He slap her when he drink, but I don' think he would kill her to kill her."

"He wouldn't do it on purpose."

"Essackly."

"Yolanda, would he kill her for money?"

"No," she said firmly. "He Evangelico. A bad Evangelico, but not *el diablo."*

"He wouldn't do it for *lots* of money?"

"No, he don' kill her for money."

I said, "What about Pasqual?"

"I don' think so."

"Martina have any *enemigos?"*

"No!" Yolanda said. "No one want to hurt her. She like sugar. Es so *terrible!"*

She began to cry. I didn't want to question her any more over the phone. A face-to-face meeting would be better. I asked her when the funeral service was.

"Tonight. *En la iglesia a la ocho.* After the *culto funeral,* we go to *cementerio.* You wan' come?"

"Yes, I think that might be best." I told her I knew the address of the church and would be there at eight o'clock sharp.

I was unnerved by what I had to do next: break the bad news to Deirdre Pollack. But she took it relatively well, never even asked about the ring. When I told her I'd volunteered to look into Martina's death, she offered to pay me. I told her that wasn't necessary, but when she insisted I didn't refuse.

I got to the church by eight, then realized I didn't know Yolanda from Adam. But she picked me out in a snap. Not a plethora of five foot eight, blonde, blue-eyed El Salvadoran women.

Yolanda was petite, barely five feet and maybe ninety pounds tops. She had yards of long brown hair—Evangelical women didn't cut their tresses—and big brown eyes moist with tears. She took my hand, squeezed it tightly, and thanked me for coming.

The church was filled to capacity, the masses adding warmth to the unheated chapel. In front of the platform was a table laden with broth, hot chocolate, and plates of bread. Yolanda asked me if I wanted anything to eat and I declined.

We sat in the first row of the married women's section. I

glanced at the men's area and noticed Pasqual with his cronies. I asked Yolanda to point out Jose. He was the man who had come to the door after Pasqual. The other two men were also his brothers. Jose's eyes were swollen and bright red. From crying or post-alcohol intoxication?

I studied him further. He wore an ill-fitting black suit and his dark hair was slicked back with grease. All the brothers wore dark suits. Jose looked nervous but the others seemed almost jocular—until Pasqual caught me staring. His expression immediately darkened, his eyes bearing down on me. I felt needles down my spine when he started to his feet, but luckily the service began and he sank back into his seat.

Pastor Gomez came to the dais and spoke about what a wonderful wife and mother Martina had been. As he talked, the women around me began to let out soft, muted sobs.

Afterward, the pastor gave the congregation directions to the cemetery. Pasqual hadn't forgotten my presence, but I made a beeline for the pastor, managing to snare him before Pasqual could get to me.

The pastor led me to a corner.

"What happened?" I asked him.

"I wish I knew."

"Do the police—"

"The police!" His green eyes flashed. "They don't care about a dead Hispanic girl! One less flea in their country. I was wearing my work clothes when I got the call this morning. I'd been doing some plumbing and I guess they thought I was a wetback who didn't understand English. They joked about her. They said it was a shame that such a body would go to waste."

I couldn't speak for a while. "That stinks."

"Yes." Gomez shook his head. "So you see, I don't expect much from the police."

"I'm looking into her death."

Gomez stared at me. "Who's paying you to do it?"

"Not Yolanda," I said.

"Martina's *patrona*. She wants her ring."

"I think she wants justice for Martina."

The pastor blushed from embarrassment.

"I would have done it *gratis*. I have some suspicions." I filled him in on my encounter with Pasqual.

Gomez thought a moment. "Pasqual drinks even though the church forbids alcohol. But he's not a bad person. Maybe you made him feel threatened."

"Maybe I did."

"I'll talk to him," Gomez said. "Calm him down. But I don't think you should come to the *cementerio* with us. Now is not the time for accusations."

I agreed.

Then he excused himself as another parishioner approached him. I met up with Yolanda and explained my decision not to go to the cemetery. She understood.

We walked out into the school yard, into a cold misty night. Jose and his brothers had already taken off their ties and replaced their suit jackets with warmer windbreakers. Pasqual took a deep swig from a bottle inside a paper bag, then passed the bag to one of his brothers.

"Look at them," Yolanda said with disgust. "They no even wait till after the funeral. They nothing but *cholos*. Es terrible!"

I observed the brothers. Something was bothering me and it took a while before it came to me. Three of them, including Jose, were wearing old baseball caps. Pasqual alone wore a painter's cap. I don't know why I found that significant. Then I remembered my first conversation with Yolanda and I decided I'd better put in a call to the bus company.

From behind me came a gentle tap on the shoulder. I turned around.

Pastor Gomez said, "Thank you for coming, Ms. Darling."

I nodded. "I'm sorry I never met Martina. From what I've heard, she seemed to be a very good woman."

"She was." Gomez shook my hand. "I appreciate your help and I wish you peace."

Then he turned and walked away. I'd probably never see him again and I felt a little bad about that.

I tailed Jose the next morning. He and his brothers were part of a crew framing a house in the Hollywood hills. I kept watch from a quarter block away, my truck partly hidden by the overhanging boughs of a eucalyptus. I was trying to figure out how to get Jose alone when I got a big break. The roach wagon pulled in and Jose was elected by his brothers to pick up lunch.

I got out of the truck, intercepted him as he was returning with an armful of burritos, and stuck my .38 in his side with the warning that if he said a word I'd pull the trigger. My Spanish must have been clear because he was as mute as Dopey.

After I got him into the cabin of the truck, I took the gun out of his ribs and held it in my lap, still aimed at him.

I said, "What happened to Martina?"

"I don't know."

"You're lying," I said. "You killed her."

"I don' kill her!" Jose was shaking hard. *"Yo juro!* I don' kill her!"

"Who did?"

"I don' know!"

"You killed her for the ring, didn't you, Jose?" He shrank back in the seat. "Martina would never tell you she had the ring: she knew you'd take it from her. But you must have found out. You asked her about the ring and she denied having it, right?"

Jose didn't answer.

I repeated the accusation in Espanol, but he still didn't respond.

"You didn't know what to do, so you waited and waited and finally, on Monday morning, you told your brothers about the ring. But by that time Martina and the ring had already taken the bus to work."

"All we wan' do is talk to her!" Jose said. "Nothin' was suppose to happen."

"What wasn't supposed to happen?"

Jose opened his mouth, then shut it again.

I continued. "Pasqual has a truck—a Ford pickup." I read him the license number. "You and your brothers decided to meet up with her. A truck can go a lot faster than a bus.

When the bus made a stop, two of you got on it and made Martina get off."

Jose shook his head.

"I called the bus company," I told him. "The driver remembered you and your brother—two men making this woman carrying a big bag get off at the stop behind the big garbage bin. The driver asked her if she was okay, but Martina didn't want to get you in trouble and said everything was fine. But everything wasn't fine, was it?"

Tears welled up in Jose's eyes.

"You tried to force her into Pasqual's truck, but she fought."

Jose remained mute.

"But you did finally get her into the truck," I said. "Only you forgot something. When she fought, she must have knocked off Pasqual's Dodgers cap. He didn't know it was gone until later, did he?"

Jose jerked his head up. "How you know?"

"How do I know? I *have* that cap, Jose." Another educated guess. "Now, why don't you tell me what happened?" I gestured with the gun to remind him of it.

"It was *assident.* Pasqual no mean to hurt her bad. Just get her to talk. She no have ring when we take her off the bus."

"Not in her bag?"

"She no have bag, just her handbag—and it not there. She tell us she left ring at home. So we took her home, but she don' fin' the ring. That make me mad. I *saw* her with ring. No good for a wife to lie to husband." His eyes filled with rage.

"So you killed her," I said.

"No—I tol' you. Pasqual did it. It was assident!"

Just then the driver's door jerked open and the gun was knocked out of my hand. Pasqual dragged me out of the truck and down to the ground, his face looming over me, his complexion florid and furious. He drew back his fist and aimed it at my jaw.

I rolled my head to one side and his hand hit the ground. He yelled, but not as loud as Jose did shouting at him to stop. Then I heard the click of the trigger. Pasqual heard it, too, and released me immediately. By now, some people had run up and were shouting, too. My gun in his hand, Jose aimed it at Pasqual.

"You kill Martina! Now I'm going to kill you!" he cried.

Pasqual looked genuinely confused. He spoke in Spanish. "*You* killed her! You beat her to death when we couldn't find the ring!"

Jose looked at me, his expression saying: do you believe this? Something in my expression must have told him I did. I told him to put the gun down, but he turned his back to me and kept the gun on Pasqual. "You lie. You get drunk, you kill Martina!"

In Spanish, Pasqual said, "I tried to *stop* you, you—"

"You *lie!*" Jose said. And then he pulled the trigger.

I charged him before he could squeeze another bullet out of the chamber, but the damage had been done. Pasqual was already dead when the sirens pulled up.

The two other brothers backed Jose's story. They'd come to confront Martina about the ring. She told them she had left it at home. But when they returned to the house and the ring wasn't around, Pasqual, in a drunken rage, beat Martina to death and dumped her body in the trash.

Jose will be charged with second-degree murder for Pasqual and maybe a good lawyer will be able to bargain it down to manslaughter. But I remembered the murderous look in Jose's eyes after he'd told me Martina had lied to him. If I were the prosecutor, I'd be going after Jose with charges of manslaughter on Martina and murder one on Pasqual. But that's not how the system works. Anyway, my verdict—right or wrong—wouldn't bring Martina back to life.

I called Mrs. Pollack after it was over. Through her tears, she wished she'd never remembered the ring. It wasn't her fault, but she still felt responsible.

There was a small consolation. I was pretty sure I knew where the ring was.

I'm not too bad at guesses—like the one about Pasqual losing his hat in a struggle. That simple image of the brothers at the church—three with beat-up Dodgers caps, the fourth wearing a new painter's cap. Something off-kilter.

So my hunch had been correct. Pasqual had once owned a Dodgers cap, too. Where had it gone? The same place as Mr. Pollack's robe? Martina had packed the robe in her bag Monday morning. When she was forced off the bus by Jose and his brothers, I pictured her quickly dumping the bag in a garbage bin at the bus stop, hoping to retrieve it later.

The ring was right where I thought it would be: among the discards that had shrouded Malibu Mike the night he had died. The Dodgers cap he had been wearing got me thinking in the right direction. If Malibu *had* found Pasqual's cap, maybe he found the bag left behind by Martina. After all, that bin had been his spot.

Good old Malibu. One of his layers, I learned, had been an old robe—and wedged into the corner of the left pocket had been a diamond ring. The police had listed it but not made the information public.

Mrs. Pollack didn't feel right about keeping the ring, so she contributed it to the burial committee for Malibu Mike. Malibu never lived wealthy, but he went out in high style.

THE GIRL WHO WANTED TO SEE VENICE

by ANTONIA FRASER

The furniture in the hotel suite was all on the grand scale: shades of turquoise, painted heavily with gold and upholstered in velvet. Above Jemima Shore's head twinkled an enormous chandelier made of glass drops, with one large central pear, and other swags of diamonds in frozen loops.

It was Venetian glass, presumably; for this was the Hotel Carpaccio, one of the most lavish (but not modern) hotels overlooking the Grand Canal. The flowers—and champagne—sent up by the manager to welcome Jemima Shore, Investigator, filming in Venice for Megalith Television, were equally imposing.

At this point Jemima, gazing at the manager's card, began to laugh. Admittedly, Megalith's current series had the overall title *The British Honeymoon with . . .* Venice forming the subject of the first episode. But he had clearly got quite the wrong idea, for the card read: "To wish you all happiness in your married life." Jemima, being unmarried, was still smiling when there was a soft, persistent rapping on the door.

She imagined it to be one of the innumerable deft waiters who had given the Hotel Carpaccio its reputation for luxury and service. Instead she was confronted by a total stranger—a dark-haired, dark-eyed young man, very handsome in an Italian way, but definitely no waiter.

"Jemima Shore, Investigator?" he inquired in an anguished voice. "It's the police. You've got to persuade them for me. You see, it was all her idea. *She* wanted to see Venice."

"What on earth—?" began Jemima.

"I'm Harry Hewling," said the young man. He spoke as though the name explained everything. "I—we're in the next-door suite. I've seen you on your balcony. I recognized you. I—we're on our honeymoon."

"Your flowers! Of course!" cried Jemima. "Your wife must have them straightaway."

The young man gazed at her. "Don't you understand? Nadia—my wife—has disappeared. And the police seem to think I'm responsible." He looked down at the Italian newspapers, lying still untouched by the champagne bottle.

Even Jemima's fairly rudimentary Italian was sufficient to translate the glaring headlines:

WHERE IS SHE, THE VANISHED ENGLISH BRIDE?

IS SHE DEAD, THE BEAUTIFUL ENGLISH HEIRESS?

And for once the story now told by Harry Hewling to Jemima in a series of agitated confidences was certainly bizarre enough to justify such press attention.

Harry and Nadia Hewling had only just got married, in England, having known each other a bare month before that.

"But it was love at first sight," Harry insisted in his low desperate voice. "Love immediately. She was so fantastic. And the reason we got married quickly was because of Nadia's loneliness. She'd come from South Africa and her parents were dead. She was alone in the world."

"And rich?" contributed Jemima gently.

"Sure, she was rich!" exclaimed Harry. "Nadia happened to inherit a lot of money from a trust fund on her twenty-first birthday. Was that my fault? Sure, she paid for everything, including our honeymoon. Sure, I'm her husband and I stand to inherit if anything happens to her. Sure, she insisted on settling money on me on our marriage—she wanted to make us equal, she said. None of that makes any difference. I keep telling the police: I love her! And she wanted to see Venice."

"So you didn't marry her for her money?"

Harry Hewling hesitated, then impulsively took a crumpled

photograph out of his pocket. Jemima stared at the slight, dark-haired girl feeding the pigeons in the Piazza, St. Mark's Byzantine façade in the background.

"Isn't she beautiful? Does a girl like that *need* two hundred thousand pounds to make you fall for her?"

"She's quite lovely." Jemima thought that together the Hewlings must have made a striking couple, with their regular dark good looks; had she known of their existence in the next-door suite, she might even have interviewed them for *The British Honeymoon* series. It would have been an amusing twist to interview a *real* English honeymoon couple for what was primarily a cultural investigation.

Jemima stared at the photograph. "You're quite alike, almost like brother and sister."

Harry Hewling smiled for the first time. "Everyone says that. Actually, I have got a sister, Gemma, but she's years older than me. She's my half sister, in fact. We're not close."

But Harry Hewling stopped smiling when he came to the subject of Nadia's disappearance. They'd had a terrific dinner —"We found this special restaurant in a funny little square off one of the small canals"—and then had walked back to the Carpaccio hand in hand. Up in their suite, Nadia had disappeared into the bedroom and shut the door. That didn't surprise Harry: she would probably reemerge modeling one of the satin-and-lace negligées she had bought for the honeymoon. Harry stood for a moment on their balcony looking out over the Grand Canal.

It was only after a while, when Nadia had not reappeared and the door was still closed, that Harry went into their bedroom. But the huge ornate room, with its double bed surmounted by a carved eagle, was empty. Harry investigated the marble bathroom. That, too, was empty.

Somewhat reluctantly, he telephoned down to the night porter. It was then that he had his first real surprise. Yes, the Signora Hewling had gone out and certainly without luggage.

And from that moment on, there had been no sight or sound of Nadia Hewling: no message, no telephone call—nothing. She had completely disappeared in Venice, wearing a summer dress and taking with her nothing—nothing, that is, except her passport. In the haste of the wedding, they hadn't had time to change her original passport in her maiden name of Nadia Dansk; but, Harry said wanly, that had hardly seemed important at the time.

The hotel staff, quite politely, had indicated that there must have been a row and that the Signora would return. Honeymoons did not always go smoothly—even in Venice. At first the Italian police had taken the same line.

It was Harry Hewling himself who insisted that there had been no row, insisted they investigate Nadia's disappearance, treat her as a missing person. Now the financial circumstances of Nadia Dansk had come to light, via her English lawyers, and the police suddenly turned their attention to the bridegroom.

Everything began to count against Harry Hewling: the fact that he had been out of work before he met Nadia, the fact that she had given money over to him on marriage, the fact that he would inherit still further funds on her death. And yet in the absence of a body, no corpse having been dredged up from the Canal, no unknown body lying in the mortuary, it was difficult for the police to proceed further than interrogating Harry Hewling daily—and suggesting very firmly that he should not leave the city.

"In any case, I don't want to leave!" Harry told Jemima. "Supposing she comes back? She *must* come back." The airports had been checked—Venice airport first of all, then Milan and the other Italian airports; the railway stations similarly and the various frontiers of the country. No one traveling under the name of Dansk had departed. As for her description—well, a slight dark-haired girl in her twenties was a common enough sight in Italy at the height of the tourist season.

"And yet she took her passport," mused Jemima. "Why does a woman, a pretty young woman on her honeymoon with a wonderful trousseau, take her passport with her unless she intends to travel?"

Out of curiosity, or perhaps to give the distraught Harry Hewling the impression she could help him (which she doubted), Jemima allowed herself to be taken next door. She was shown the whole suite. It was, in fact, identical to her own, except for the rather macabre sight of Nadia Hewling's belongings still hanging in the ornately gilded cupboards, including the Janet Reger-style satin negligées. Then there were her shoes—lots of shiny new high-heeled sandals, totally unworn.

"What shoes was she wearing when she disappeared?" Jemima asked suddenly, her feminine curiosity aroused by this pathetic array of untouched splendor.

"I don't know," said Harry wretchedly. "I remember the dress very well because she was wearing it at dinner—turquoise blue, her favorite color. But the shoes—well, she had so many shoes, didn't she?" He pointed. "How can I remember which are missing?"

Jemima reflected that Nadia Hewling must have been very fond of them, for she'd worn the same ones throughout her entire sojourn in Venice. Or did all the beautiful new shoes pinch her?

The next day, Jemima found that Harry Hewling, in the nicest possible way, was clinging to her company, as though he was still somehow convinced that she would come up with a solution to his problems.

His grief and bafflement at his wife's disappearance was so constant and so evident that Jemima didn't like to turn him away from her side. She allowed him to accompany her when she went to the Piazza for a cup of coffee, even though she had craved a few days' solitude.

After a while Jemima began to have an uncomfortable feeling that Harry Hewling, for all his recent loss, was finding her increasingly attractive. Then Harry revealed, shyly, that he was an out-of-work actor—and matters became clearer. Presumably, he hoped that the magic of Jemima Shore would somehow help to secure him a job in television.

They sat outside Florian's, looking at the pigeons and the passers-by.

"All this," said Harry Hewling in a broken voice, waving his hand rather wildly in the direction of St. Mark's and the

Campanile, "all this was what Nadia wanted to see so much. She wanted to see Venice. And she never did."

"Except for a very short time," corrected Jemima.

"*Too* short. Everything about our life together was too short." There was something about Harry Hewling's melodramatic turn of phrase that made Jemima wonder what kind of actor he was on stage.

Afterward, Jemima could hardly prevent Harry Hewling from walking back with her to the Hotel Carpaccio, although by this time a rather odd train of thought had started in her mind—a train of thought she really wanted to explore by herself without the benefit of the company of the attractive Harry Hewling—for attractive he undeniably was. Jemima could see how Nadia Dansk, alone in a strange country, might have fallen for him.

So Jemima was actually standing with Harry Hewling at the desk as they were asking for their keys when the hotel manager, Fulco Montevecchi, stepped forward and in his excellent English said: "Signor Hewling, would you come with me?"

The last Jemima saw of Harry Hewling was his back view disappearing, somewhat dwarfed by two rather burly visitors on either side of him. But Jemima was well able to hear Harry Hewling's next utterance, because it was in fact a scream—quite a piercing scream—followed by the noise of someone falling.

Jemima, in spite of an instinct which made her want to rush into the manager's office, was obliged to rein her curiosity and depart—rather slowly—up the grand hotel staircase.

Once in her rooms, however, she could hardly settle amid the turquoise and gilded grandeur, the profusion of the manager's scarlet gladioli in honor of a happy married life—which had somehow never been removed—without wondering what had now happened to Harry Hewling. Her curiosity was not gratified for some hours.

Then the figure of Harry Hewling, looking extremely pale and shaken, reappeared at the door of her suite.

"She's dead," he said in a blank voice. "Nadia, I mean. I can't believe it. They're saying she drowned herself. She must have gone back to England somehow and killed herself. I don't believe it. You know, I fainted when I heard the news. Her body has been in the sea all this time but they think it's her from dental records. But I suppose"—his voice broke—"I shall have to identify her. There's no one else."

"Your sister—your half sister, I mean?"

Harry Hewling looked at Jemima in some surprise.

"Oh, no. You see, Gemma never even met Nadia. She didn't even come to the wedding. I told you, we don't get on." By now he was openly crying. "Poor, poor Nadia. I shall *never* understand."

But Jemima Shore, with a chill feeling, thought that perhaps she *did* understand.

That instinct which nagged at her was telling her that she must go and talk to the detectives who had arrived from England. There must be some clue they could give her.

"Jemima," Harry Hewling was saying, "you will have dinner with me tonight? I suppose I'll have to go back tomorrow, but—well, I don't know how to put this, but I'd like to have one evening with you."

"This has all been a terrible shock," Jemima replied. "Why don't you go to your suite? And I'll be in touch with you later."

It was after a few rapid telephone calls involving the name Megalith Television and that of Jemima Shore, and the mention of little ways in which she had helped the police in the past, that Jemima tracked down her quarry.

An hour later she was having a drink in the Piazza once more, but this time at Quadri's on the opposite side of the square, with Detective Chief Inspector Ronnie Tree, one of the two detectives who had flown out from England to break the news of Nadia Hewling's death to her husband and accompany him back to England to identify the body.

"Thank you, Jemima; I'll have a Campari soda. Make that a double Campari soda," said the Inspector. "I loathe the stuff, mind you, but I've always wanted to see Venice and it's not worth coming all this way to drink beer, is it? Particularly as we've lost our man."

"Harry Hewling?" Jemima was drinking Italian white wine with a great deal more relish than the Inspector was displaying over his Campari.

"None other. A slippery customer. Oh, a pretty face and all that, I'll grant you he's good-looking—if you like the type, as obviously the late Mrs. Nadia Hewling did. But it's all too neat, much too neat. And now he's got away with it."

"Explain—"

"I'd better explain after I've finished this." The Inspector wrinkled his nose as he drained a huge red glass which looked, and evidently tasted to him, like medicine. "The things I do for England," he added. Looking grave, he continued: "We had it all worked out: bright young out-of-work actor meets up with shy South African heiress with no relations. He seduces her, marries her. She makes a will, leaving him everything and makes a settlement on him straightaway. The lawyer doesn't like it very much—*he* doesn't like Mr. Hewling's pretty face—but there's nothing he can do.

"Then the wife disappears on honeymoon in Venice, and the husband begins to scream blue murder. Well, it stands to reason there's something very fishy there, doesn't it? When she does turn up, she's dead. And that's where the trouble starts. Mrs. Hewling is dead as a doornail in the English sea, and Mr. Hewling is alive and well with an unbreakable alibi in the Hotel Carpaccio, Venice. What's more, everyone testifies that he'd been there all along, in constant touch with the police. No way he could have followed her and done it."

"There is a way it could have been done," said Jemima slowly. "I'm thinking about some unworn shoes—masses of shoes—and a photograph of a dark-haired girl feeding the pigeons in the Piazza."

Several hours later, Jemima Shore, having returned to her suite, received the call she was expecting. "Quite right, my dear, quite right," boomed the voice of Detective Chief Inspector Tree. He sounded remarkably jovial, considering the amount of Campari soda he had imbibed. "How did you guess? The name's Kenyon, by the way, and there's a theatrical background there, too. The Italian police will be coming to get him shortly. So how did you guess?"

"First of all, the disappearance of the passport," said Jemima. "The point was being made to us: Nadia Hewling was able to travel away from Venice because she had taken her passport. Yet there was no record of Nadia using the passport to go home. Then Harry Hewling impulsively showed me a photograph of a pretty girl—Nadia as he called her—to prove that he had not been fortune-hunting. I pricked his vanity.

"The first thing I noticed was that it was crumpled—quite old, in fact. Secondly, that it was taken in the Piazza. When I commented that they looked so alike Nadia might have been his sister, Harry told me very firmly that although he did have a sister she was much older and he hardly knew her. He made a point of it—just as later he insisted that the sister had never met Nadia."

"Gemma Kenyon," said Detective Chief Inspector Tree. "His half sister, and in fact a few years younger—another would-be actress and much the same facial type as the wife. She was in it up to the neck. She traveled out with Hewling on Nadia's own passport under the name of Dansk, then went home under her own—knowing it was extremely unlikely that anyone would remember her among the many dark-haired girls traveling at holiday time. She must have destroyed the Dansk passport en route."

"But it was the shoes," pursued Jemima, "which really made me suspicious—all those totally unused shoes from poor Nadia's trousseau. Gemma must have traveled to Venice and gone out to dinner and left the hotel all in the same pair. Shoes are very personal things. You can always trust a woman to look at shoes. Gemma could wear Nadia's clothes but not her shoes, which were too small. She presumably just brought one pair of her own and wore them all the time. So when Harry Hewling told me Nadia had never even seen the Piazza, forgetting that he'd rashly shown me that photograph, then—"

"Then Jemima Shore, Investigator, became most suspicious," concluded the Inspector. "Well, they did for her all right, the pair of them—did for her in the sea somehow and made sure that the body wouldn't be washed up for some time. And then went straight off to Venice to give him the alibi he needed. We're still working out the details."

About twenty minutes later, Jemima was standing on her balcony gazing at the great dome of Santa Maria della Salute across the Canal, listening to the evening bells and thinking that they were sounding their own kind of memorial to Nadia Hewling. Then she was aware that Harry Hewling had stepped out onto the balcony next door. He was looking at her.

"What are you thinking about, Jemima?" asked Harry. He was smiling. "Are you thinking about having dinner with me?"

"I am thinking about a girl who wanted to see Venice," responded Jemima in a peculiarly expressionless tone, which some at Megalith Television would have recognized as the "trap" interview voice she used when she wanted to avoid arousing the suspicions of her intended victim. "And never did see it, not even for one day—*not even for one day!*"

Harry's dark eyes met hers for one instant. For one instant the mask of the actor seemed to drop—the shy young man vanished to be replaced by some more rapacious kind of animal. He took a step forward, toward her.

Whatever Harry Hewling would have done, Jemima Shore would never know, for at that point she heard a loud knocking at the door of the next-door suite. Harry Hewling continued to look steadily at her.

"You know, you really shouldn't have tried to pick me up as well," said Jemima. Her voice was now openly hard and cold. "Otherwise, without a woman's instinct, who knows, you might have actually got away with it."

CHAIN OF TERROR

by PATRICIA McGERR

Selena encountered Senator Stein in the lobby of the King David hotel on what was to have been her last evening in Israel. She had stopped at the desk to ask for messages when a familiar voice called her name. Turning, she took a step forward to meet the tall white-haired man who was hurrying toward her with arms outstretched.

"Selena, my dear, what a happy surprise!" He clasped both her hands and gave her a hearty kiss on the cheek. "I had no idea you were in Jerusalem. Is your husband with you?"

"No, this is a business trip," she explained, "and made on very short notice. My magazine set up interviews with the prime minister and several cabinet ministers. Then the Middle East correspondent was hit by appendicitis. I was sent over in his place."

"A wise choice," he approved. "There's nothing for you to cover in Washington after Congress adjourns."

"Only the White House and the Supreme Court," she replied with a smile. "How about you? Is your trip business or pleasure?"

"Entirely pleasure. And paid for, every penny, out of my own pocket." He shook an admonitory finger. "So don't you put me in one of those exposés about Congressional junkets at taxpayers' expense. Rachel and I are on holiday and I don't even intend to touch base with our Embassy. And speaking of Rachel, she'll be as delighted as I am to see you. How much longer will you be here?"

"I fly home tomorrow. At least—" She turned round to pick up the message slips the clerk had placed on the counter and glanced at the one on top. "Oh, no!"

"Not bad news, I hope."

"Disappointing. I expected confirmation of my plane reservation. Instead they say there's nothing available until the next day."

"Then you can come with us tomorrow," the senator said. "I've rented a car and we plan to drive down into the Negev. We'll visit Masada and the Qumran caves, maybe swim in the Dead Sea. How does that sound?"

"Wonderful," she responded. "I'm almost glad there's no space on the plane."

They got an early start the next morning. Selena and Rachel Stein, in the back seat, exchanged news of mutual friends at home while the senator maneuvered the car through the traffic-clogged streets. There was a faint chill in the November air, but the sun was bright in an almost cloudless sky. They circled the walls of the old city and crossed the Kidron valley to reach the Jericho road.

In less than an hour signs of modern civilization were left behind as they drove into the Judean wilderness along the shore of the Dead Sea. From a capacious handbag Mrs. Stein brought out a map and a guidebook. Selena joined her in tracing their route and picking out points of historical or current interest along the way. Most of the land was hilly and rock-strewn, sparse in trees or other vegetation, but occasionally they passed an Israeli settlement where irrigation and hard work had made the desert bloom with fields of eggplant or tomatoes and orchards of date palm. The senator slowed the car while his wife pointed out the caves of Qumran where the Dead Sea scrolls had been discovered.

"We'll stop on the way back," he promised.

Ahead of them in the distance rose the mountains of Moab where, according to tradition, Moses was buried. Behind them rusting tanks recalled the 1967 war. Near the oasis of

Ein Gedi, where David hid from Saul, they crossed the border from the West Bank of Jordan and were waved through a checkpoint by Israeli soldiers. Farther on the senator slowed again to call their attention to three tents of black goatskin which marked a Bedouin camp. Nearby, women and children on camels tended a small flock of sheep.

"Where are the men?" Mrs. Stein asked.

"In their tents, of course," her husband replied. "Drinking coffee and solving the problems of the universe."

"Sounds like a Senate Committee," she remarked.

It was then that Selena first noticed the dust-covered Fiat behind them. Since leaving Jerusalem they had passed a number of buses but few private vehicles. Now, with their car slowed to a sightseers' crawl, Selena expected the other car to pull out and pass. Instead it dropped back, widening the gap between them. When the senator accelerated, the Fiat also increased speed.

Are we being followed, she wondered, and immediately derided herself for an over-active imagination. That's what comes of working with an intelligence organization. I see spies and shadows everywhere. But I'm not on a Section Q assignment now and there's no cause for suspicion. The people in that car are no doubt tourists too and have the same reason we have to slow down at interesting places. A few minutes later they turned off the main highway to a narrower road that led to Herod's ancient fortress of Masada.

"Impressive, isn't it?" the senator said as he stopped in the parking lot near the great flat-topped mountain. "Remind me to fill up with gas when we finish here. The gauge shows nearly empty."

They left the automobile and walked past souvenir shops to the cable-car station. Soon, with a group of other visitors, they boarded a bright red car and were swiftly transported upward to a point near the summit. Looking down from the swaying car they could see a few energetic travelers starting the climb by way of the Snake Path.

Selena's eyes were drawn to the parking lot where a small car had pulled up beside the senator's. The Fiat again? And if so, what did it signify? Only that, like ourselves, they've come to view Masada. Shaking off a sense of foreboding, she turned back to Rachel who, guidebook in hand, was pointing out the restored walls of a Roman camp.

From the place where they left the cable car it was a short but steep walk up rocky steps to the summit. Sighting benches at the top, Mrs. Stein gave an exaggerated sigh of relief.

"Ah, good! We can sit down for a few minutes. That climb really wore me out."

But it was the senator who was breathing hard, his face flushed, and Selena suspected that his wife's pretense of exhaustion was meant to give him a chance to rest without an admission of weakness.

When they were seated the older woman drew from her bag another small book and read from it the story of Masada. The words took them back 19 centuries to the final revolt against Rome when Jewish zealots had captured this stronghold and held it for three years after the fall of Jerusalem. Surrounded at last by 10,000 Roman legionaries, the defenders—960 men, women, and children—chose to die by their own hands.

"I learned the speech of their leader Eleazar as a boy," the senator said, "though I've forgotten most of it." He closed his eyes, and bringing up snatches of memory he recited slowly, "Long ago we vowed never to serve the Romans nor anyone else but God. We were the first to revolt and we shall be the last to break off the struggle. Daybreak will end our resistance, but we are free to choose an honorable death with our loved ones. And I think it is God who has given us this privilege that we can die nobly and as free men."

"The site was excavated about fifteen years ago." Mrs. Stein turned to the last page. "And today, right where we're sitting, young Israeli soldiers come to receive their weapons and swear allegiance to the state and the flag with an oath that ends, 'Masada shall not fall again.' " She glanced sharply at her husband, saw that his breathing was steady, his color normal. "Well!" She closed the book and rose briskly to her feet. "I'm rested now. Let's see the sights."

There were many sights to see, starting with a series of

rooms where food and wine were stored. Behind and in front of them as they made the circuit were many other tourists, most of them in bands of 20 or more led by a guide. They were on the upper terrace of Herod's palace when Mrs. Stein leaned close to Selena to whisper, "I think you have an admirer. Near the wall at your left. The young man in the yellow shirt."

Selena glanced in the direction indicated, then shook her head. "I've never seen him before."

"He keeps looking this way," Mrs. Stein told her. "I first noticed him when we came out of the synagogue. He was standing near the entrance, almost as if he were waiting for us."

"If he has his eye on either of you girls," the senator joked, "I can only say I admire his taste. But I think it's time we started down. I've worked up quite an appetite."

They descended from the mountain and ate a leisurely lunch in the restaurant at its base. They were starting back to the car when members of a tour group caught up with them.

"You're Senator Stein, aren't you?" one of the women asked. "See, Rose, I told you that's who it was. You spoke to our sisterhood luncheon last year and—"

His wife and Selena walked on ahead, leaving him to shake the outstretched hands and answer questions.

"I hope this trip hasn't been too strenuous." Rachel looked back with a frown of concern. "It's so hard to keep him from overdoing."

"You're worried about him, aren't you? Is he ill?"

"Not really. Not if he's careful. He had a heart attack last spring. A mild one, so we were able to keep it out of the papers. The doctor said he'll be fine as long as he follows the rules. A proper diet. Plenty of sleep. No unusual exertion or excitement. It's the last part that's difficult. Dan's used to an active life. But he'll be seventy in a few weeks and he's promised me that when his term ends next year he won't run again."

They reached the car and stood beside it to wait for the senator. He had taken leave of the tour group and was crossing the parking lot when two young men came up behind him. One, Selena noted, was the man in the yellow shirt to whom her attention had been called on the upper terrace. As she watched they caught up with the senator, one moving to his left, the other to his right, so close that the three bodies were almost touching. The yellow-shirted one spoke and when Senator Stein replied, Yellow Shirt's arm went round his back so that he almost seemed to be supporting him. The senator's movements became mechanical, his body stiff, his legs leaden, as if each step was taken under duress.

"Something's wrong." Rachel Stein, alarmed, started forward. "Dan, aren't you feeling all right. What is it?"

"I'm all right, Rachel. Be calm."

There's a gun at his back, Selena thought. Instinctively she moved closer to the other woman and laid a restraining hand on her arm.

"Everybody get in the car," the yellow-shirted man said. His English was precise, the accent faintly British. "Be nice and quiet and nobody will get hurt."

Mrs. Stein shook off Selena's hand and continued her rush forward.

"Who are you?" she demanded. "What are you doing to my husband?"

She was about to throw herself on the spokesman when his companion stepped forward and, grasping her arm, twisted it behind her back to turn her fully around until she was again facing Selena. Tears started in her eyes but did not stop her angry protest. The senator hurled himself on his wife's assailant and the gun was for an instant visible in the second man's hand as he moved close to the entangled trio.

In that instant Selena weighed alternatives. To run for shelter behind the car and summon help by shouting? To take advantage of the gunman's distraction and try to seize his weapon? The restaurant was a long way off and a bus had moved in front of it, cutting off the view of the touring Americans, so the latter option seemed more practical. But as she poised to spring, the senator gave a low moan and sank to the ground.

"Pills," he gasped. "Pocket."

His wife broke free of the young man. He reached out to grab her again but was stopped by his partner.

"Don't hold her, Rahim. The old man needs help. You take care of the other one."

Rahim moved to Selena's side while Mrs. Stein dropped to her knees and quickly took a small bottle of pills from the senator's coat pocket. With trembling fingers she shook out a tiny pellet and placed it on his tongue, then cradled his head on her arm. Selena and the two men watched in silence until the senator opened his eyes and raised his head.

"I'm fine now, Rachel," he said. "No cause to worry."

"Then get in the car," Rahim ordered. "We've wasted enough time."

Selena moved to her friend's side, assisting her to rise, and she, in turn, gave a helping hand to her husband.

"Look at the old man, Abdul," Rahim said. "He's not in shape to drive."

"We'll have to change the plan," Abdul returned. His eyes fixed on Selena. "Can you handle the car?"

"I can drive," she answered. "But if it's money you want—"

"You think we're common robbers?" He drew himself up haughtily. "We are Palestinians and patriots. It is the man we've come for, not his money."

"Then take me." Strength had returned to the senator's voice. "And let the women go."

"Never, Daniel." Rachel clung tightly to his hand. "Whatever they do to you, they must do to me. I'll not be parted from you."

"Don't worry, lady. We'll keep you all together."

"My husband and I will go with you," she said firmly, "if you'll free our friend. Whatever your plans for us, she shouldn't be involved. She's not even Jewish."

"Then it's her bad luck she's traveling with you. We can't let her loose to call the police, can we? Come on, let's get out of here."

Soon they were all in the car. Rahim sat in back with the Steins as Selena took the wheel with Abdul at her side.

"I have a gun." He spoke matter-of-factly, without menace,

as she started the engine. "My partner has a knife. If we need to use them, we will. But if everyone behaves with common sense, you will be treated honorably as prisoners of war. And if all goes well, you will be able to return home alive and unharmed in a very short time. Now, miss, please return to the main highway and then turn right."

Selena did as she was told. The tour bus, its passengers having boarded, followed them on the road leading from Masada. She tried to think of some way to signal them but too soon she reached the highway where, turning south, she watched in the rear-view mirror as the bus went in the opposite direction, back toward Jerusalem. Scanning the dashboard instruments, she confirmed the senator's earlier comment about needing gas. If this was to be a long journey, they'd have to stop and that might provide her with a chance to pass on a message. But for the moment she could only follow orders and keep driving.

It was a silent ride. The Steins exchanged a few words, cut off by Rahim's command to be quiet. Selena darted frequent glances from the road ahead to the instrument panel to see the kilometer numbers mount slowly upward while the needle on the gas gauge hovered near empty. If we do stop, she asked herself, how will I let the attendant know we're in trouble? They won't let me talk to him alone, that's certain. If it were like service stations at home, I could ask to use the restroom and write a note. But out here in the desert, there'll be nothing but a pump. And the man may be an Arab and in sympathy with our captors. But that will be our last chance to call for help, so when the time comes I must be ready.

"Slow down," Abdul broke in on her thoughts. "We're near our turnoff. Yes, here it is. Turn right."

The road to which he directed her was narrow and unpaved, hardly more than a trail. If they met another car, one of them would have to pull off to the side. But they met no one and passed no other signs of life. They were headed, it appeared, into a part of the desert that was isolated and uninhabited. The nearly empty gas tank was no longer a good omen. Running out of fuel here might inconvenience the Palestinians, but it would not improve the plight of their victims.

The suspense at any rate was soon ended. She had followed the trail for about ten minutes when she saw ahead, a few yards from the roadside, two goatskin tents. Standing beside them was a man in the flowing robes and headdress of a desert Arab.

"We've arrived," Abdul told her. "Stop the car."

She obeyed, noting as she did so that the needle on the gauge had passed the gauge-line indicating empty. They could probably have traveled only one or two kilometers farther. But that was no longer cause for hope. Instead it meant that, even if there was an opportunity, the car was useless as a means of escape.

The stranger approached and spoke through the window to Abdul.

"Did everything go as planned?"

"Yes. Except that they took someone with them to Masada."

"So we have an extra guest. No problem." He opened the rear door with a bow that was almost courtly. "Senator Stein. Madame. Will you please alight?"

"Who are you?" the senator asked. "Why have you brought us here? What do you hope to gain from kidnaping three United States citizens?"

"A great deal." He answered the final question. "Our hospitality, I fear, is less than you are used to, but you will not have long to endure it. If you get out of the car, I will be pleased to introduce myself and, as far as possible, to satisfy your curiosity."

"It appears we have no choice." The senator climbed from the car, then leaned back to assist his wife. The others followed, forming an awkward group with the three Americans confronting the three Arabs.

"I am Hassan el-Fattah." The speaker was an imposing figure, taller and older than the other two and clearly the one in command. "I shall be your host for as long as it takes for the Jews to comply with our requests."

"So we're hostages," Senator Stein interpreted. "And you're members of a terrorist gang."

"Terrorists or freedom fighters." Hassan shrugged. "It depends, doesn't it, on who is speaking. We are not at war with you, Senator, and we will do our best to make you and your ladies comfortable. Abdul, move the car out of sight. And you, Rahim, can let our comrades know that the first step is accomplished."

The two young men moved quickly. Abdul got back in the car and drove it under an overhanging cliff while Rahim scurried into one of the tents. They must have a short-wave radio, Selena thought. If I can get to the transmitter when no one is watching, maybe I can send an S.O.S. But to whom? Even as the idea formed, she realized its absurdity. This isn't Citizen's Band land. I'd only reach the people with whom Rahim is communicating—a Palestinian command post. There has to be another way to get word to the outside world about what is happening to us.

There's a seven-hour time difference between Israel and Washington, so it was still morning when word was received at the White House that an American senator and his wife had been abducted. The price of their release, according to a message delivered to the American Embassy in Israel, was freedom for five Palestinians who had been jailed for a series of bombings in which nine Israelis had died.

The news, routinely circulated to all intelligence agencies, reached Hugh Pierce in his Georgetown studio. Section Q, the small secret security branch that he headed, was not directly involved, but it was asked to stay alert and contribute any relevant information. That his wife might be in danger did not occur to him. Selena's cable the night before had advised him of her delayed departure and he thought of phoning to tell her about the Steins. But she might take that as encouragement to stay and join in the search. Since he was unwilling to do anything that might delay her homecoming, he took no action but remained in his studio to await developments.

At first there was hope, shared by the Israelis and Americans, that the message was a hoax. This was bolstered by inquiries at the King David Hotel from which it was learned that the Steins had set out in the morning on an all-day tour of the Dead Sea area. Tour agencies were checked until a guide was found who reported that several members of his group had actually spoken to Senator Stein after lunch at Masada. There was reassurance in the knowledge that, only a short time before the report of his kidnaping, he had been free and following his intended itinerary.

But it grew late and the Steins did not return to the hotel, and later still friends whom they had invited to dinner had waited in vain in the lobby. Agents fanned out to question all members of the tour who had seen them at Masada. A couple riding in the front seat of the bus recalled following the senator's car back to the highway.

"But he wasn't driving," the woman volunteered. "You remember, Joe, there were three people in the back seat, a woman and two men. I'm sure one of them was Senator Stein. That thick crop of white hair couldn't belong to anyone else."

"That's right," Joe agreed. "We figured he must have a chauffeur."

The rental agency quickly refuted that guess. The senator had hired a car, not a driver, and the hotel porter confirmed that, when the party left the hotel that morning, the senator was at the wheel. So the conclusion was at last unavoidable. The Steins were at the mercy of terrorists and the government was faced with intolerable alternatives.

Even more disturbing to Hugh was information that was included in the report as a minor footnote. Several of the tourists said there were two women lunching with the senator. One they assumed was his wife, the other was much younger. The professional concern that Hugh had felt since the reports began was suddenly raised to white-hot anxiety. If Selena—no, it couldn't be—but she was in Jerusalem and at the same hotel—with a free day—and the Steins were old friends of Selena's parents.

With a hand that was barely steady, Hugh picked up the phone and put through a call to the King David. The wait seemed interminable, and when he was finally connected, the clerk's answers did nothing to quiet his fears. Selena was not in the hotel. The key was in her box, along with a teletype from the airline that had been received at 9:50 a.m. It appeared, therefore, that she had left the hotel soon after breakfast and had not yet returned.

"And in Jerusalem"—Hugh looked in despair at the bright sunshine streaming through his skylight—"in Jerusalem it's nearly midnight."

In the desert Hassan had provided his captives and his two associates with garments like those he was wearing. The road, he explained, led to a long abandoned archeological dig. Now nobody had reason to come within miles of the site. But in case anyone did, or if one of the low-flying Israeli patrol planes passed overhead, they would see a small Bedouin encampment, one of many that dotted the area. As long as they were properly costumed and stayed within specific boundaries, the captives were free to roam about or to rest in the smaller tent. It was, Selena realized, perfect camouflage. And to stifle any thought of flight, either Abdul or Rahim—the gun inconspicuous but not invisible—was at all times on guard.

At nightfall Abdul built a wood fire to heat a mixture of lamb chunks and rice which he ladled onto tin plates.

"Eat your fill," Hassan urged them. "We have rations and water for two days. Enough even"—he nodded to Selena "—for an unexpected guest."

"And after two days—" Selena ventured the question.

"We break camp," he said. "They have forty-eight hours to let our brothers go."

His tone was mild but his face, lit by the flickering flames, showed a fanatic determination that made it unnecessary to ask what would happen if the deadline was not met. It was not surprising that none of his guests had much appetite.

At bedtime a new complication appeared. It had been planned to put the Steins in the small tent and the Arabs in the larger one, which also contained the radio equipment. That left no place for Selena.

"I can sleep in the car," she suggested.

"Let both the ladies have the car," the senator said. "The

cushions are softer than the ground and they'll be sheltered from the wind."

"But I'd rather stay with you," Mrs. Stein said.

"And let Selena be off by herself?" His quick glance at the other men was meaningful. "No, dear, that's not wise."

"I hope you're not so foolish as to think you can use the car to escape," Hassan said. "You would first need boards to lift the back wheels out of the sand. And of course one of us will be on watch all night. But if, for comfort, you choose the car as a sleeping place, I do not object."

So it was settled. Rachel Stein stretched out on the car's back seat while Selena curled up in the front. At ten o'clock she switched on the car radio and found an English-language news broadcast. The Israeli cabinet, they heard, had been called to an emergency meeting and would probably remain in session through the night to decide on a response to terrorists who held hostage an American senator, his wife, and an as-yet-unidentified female companion. The senator and the two women, according to the announcer, had last been seen when their car, driving away from Masada, had turned south on the road to Sodom.

"Sodom!" Mrs. Stein exclaimed. "That's appropriate. We couldn't be any harder to find if we had all turned to salt. My dear, I'm so sorry we got you into this."

"We're in it together," Selena answered. "What we need to find is a way out."

But as she lay awake, her mind busy, every avenue of escape seemed blocked. From time to time the sound of wood being placed on the fire or the footsteps of someone walking near the car spoke of their captors' unbroken vigil. Finally, from exhaustion, she slept.

When she woke, the fire was out and the camp dimly lighted by the rising sun. She pulled herself upright in the seat and looked back to see that Rachel was also awake. Rachel's carryall had yielded another book which she was reading with the aid of a miniature flashlight. She looked up to greet Selena.

"I'm sorry if my moving around disturbed you. You seemed so peaceful."

"I hope you were able to get some sleep too."

"Enough." Her eyes went back to the book and she read aloud, " 'The Lord is my light and my salvation, whom shall I fear? The Lord is the stronghold of my life, of whom shall I be afraid?' "

"The Psalms?"

"Yes. I like to have them with me. Somewhere in here"—she tapped the book's cover—"there are words of strength and solace for every crisis."

They breakfasted on bread and dried fish and then began a long stretch of waiting. Selena, covered from head to foot as a Bedouin woman, roved restlessly about the camp, followed always by the eyes of one of the Arabs. The Steins were more passive, staying close together as if each drew comfort from the other's nearness.

In mid-morning Hassan came out of the communications tent to tell them of a new development. The Israeli government had announced that they could not reach any decision without proof that those making the demands had actually taken Senator Stein and that he and his companions were alive and well.

"So they're ready to deal with us." Hassan was exultant. "You can speak over our radio, Senator. Headquarters will put your voice on tape and play it for the government. If all goes well, our brothers will be in Damascus tonight and you can sleep in real beds. Is that not good news?"

"No," the senator said. "I will not speak on your radio."

Hassan stared at him in surprise, then he said, "Nobody is asking you to speak in support of our cause. All you have to say is that you and the ladies are our prisoners and that you are well. That's true, isn't it? And the sooner they hear you say so, the sooner we can all go home."

"The Israelis won't give in to blackmail," the senator declared. "They never have. They never will."

"Maybe not before," Hassan conceded. "But our side has never had a United States senator as a bargaining point. You're an important man and a popular one. How do you think the American public, and especially the other senators, will feel if the government here says they'd rather keep a few Palestinians in jail than save your life?"

"Those Palestinians," the senator snapped, "are murderers. If they're released, there'll be more bombs—and then more kidnapings to free the bombers—and on and on in an endless chain of terror. If you need my voice on your radio to convince the world that you have me, then perhaps I've found a way to stop you."

"At what cost, Senator?" Hassan asked. "You may be willing to die for Israel, but what about your wife and her friend? You talk to him, ladies. I'm sure you can persuade him to cooperate and save your lives."

Deliberately he walked away, out of earshot.

"You're right, Dan." Mrs. Stein reached for his hand. "They're counting on outside pressure to weaken Israel's resolve not to deal with terrorists. You must do nothing to help them."

"They won't deal, no matter what I do or say," he answered. "Asking for proof that we're alive—I'm sure that's just a way to gain time, to keep the negotiations open. The Israelis don't ransom hostages, they rescue them."

"Like at Entebbe." Eagerly Rachel seized the hope he held out. "Certainly it should be easier to pluck three people from an open space than it was to invade an airport guarded by soldiers in a hostile country."

"Much easier," Selena agreed. "If only they knew where we are."

"That's the rub," the senator said. "After we left Masada we vanished as if the earth had swallowed us up. I might even make their broadcast if there were some way to sneak in a clue to our location."

"Just say we're disguised as a sheik and his harem not far from the Dead Sea. Can you get that past the censor?"

"Not a chance," he replied. "But it makes an interesting fantasy."

Their spirits, Selena noted, seemed buoyed by the discussion. Although the hopelessness of their situation had not changed, the senator was no longer a passive figure. By refusing to speak, he had shown himself free to choose, to make a decision and hold to it, to take command of his fate.

"Well, Senator?" Hassan had come back to them. "Have you decided to listen to reason?"

"My position remains the same."

"And it won't change," his wife added.

"You are stupid!" Hassan exploded. "If we don't prove you're alive, your people will think you have already been killed. Then they will have no cause to deal with us."

"That's just how I see it."

"If they don't meet our terms, you will die." His gaze moved slowly around the circle. "All of you. Be sure you understand what you are doing. By refusing to cooperate, you commit suicide."

"And that"—Rachel echoed the words recited on the mountain top—"that can be an honorable death."

The midday meal was again a mixture of lamb and rice. Later Selena went to the car to tune in another news broadcast. She learned that there was no further word from the alleged kidnapers of Senator Stein, but Jerusalem and Washington were in constant consultation about what action to take. She learned also that her own identity had been established. But the announcer's final line was, to her, the most interesting.

"The husband of the third hostage, the well-known American artist Hugh Pierce, arrived today in Jerusalem to await news of his wife."

Hugh! Her heart bounded. Hugh was in Jerusalem. So short a distance away. Hugh would find them. She projected her thoughts northward as if she might, by willing it, force them into his mind. But that's insane. She brought herself back to reality. There was between them a depth of understanding that made them able to convey much in few words. But not, she thought wryly, in no words at all. If I'm to send a message to Hugh, I'll have to use means more substantial than telepathy.

She turned off the radio and weighed the possibilities. Then she left the car to join the Steins who were strolling arm in arm at the other end of the cliff. She asked Mrs. Stein if she might borrow her book of Psalms.

"Of course, dear. I left it in the car. I hope you'll find a verse to answer your need."

"I'm sure I shall." She returned to the car and began to read. A short time later she went to Hassan who was resting in the sun, his back against a rock outside the larger tent.

"I've been thinking." She sat down beside him. "The senator is determined not to help you. And Mrs. Stein agrees with him. Nothing will change their minds."

"There are ways to persuade people," he said darkly. "I think he would not like to see his wife hurt."

"Oh, no!" She drew back. "You wouldn't—you couldn't!"

"We do whatever is necessary for our cause. I am waiting now for instructions."

"But public opinion is important to your cause too. You've treated us kindly. I can report that to the world when we're free. I'm a journalist."

"I know. The radio told us who you are. Perhaps when you go back you will write that we are not monsters, that we fight only to regain our land."

"But when you threaten to hurt a helpless woman—"

"Her husband will be to blame, if he remains stubborn."

"There's another way. That's what I came to talk to you about. All you need is proof that the three of us are in your custody and well. So why not let me make a tape? I'll say what you want me to say—that Senator and Mrs. Stein and I are well and that you're taking good care of us. If you like, I'll even explain that I'm talking instead of the senator because he'd rather die than help you. People who know the kind of man he is will believe that. Then you'll have no need for his voice."

"Hmm." He frowned, thinking. "Yes, that may serve. I will pass on your proposal and see what the leader thinks. You wait."

In a few minutes he was back. "There is a difficulty," he told her. "The senator's voice is well-known. When he speaks, people recognize him. But if you make a tape, they cannot be sure if it is really you or someone else merely using your name."

"Ah, yes, I see." She did not add that if he had not raised that objection, she herself would have pointed it out to him. She remained silent, her eyes focused on the ground as if in deep thought. "But wait—" She looked up, brightening. "I have an idea. My husband is in Jerusalem. If I add a special message for him, one that he'll know can only come from me, that will solve the problem."

"What kind of message?"

"I often quote the Bible to him. There's one verse in particular that he'll associate with me."

"I will check."

Again he went into the tent. It was a long time before he returned, but when he did he was beaming his approval. "The leader is pleased that you will work with us," he told her. "He says to tell you that you will not be sorry. Now here is what you must say."

He handed her a slip of paper on which were written three short sentences. She was to identify herself, say that she and Senator and Mrs. Stein were well cared for by Palestinian patriots, and urge the government to save their lives by meeting the demands. "After that," he said, "you say the Bible verse that will make your husband certain it is you."

This time she went into the tent with him and sat quietly while he spun dials to renew radio contact with his headquarters. After a brief exchange in Arabic he handed her the microphone.

"Go ahead. They are ready to start the tape."

She read the message exactly as it was written, then added, "I heard on the radio that my husband is in Jerusalem. Please tell him that I quoted my favorite verse from the Psalms, 'The Lord is in his holy temple, His throne is in heaven. His eyes behold the children of men.' "

While government ministers held round-the-clock sessions at the Knesset, officers of an elite commando unit of the Israeli army met in the basement of a bank a few blocks away. They had planned and practised techniques for air and sea rescues from a wide variety of open and enclosed spaces—airfields and farms, offices, hotels, theaters, schools, houses—every conceivable place where hostages might be taken. But all these preparations were nullified by the total disappearance of the Steins and Selena. Known and suspected members of the Palestinian underground were under strict surveillance, but nothing was discovered. The demand for proof had been made on the chance that, in supplying it, the abductors might make a slip that would reveal their hiding place. But that was another dead end.

The tape bearing Selena's message had been played over the phone to the American ambassador who, in turn, made a tape that was passed to the commandos. Hugh, joining them in the basement, identified his wife's voice but scowled in bafflement as she recited her "favorite psalm." They played it several times, hoping to hear background noise that might furnish a clue. But there was nothing. Half of the 48 hours given in the original ultimatum had already elapsed.

"What I need," Hugh said suddenly, "is a rabbi."

The soldiers looked at him, startled, as if suspecting that he had cracked under the strain. But they acceded to his request for one more replay of the tape. He noted Selena's exact words, then went into an adjoining office to use the telephone.

"He may be right," the major commented. "There's not much left to do except pray."

But a short time later Hugh was back in the commando room and the atmosphere was dramatically changed. A large map hung on the wall and Hugh stood beside it with the officers clustered close to watch each movement of his pencil.

"Here—" He tapped the point at which the Masada road joined the main highway. "This is where they were last seen. We know from the tourists that they headed south. So we move along this route not less than eleven and not more than twelve kilometers." He measured carefully and put two dots on the map. "This is where they turned, either left or right."

"A left turn," a lieutenant commented, "would put them in the Dead Sea."

"Correct. So they went to the right. Not less than four or more than five kilometers." From the dots he drew parallel lines into the desert and then, checking his measurements with care, drew a square to enclose an area one kilometer in each direction. "That's where they are."

"We'll do an aerial rec," the major said, "and make sure."

"Be careful," Hugh warned. "If they guess they've been spotted, they may find another hole to hide in."

"We know our job," the Israeli answered. "We won't scare the birds. One pass with a wide telephoto lens will be enough. It will look like a routine desert patrol."

When the plane flew over, Selena was walking with Rachel Stein. She had told them at once about making the tape but had not explained her motive. It was possible that nothing would come of it and she did not want to arouse false hopes. Now Mrs. Stein, concerned that Selena might feel guilty, was trying to reassure her.

"Daniel and I both think you did the right thing," she said. "He couldn't help them. It would betray all his principles. But Israel doesn't mean to you what it does to us. And I was worried that they would use force on Dan, torture even. I don't know how long Dan could have held out. With his heart condition, he might—" She broke off, unwilling to complete the thought. "You spared us that, Selena, and I'm thankful. Also it should make the Arabs more friendly to you. In the end, if it comes to that, it may save your life."

"Oh, no! Mrs. Stein, that isn't why I made the tape."

"Of course not!" She was equally emphatic. "My dear, we know you too well to think that for one minute. But if it has that effect—well, it eases my mind to believe that whatever happens to us you'll survive. Daniel and I have lived a long time, the years have been full and happy for us. And there are worse ways to die than for a cause one believes in. But you're young and you were caught up in this by accident. We're to blame for your being here and if harm comes to you —ah, look!" She was distracted by the sound of an approaching plane. "Isn't there some way we can signal, let them know we're here?"

But the plane, staying high in the sky, had passed over them and was gone before she could finish the question.

In the commando room the series of pictures, greatly magnified, was spread out for inspection on a large table.

"A Bedouin family is great cover," the major said, "and all very authentic. Except for this." He pointed to a shiny surface near the ground close to the cliff. "What do you make it to be?"

"Something metal," his aide answered. "From the shape and location, I'd say it's the end of an auto bumper."

"So we've trapped our birds." The major smiled his satisfaction. "The pictures show five people. Three of ours, two of them."

"There may be one or two others out of sight," the aide suggested.

"Sitting ducks. We'll go in tonight, land behind this hill, and implement Plan D."

"There'll be a dangerous minute or two when we go over the hill," Hugh said. "If they hear us coming, they'll have time to grab one of the hostages to use as a shield."

"We're fast and silent in the dark," the major said. "Anyway, that's a risk we have to take."

"It's a risk we can minimize," Hugh countered. "My wife's tape said she has access to a radio. She told us where they are, so she's expecting us to mount a rescue. If I let her know exactly when we're coming, she'll figure a way to put space between them and their guards at the crucial moment. Can you arrange for me to put a message on every English-language newscast for the rest of the day?"

"Are you crazy?" the major asked. "Those fellows speak English. There's no way you can brief our people without tipping off the other side."

"You work out your strategy," Hugh retorted, "and tell me the exact hour and minute you start over the top. Then I'll get word to my girl."

Selena waited impatiently for night to fall. Had Hugh, she wondered, understood her message? How and when would they act on it? Surely not until after dark. Probably in the predawn hours when guards are least alert. By ten o'clock the women were in the car, the senator was in his tent, and Hassan was keeping lonely vigil by the campfire.

Again Selena switched on the radio. Most of the news was repetition. Senator Stein and his party were still missing. The officials were still debating. The public was demanding action.

Then came an announcement that quickened her pulse. "Hugh Pierce, husband of one of the hostages, was interviewed this afternoon. Asked if he had any message for his wife, he replied, 'Only this. Be brave, darling, and remember what the Psalmist said. 'You, O Lord, are a shield about me, my glory and the lifter up of my head.' "

"What a sweet thought." Mrs. Stein leaned over the back of the seat to give Selena's shoulder a gentle pat. "I didn't know Hugh was a religious man. But of course in times of trouble—"

"Yes," Selena concurred. "It makes a difference."

With the flashbulb sheltered to show no light outside the car, she scanned the pages of the book of Psalms until she found the passage Hugh had quoted.

"They're coming for us. We must be prepared."

"What shall we do?" Rachel asked.

"Our part is to be out of harm's way. This car is the safest place, so you and I are all right. But we have to find a way to get the senator in here with us without making them suspicious. There's no hurry, though. We've several hours to think about it."

They discussed and made plans, discarded them and devised others, finally arrived at a firm arrangement. Then they were silent, waiting. At midnight Abdul relieved Hassan. The fire burned low, the camp was quiet. The hours dragged on, but neither of the women slept. At last the luminous dial of Selena's watch showed 3:00 A.M.

"It's almost time," she whispered.

"I'm ready," Mrs. Stein replied. "Just tell me when to start."

She watched the second-hand sweep round.

3:01.

3:02.

"Now!" Selena said.

"Oh-o-oh!" Rachel broke the silence with a long drawn-out cry of pain. "Daniel, help me!"

"What's going on?" Abdul, dozing by the fire, sprang to his feet.

"Rachel, what is it?" The senator burst from his tent but was caught and held back by Abdul.

"It's Mrs. Stein." Selena called across the open space. "Chest pains—her heart. Her husband has pills."

"Let him go to her, Abdul." Hassan came out of the other tent. "We don't want the old lady to die on us."

Released, the senator hurried toward the car. Mrs. Stein pushed open the back door.

"Rachel, what—"

"I'm all right, Dan. Get in. Hurry!"

He scrambled in beside her. Selena pulled the door shut, pressed down the lock. Hassan at a more leisurely pace was moving toward the car.

"What's this all about?" the senator asked. "Why—?"

Before he could say more there was a sound of movement on the hill to their right. A rock, dislodged by running feet, rolled to the bottom. Hassan whirled around, drawing his gun. Then a spotlight shone in his eyes, blinding him, and other lights illuminated the whole camp.

"Drop your guns," a voice out of the darkness ordered. "You're surrounded."

Hassan fired toward the light but an answering shot struck his arm and the gun fell to the ground. Abdul and Rahim were less militant. Within a few minutes the commandos were in the camp and had taken the three men prisoners. The Steins and Selena emerged from the car.

"Senator Stein?" The major introduced himself and his unit. "I hope you and the ladies are all right."

"We're fine, young man. And very grateful to you. That was a remarkable performance."

"Standard operating procedure," he replied. "There's a helicopter waiting to take you to Jerusalem."

Selena, spotting a familiar figure behind the major, had not listened to their exchange. Only when Hugh's arms were tightly around her was she able to release the emotion that she had, for 36 hours, held so tightly in check.

Later, riding in the helicopter, they reviewed what had happened.

"It was like a miracle!" Mrs. Stein exclaimed. "The way they suddenly swooped down and set us free. But what I don't understand"—she turned to Hugh—"how did you know where to find us?"

"Selena sent me a message."

"I watched the odometer while I was driving to the camp," Selena explained. "It showed a little over eleven kilometers south and about four west. When they let me tape a message, I added a verse from the Psalms."

"Psalm 11, verse 4," Hugh said. "As soon as a Bible scholar identified the passage, I had the numbers I needed."

"And the quotation Hugh sent back—Psalm 3, verse 4—told me when to expect them."

"Then the commandos," Hugh concluded, "did the rest. It was a by-the-book rescue operation."

"Exactly," Selena echoed. "Rescue by the Book."

TANIA'S NO WHERE

by AMANDA CROSS

My name is Leighton Fansler. I have long wanted to publish some of the cases of my aunt, Kate Fansler, who, while never a private investigator in any professional sense—she certainly never had a license nor was she paid—took on, like Sherlock Holmes and Peter Wimsey, many interesting cases. She has been adamant until now about her refusal to let me tell the stories of any of her cases, and no one can be more adamant than Kate Fansler. I finally got her to admit, however, that this case was an exception. All those intimately concerned with it are now dead, and no harm could be done to anyone in the telling of it. Indeed, she mused, it might be of help to some.

What was clear to Kate at the very beginning of the case was that by the time Tania Finship was sixty-two, and almost the oldest member of the faculty in her department or anywhere else, she had become beloved. After her disappearance, it became clear that, in the opinion of her colleagues and students, she had not known this. She had done her job efficiently, curtly, honorably, and without notable tact, and had undoubtedly considered, if she reflected on the matter at all, that the outrage and anger she heard from students who had not done well in her courses represented the general opinion. As is, alas, so often the case among human beings, who tend, whatever their profession, to substitute tardy regret for timely expressions of appreciation, Tania Finship was gone before anyone had told her that they loved her.

If she was dead, there was no evidence to say so. Had her husband wished to claim her savings and remarry, he would have been hard-put to do so before the statutory seven years. As it was, he mourned her, having always loved her and made his affection clear, if unspoken. She may have kept her professorship through tenure, as many disgruntled younger professors had been heard to mutter, but she kept her marriage because it suited them both: in the United States in those years one did not stay married unless one chose. Her children, grown and moved away, had come East when she disappeared, and finally returned to the West Coast, keeping in close touch with their father. As to her savings, all she and Tom, her husband, owned they had owned jointly. It was already his, but, as he often made clear after the disappearance, sharing it once again with her was his only, his fervent wish.

No one could imagine what had become of her. The police were as puzzled as the F.B.I. and the C.I.A., who had entered the case on the thinnest of suspicions that she had been part of a spy ring. Her parents had been Marxists and Trotskyites in the 'twenties and 'thirties, and one never knew for sure that they had not become Stalinists and planted Tania for future spying at birth. Unlikely, but the C.I.A. is nothing if not expert at the unlikely. She might have waited all those years, until her children were grown, and then taken off with her ill-gotten information. What information a professor of Russian literature could have acquired in a blameless life was at best unclear, at worst nonsense. Still, she did read and speak Russian, and what is more she had been clearly heard to say critical things about the United States Government. Anything might be suspected of someone as profoundly anti-nuclear and anti-war as Tania.

"Which," as Fred Manson said to Kate Fansler, "is just the problem. The C.I.A. has got this ridiculous bee in their bonnet, but the result is everyone has just decided she's in Russia and stopped looking—everyone who had the ghost of a chance of finding her, that is. And the students are getting restless. They've heard her hold forth, and they're perfectly sure leaving this country or even her penthouse for more than a few hours was the last thing she wanted. If Tania had ever had any wanderlust, she had long since lost it, or so the students and her husband reported. The point is, can you help us? I've heard a lot about you."

"What do you think happened?" Kate asked.

Fred Manson heaved a great sigh. "I try not to think," he said. "The fact is, Tania was a bit of a burden in the department; conscientious, heavens yes, and hard-working, and highly intelligent. But she had taken to cultivating a crusty manner that was as hard on her colleagues as it was on her students. You want an example? All right: at a meeting of the curriculum committee some weeks ago, when we were discussing next year's catalog, I had to report that some man who had promised to teach the survey course next year was now refusing to do so. Tania was in charge of survey courses, and was considerably annoyed, as anyone would be at that news that late. What she said was: 'Couldn't we just tell him to go pee up a rope?' "

"I see what you mean," Kate said. "You're not suggesting that the man in question heard about it and abducted her?"

"I'm not suggesting anything; certainly not that. But it's hard enough to run a language department. They're the worst kind: for some reason those who teach languages become ornery from the moment they learn about inflected nouns, without having them talk nothing but mayhem, kidnaping, and worse. Find out what happened to her, please, for the sake of the academic world and my sanity. The department has discretionary funds, and the university will help, all on the q.t., of course. The university position is that she needed an emergency operation and doesn't want anyone to know. They may have to admit a scandal, but not before it's absolutely necessary."

"I should think," Kate said, "that the feelings of the university were not anyone's prime concern. They certainly wouldn't be mine. You've checked the hospitals?"

"Everything has been checked," Fred Manson said. "Everything. When my mother used to lose things, she always said they had disappeared into thin air. Of course, they always turned up fifteen minutes later. If there's one thing I can't stand, it's cliches enacting themselves. Tania's no where, God damn it, no where."

"I'll think about it," Kate said. "I'll let you know my decision in a few days. Meanwhile, may I talk to Tania's husband? Will he see me?"

"I'll damn well make sure he'll see you," Fred Manson said. Kate could not but reflect that, chancy as the Chair's disposition clearly was, this disappearance had done nothing to improve it. Could Tania have simply decided to vanish for the sheer joy of ruining Fred Manson's life and temper? Or could the husband, however devoted he was reported to be, have also inspired such retribution?

One hour with Tom Finship proved that supposition as unsubstantial as all the others had been. He greeted Kate in the penthouse on Riverside Drive he had long shared with his vanished wife. They had bought it many years ago, for a now (given the state of New York City real estate) ridiculously low sum. As their penthouse had risen in value, they had always talked of selling it and buying a house in the country where their gardening joys might really have scope. But the moment had never arrived. The terraces on the penthouse were large, and while Kate Fansler could scarcely tell a lilac from a rhododendron, there was no question even to her ignorant eye that this was an extraordinary rooftop garden. "The house in the country never quite worked out," Tom said when they were once again seated on the terrace after the tour. Kate, looking over the Hudson River to New Jersey and sipping the ice tea with which Tom had served them, did not try to hide her scrutiny of Tania's husband from him. He was in that state of calm which follows upon terrible news, but also in the state where talk is necessary and all but ceaseless. Kate, glad to serve as an audience to one who would be helped simply by talking, also needed to learn all he could tell her, which was the story of their lives.

"We would have had to trade this"—his arm swept to indicate the whole terrace with its rich plant life—"for a small apartment and a house, and somehow the whole thing never fell into place. God knows we had great offers for this place, but when we looked at the small apartments we could by then afford we began to feel cramped, cabined, cribbed, and confined, as Hamlet said, before we had even tried it out. And with a house in the country, Tania would have been there only weekends and in the summer. So we just kept talking about it. Now, without her—" He did not complete the sentence.

"It was Macbeth," Kate said. "Hamlet talked about being bound in a nutshell. When did you retire?"

"Five years ago," Tom said. "I was a professor at City College, and I just couldn't take it any more, teaching remedial English and being mugged in the parking lot. A lot of us took early retirement when the system, in order to get rid of us, made it especially attractive. And it wasn't really the remedial English and the parking lot, it was just that I'd been at the same game too long. As you can see, I've even forgotten my Shakespeare—not that I'd taught him since open admissions."

"Have you enjoyed the retirement, until this came along?"

"Moderately. The days pass. I like working around the house. I have a few investments, and they need looking after. I've always wanted to write a novel, but having all day isn't particularly conducive to creation, or so I've found. Funny thing, though, I discovered I really liked cooking. Tania always said she had the oldest kitchen boy in town. We had people in a lot, for dinner, drinks out here. It was a good life. Regular. It doesn't make any sense."

"What do you mean by 'regular'?"

"Every day was just like every other. Well, not exactly, of course. The days Tania taught were different from the days when she didn't teach. We joked: if Tania's teaching Chekhov, it must be Tuesday. And then every afternoon, when she'd come back from the university—she taught in the morning and advised from one to three—or just when the hour came round, on the days she didn't teach, she'd take her walk. Down Riverside Drive, across Seventy-second Street to Broadway, down Broadway to Fifty-ninth, and across to Fifth

Avenue. Then she'd turn and come back, without the carrots."

"Carrots?"

"For the horses, the ones that pull the carriages through the park. For tourists, I suppose. Tania loved to offer them a carrot each, brightening their lives. It's funny how it began, really." Tom seemed lost in thought.

"How?" Kate urged him.

"She was crossing Fifty-ninth one day, she told me—going somewhere, not on her exercise walk—and a little girl got out of one of the carriages she was riding in with her family, to have her picture taken with the horse, and she tried to feed the horse a carrot, holding it upright, by its end. Of course, the horse took her hand with the carrot and the girl dropped it, screaming. To the rescue, Tania. She showed the girl how to hold her hand flat with the carrot on it, and calmed her down, although, Tania said, she couldn't convince the child to try again. That's what put the idea of carrots for the horses in Tania's mind. Also, it gave her a destination for her walk and made it possible for her to say she walked almost three miles every day—warding off osteoporosis, and other dangers of aging."

Tom fell into a sort of trance, staring out over the Hudson River. "I've been thinking," he finally said, "how we work so hard to avoid the dangers of old age, now that we live so long, and then, suddenly, we're gone."

"There's no real evidence she's 'gone,' " Kate said.

"I can't believe she wouldn't have let me know, if she was able to. Something terrible must have happened."

"You've been married a long time then," Kate said, not making it a question.

"We were married in the war. We both finished graduate school, and then the children were born. Tania taught all through those years; we needed the money. It was a busy life, but a good one. The children keep calling," he added, reminded of them. "I've gotten to dread the phone calls. 'No news, Pop?' And I always have to say, 'No news.' She can't just have disappeared into thin air," he concluded in an unconscious echo of Fred Manson.

"What have the police done?" Kate asked, more to have something to ask him than because she needed to be told. The police had put Tania on their Missing Persons computer, and had made inquiries—perfunctory, Kate felt sure. There had been no ransom notes, no signs at all. Either she was dead—though in that case where was the body?—or she had chosen to vanish. The police admitted that, in the case of aging wives, this was unlikely. Amnesia? Possibly. But the hospitals had received no one of that sort, nor had the shelters for the homeless. Weren't there a lot of homeless women on the streets? God knows there were, and one could hardly question all of them, though most of them were well enough known in their neighborhoods. Still, no one was likely to report a new bag lady. The police shrugged, officially and metaphorically. Call them when there was a body.

After a while, Kate ran out of questions and Tom fell into silence. She left him finally with sympathetic reassurances, but without much hope on either side.

Later that week, Kate called Fred Manson and told him that frankly she didn't think there was much she could do. Just for the hell of it, she had walked Tania's exercise route, but no inspiration followed. It was a rainy day, and there were not many horse carriages lined up—just a few across from the Plaza, the horses, under their blankets, looking sad, and the drivers, under their raincoats, looking sullen.

Fred Manson was not in the best of humors when Kate reached him, and he told her, far from tactfully, that she had been their last hope but not, as far as he was concerned, a very likely one. He'd been told she had a reputation as a detective, but in his view detectives had their being exclusively between the covers of books highly suspect as to quality. Only Dostoyevsky had been able to write intelligently of crime, and he showed you the murder taking place—no nonsense about clues. Kate wanted to say she vaguely remembered a detective in that novel, but resisted the impulse.

"Well," Manson said, "I'll have to hire a substitute for her in the fall if she isn't back by the end of this semester. I've got an assistant professor filling in her classes, but it's hardly fair to anyone. Do let me know," he added unkindly, "if you're inspired with any knowledge of her whereabouts. I certainly hope she returns, but I don't mind telling you, it's the uncertainty that's killing us all." And that was the end of the story as far as anyone knew.

Then, just about at the end of that semester, Tania called Fred Manson and said she was back, she'd just been away a while, and she'd be teaching and everything as usual in the fall semester. Naturally, Fred wanted to know where she'd been and how she was, but she wouldn't say much, just that she was back and that it was good to see Tom, who was glad to have her back, the children were also relieved, and they could all now forget the whole thing and enjoy their summer.

Except, Tania added, Fred ought to call Kate Fansler and thank her, and apologize for being such a prick (obviously Tania's language hadn't been changed by her absence), because it was due to Kate she was back. She was never, Tania announced, going to say another word about it, but she didn't think Fred ought to have sneered at Kate as a detective. Kate didn't identify with criminals, like the detective in Dostoyevsky and other deep types, but she was damn good and Fred might as well say so. Fred did write Kate a rather gracious letter, and that was that for a long while. It was only many years later, when Kate told me about Tania, that I learned the part of the story nobody else had ever been told.

Tania and Tom were both killed in a car crash years after Tania had retired, and it was when Kate heard that she finally told me the whole story. Kate doesn't often fall into a reminiscent, storytelling vein, but she did that day.

Kate said it was the most patient, foot-slogging work she'd ever done. I like this case because I think only Kate could have solved it. Policemen and tough-guy detectives don't bother with cases where they haven't got a body and a bellyful of hate in at least five suspects. That's what made this the perfect Fansler case. At least, pointing that out was how I got Kate to let me publish it.

Somehow, Kate kept finding herself across from the Plaza, studying the horse-drawn carriages. She seemed to have developed a new consciousness of the things; they stopped being a familiar background and moved into the foreground of her awareness. Many years before, she and Reed, when they were newly met, had hired a carriage and tried to imitate the proper romantic attitudes connected with them. They had ended up dissolved in laughter, at their own antics and the prattle of the driver, who took them for newlyweds and tourists, pointing out features of Central Park that Kate had known since birth. The ride had cost five dollars, which indicated how long ago that had been. The notices on the carriages Kate observed informed the romantic and unwary that the price was seventeen dollars for the first quarter hour. Despite these prices, business was good, to judge from the number of carriages lined up, especially on the weekends.

On a warm spring weekday afternoon Kate hired one. The driver was a young girl in a top hat, her blonde hair seeming to pour out below it to the middle of her back. Kate had approached the girl because she looked somehow easier than the male drivers to induce into conversation as opposed to barker talk. Her other attraction was that she had tacked onto the front of her carriage a neat placard announcing that she took American Express cards. The combination of the girl's attractiveness and Kate's lack of cash confirmed the matter.

"I'm not a tourist," Kate said, when they had turned off into the park at Sixth Avenue. "I really wanted to ask you about driving these things. It looks like every child's dream. Do most of the drivers like horses? Do they always drive the same horse?"

"Even tourists ask that," the girl said, smiling to make the words pleasant. "Some of us do, some of us don't, to both questions. Mostly we drive the same horse, but if we aren't going to be out, someone else takes over, on a weekend, say. I always try to drive this horse; her name, though you might never guess, is Nellie. She's one of the few mares; mostly they're geldings."

"Do any of you own your horses?"

"Not many any more. You writing a book or something?"

"Not even 'or something,' " Kate said. "I've just got interested."

"Why don't I give you the usual spiel without your having to ask the questions; would that help?" Kate laughed, sitting back, enjoying the slower pace and the sound of the hoofs on the road. The park was closed to cars in the afternoon, and the forsythia was out. Kate couldn't think why she hadn't done this before. Because, she guessed, one thought of it only as a couple or family thing, while it was (though she saw not a single other carriage with only one person in it) an ideal solitary experience. Kate asked for the "usual spiel."

"We all keep our horses in the same stable," the girl began. "The carriages, too. There's a good bit of turnover in drivers. As I said, we like horses—or if we don't, we pretend to. It would never do to be mean to a horse in the public eye, and we're always in the public eye. That last was not part of the usual spiel, as I'm sure you've guessed. There are rules regulating the treatment of the horses. On the hottest days in summer, they can't stay out too long, and they have to have water, and blankets in the winter. People worry a lot more about the horses than the drivers: I don't usually say that, either."

"There's a novel by Aldous Huxley," Kate said, "in which some animal lovers take an ill-treated horse away from the man who works it, and as a result the man starves to death together with his family. Nobody notices that."

"You a professor or something?"

"Do only professors read?" Kate asked.

"Nobody ever mentioned a book to me before—at least, not a book like that. In the summer when there are more carriages to go out, we get some guys from college as drivers. They don't last very long, but they've read a book. Probably some of the customers are readers, but they don't have books on their minds. You'd be surprised what goes on in these carriages sometimes, particularly at night—I mean, people make out anywhere. I like a little privacy myself, but it all goes with the territory, I guess. Anything else I can tell you? This trip's going to cost you already."

Kate agreed to return, and watched the driver pull out her

charge-card machine and then write out Kate's charges. Kate signed the slip, adding a generous tip. "Thanks a heap," the young woman said; "any time."

"Do many people feed the horses carrots?" Kate asked as an afterthought, pocketing her receipt.

"A lot. Occasional children, though mostly they don't know how, and old ladies who are pretty regular about it. People used to feed the horses sugar, which was bad for them, although they loved it, of course. But the new diet mania in America has helped horses. Most people don't seem to have lumps of sugar any more; it's more carrots now, much better for the horses."

Kate thanked her again. "It's been a pleasure meeting you," she said. "I may be back." And she was the next day, and the day after that.

Kate got into the way of coming almost every afternoon with carrots for the horses, and sometimes an apple. After a while, she began to distinguish between the horses and to recognize the drivers, who tolerated her and even greeted her, a not untypical female animal lover of the sort they found familiar. But this one distinguished herself by occasionally hiring a carriage and taking a ride—not often, but often enough to keep hopes and tolerance high. The regular carrot ladies never rode.

Kate, of course, could come only in the afternoon, and not every day. Unlike amateur detectives, whether the effete upperclass English variety or the tough American kind, Kate had a full-time job. I've never really understood what a professor does who teaches only four to six hours a week, though Kate tried to explain it to me once. There are committee meetings and office hours and the need to go on writing and publishing and presenting papers at conferences. That spring, though, Kate devoted a lot of time to horse-drawn carriages. She's an animal lover, like all the Fanslers—I sometimes think it's all she and I share with the rest of the family—and she became quite fond of the horses after a couple of weeks.

There was one driver she noticed, indeed everyone noticed, who worked almost every day, including weekends, and who stood out because he dressed up for the part. He looked exactly like a cabbie from a Sherlock Holmes movie. He wore a black suit, a white tie and shirt, and a top hat. You almost expected someone to get into his carriage, hit the roof (there wasn't any roof, of course) with his cane, and say: "Victoria Station, driver, and hurry."

Kate took a ride with him one day. This was not as easy as it sounds, because you couldn't just pick out the carriage and driver you wanted. They lined up in order, and you had to take the next one. Kate thought free enterprise would have been better demonstrated if the customers were allowed to choose their carriages; certainly the competition would have spruced up the carriages and done something for the drivers' appearance; most of them wore old pants and T-shirts, which is what made the elegant man so noticeable. He probably would have had all the customers if the customers had had the choice.

But one day, when Kate came and began her offer of carrots to the horses, the "Edwardian" driver, as she had come to think of him, was third in line. So she sauntered along, feeding and greeting the horses, and chatting with the drivers, until her man was first. Then she hired him.

His spiel turned out to be as unusual as his costume. He began by wishing her goodday and asking if she had any place she especially wanted to see. When Kate said no, just around the park, the driver asked if she would prefer that he talked or kept silent. "And if I keep silent, ma'am," the driver said with, Kate was amused to notice, just the hint of a cockney accent—one expected him to say "Right you are, Gov'ner," but of course he didn't—"I'll still be here to answer questions, if any."

"I'd rather hear what you have to say," Kate said.

"Righto, ma'am," he said, turning sideways in his seat so that he could talk to Kate and at the same time keep an eye on the road and the horse. "This is the carousel. Been here over seventy-five years; they give the horses a bit of paint every so often, and change the tunes. Fifty years ago they still had rings you caught as you went by, silver rings but one gold, and if you got the gold they gave you a free ride." The man seemed to embrace all the park as he spoke of it, as though it were his creation; certainly it was his special pride.

"How long have you been driving a carriage?" Kate asked.

"Oh, most of my life, ma'am, one way or another. I was driving in the park before they ever closed it to cars. I remember when people were married at the Plaza and they would have a horse-drawn carriage ready to start them on their honeymoon. There were fewer of us in those days, and a different type, ma'am, if you take my meaning. I sometimes try to imagine what New York was like when there were only horse-drawn vehicles about."

"It probably smelled of horse manure and not carbon monoxide," Kate said, sitting back and enjoying herself as the description of the passing park scene continued. She didn't interrupt with any more questions; she mused. Wherever Kate is, if she's into musing, she muses. I like to think of her riding around the park on that spring day.

In the end, Kate paid the driver with cash; he did not have a charge-card notice on his carriage and she had come equipped with enough cash. "I like the way you drive," Kate said. "Is there a time I can come when I'll be fairly certain of getting you?"

"This is a good day," he said. I think it was a Tuesday. "If you come about the same time you did today, we ought to connect. Sometimes business is brisker than other times, so you might miss me, or you might have to wait. The other drivers are all good chaps," he added.

"I'm sure they are," Kate said. "I like your top hat and your line of patter, and your spruced-up carriage. Maybe I'll try again."

And she did try again, a week later. The spring semester was coming to a close, and Kate had to all but walk out on a meeting to get to Central Park South in plenty of time. It was not a particularly fine day, and the Edwardian driver was fourth from the head of the line. Kate sat on a bench with the other drivers—those were the only benches on that block—and corrected term papers while she was waiting. To her astonishment, she looked up to see "her" driver pulling his horse out of the rank of waiting carriages and driving off.

Kate leapt into the carriage at the head of the line: "Follow that carriage!" she said to the driver.

"What? The horse-drawn one?"

"Yes. Hurry!"

"I can't follow him, lady. He's off back to the stables. I can't take no customers there."

"For a hundred dollars?"

"I might make an exception," he said, whipping up the horse. "But I want to see it."

Kate leaned forward and handed him three twenties. She'd really learned about cash and horse-drawn carriages. This was no moment for American Express, even if it had been the blonde young lady. "Here's sixty. You'll get the other forty when we're there."

But, as it happened, they soon caught up with Kate's Edwardian driver, who pulled over and acknowledged defeat, more with a gesture than anything. Cars started honking. Kate handed her driver the other forty, thanked him, got into the other carriage and said: "Back to the park, my good man."

The man had to go around the block to Sixth Avenue and head toward the park. Kate waited until they were through the traffic and back on the park road. Then, "Why did you take off like that?" she asked.

"It was the papers you were correcting, waiting for me. They rang a bell, somehow. Suddenly, I remembered having heard about you and knew who you were. They hired you, I guess."

"I wouldn't say 'hired'," Kate said. "I haven't promised anything. I can forget I ever rode in a carriage. I've forgotten less forgettable things."

"After all your trouble?"

"No trouble; a pleasure, in fact. And I remembered the gold rings. My brothers used to brag about knowing how to get them. They were already gone in my day. Is this the life you want really, from now on? And of course, there's Tom."

"What made you guess?"

"Lots of things. His quoting Macbeth mainly, though he thought it was Hamlet. Hamlet may really have been closer: 'I could be bounded in a nutshell, and count myself a king of infinite space, were it not that I have bad dreams.' Was that it, or was it Macbeth: 'cribbed, cabined, confined'?"

"You mean you understand?"

"Lord, yes. But most of us don't have a dream to step into; we don't have a job to go to."

"I got to know this old man who drove. Met him when I was feeding the horses. I've always loved horses, not race horses or riding horses or herding horses, but horses that pull carriages. He wanted to quit, and I offered him enough for his carriage and horse really to tempt him, if he could get them for me and the right to keep them where he did, to live where he did, right close to the stables. He said at first he couldn't manage it, but in the end he did. I was offering to exchange my escape for his and I knew it would work if I was patient."

"Is that his suit?"

"No. This outfit is all mine. He was a much smaller man, wizened and disillusioned about the carriages working the park these days."

"What about Tom? The worry it's been to him?"

"He's been worried, but I bet he's also felt alive; something to think about, to plan beyond. It's brought a change to his life, too; it was getting too predictable. As to the department—"

"I know," Kate said, "they can all pee up one rope. When will you decide about going back? Not that I want to rush you."

"Once more around the park; on me."

And so they rode around in silence. The evening was drawing in. "You mean I have a real choice?" the driver said, looking back at her, and when Kate nodded turned around and continued driving in silence. Until they were leaving the park:

"Mine has been such an orderly life," Tania said. "I married when my mother and everyone else thought I should. Not that it wasn't a good marriage. We had children at the right time; they were good children. I guess working was the only unusual thing I did, and of course I became a language teacher, which was okay for a woman. Somehow, except when I was very young, there wasn't time for a dream, for an adventure. Suddenly, this seemed the perfect thing. A carriage, a horse, an outfit."

"You weren't afraid of being recognized?"

"Not in this outfit. People see what they expect to see. And I've always had a deep voice and a flat chest. Very good legs, though," Tania added.

When they pulled up at the curb on Central Park South, Kate said: "I get off here. I understand more than you'll ever know about how you felt. You decide it the way you want. I shan't say a word to anyone. And I won't bother you with any more rides if you decide to stay with the carriages and horses. But if you decide to go back, just call your Chair, dear Fred Manson, and announce your return next semester. 'Never apologize, never explain.' A good Victorian piece of advice."

As you know, Tania decided to return. And from that day to this, no one ever knew where she'd been and no one ever guessed. They were all glad to see her back—Tom, and the students, and even her colleagues—so she found out she was loved. Maybe that made her return more rewarding.

OLD FRIENDS

by DOROTHY SALISBURY DAVIS

The two women had been friends since childhood, their mothers friends before them. Both were in their late twenties; neither had married. Amy intended not to, although she was beginning to lose some of the vehemence with which she declared that purpose. Virginia was still saying she was waiting for the right man to come along. She admitted herself to be an old-fashioned girl. One of the sadnesses in her life was that the men she liked most were already married. It made her furious when Amy would say, "Happily?"

"I suppose you think I should have an affair," Virginia said.

"Yes, as a matter of fact, it would be good for you."

"How do you know?"

"Well, let me put it this way," Amy would say, and the same conversation had occurred in some form or other a number of times, "it would be better than a bad marriage just for the sake of being married."

"According to you," Virginia would say, "there are no good marriages."

"Not many, and I don't know of a single one that came with a guarantee."

One might have thought that it was Amy who had grown up in the broken home. Her parents had only recently celebrated their thirty-fifth wedding anniversary. Whereas Virginia's mother had divorced her third husband, each of whom had left her better off financially than had his predecessor. She and Virginia were often taken for sisters. But so were Virginia and Amy. Or, to make Virginia's own distinction, she was always being taken for Amy's sister.

At one time they had worked for the same New York publishing house, Virginia as an assistant art director, Amy as an assistant to the senior editor. Amy's father, a retired executive of the firm, had arranged interviews for both girls after they finished college. The jobs, he insisted, they had got for themselves. Virginia stayed with hers. More than anything in the world, except possibly a husband who loved and respected her, she wanted her independence of her mother. Amy, to cap the interminable subject, once suggested that was why Virginia wanted a husband, to protect her from her mother.

"I am perfectly capable of protecting myself."

And that of course, Amy realized in time, was her friend's trouble. Nobody could do anything for her. She resented anyone's attempting it. Which made her yearning for a husband suspect: what Virginia really wanted, Amy decided, was a baby. This insight, as well as others just as profound if true, had slipped beyond Amy's conscious reckoning of her friend's character long before the weekend Amy reneged on the invitation to the country.

Sometimes months went by when they did not see each other. Amy, on inheriting an ancient cottage from an aunt, gave up her regular job for freelance writing, copy editing, and restoring the cottage. While not far from the city and not actually isolated, the cottage retained a rare privacy. It had settled deeper and deeper into the ground with the decades, and the mountain laurel that surrounded it was as snug as a shawl.

Knowing Virginia to be a Sunday painter, Amy thought of her whenever there was a change in nature. Such a change had come that week with the sudden November stripping of the leaves. The light took on a special quality and the long grass in the meadow quivered glossily golden in the sun and turned silver under the moon. She called Virginia on Thursday.

"Well, now, I would like to," Virginia said, mulling over the invitation aloud. "I half promised Allan—I don't know if I've told you about him, the architect?—I didn't actually commit myself. Thank you, Amy. I'd love to come."

Amy was on the point of saying she could bring Allan, the architect, and then it occurred to her that he might be an invention of Virginia's, part of that same old face-saving syndrome which, when they saw too much of one another, made their friendship dreary. She almost wished she had not called. However, they discussed the bus schedule and settled on a time for Virginia's arrival.

"If I miss that one, I'll take the next," Virginia said. There was always a little hitch to allow room for independence.

That very afternoon Amy received a call from Mike Trilling, one of the few men with whom she had ever been deeply in love. A newspaper correspondent, Mike had been sent overseas just when they had become very happy together. If he had asked it, she would have followed him, but he had not asked it, and she had been a long time getting over the separation. Except that she was not over it. She knew that the moment she heard his voice.

Her end of the conversation was filled with pauses.

Finally Mike said, "Are you still hung up on me?"

"What humility! Yes, damn you."

"You don't have to swear at me. I've got the same problem —once in love with Amy, here I am again. I'd come out for the weekend if you'd ask me."

"All right, you're invited."

"I'll rent a car and be there early tomorrow evening. We can have dinner at The Tavern. Is the food as good as it used to be?"

"I'll fix us something. It's not that good. You can bring the wine." She refrained from saying that he could take the bus, an hour's trip. There was no better way to put a man off than to try to save his money for him.

She postponed the decision on what to say to Virginia, and while she cleaned house she let her memory of the times she and Mike had been together run full flood. She washed her hair and dried it before the blaze in the fireplace. Mike loved to bury his face in her hair, to discover in it the faint fragrance of wood smoke; he loved to run his fingers through it on the pillow and to give it a not altogether gentle tug, pulling her face to his.

She could not tell Ginny that Mike was the reason she was asking her to postpone until the following weekend. It would be unkind. Anyone else might understand, but Ginny would understand even more than was intended: she would re-examine the whole of her life in terms of that rejection. Amy did not call her until morning.

"Ginny, I've had the most tremendous idea for a story. I was up half the night thinking about it, afraid to lose it, or that it wouldn't be any good in the morning. But it's a good one and I want to dash it off fresh. Will you come next week instead? I know you understand . . ." She made herself stop. She was saying too much.

"Of course," Virginia said, and her voice had that dead air of self-abnegation. "I envy you."

"Bless you for understanding," Amy said. "The same time next weekend. I'll be watching for you."

Once off the phone she gave herself up to the pleasure of anticipation. Almost a year had passed since she and Mike were last together. She had had a couple of brief encounters since, but no one had taken his place. She had worked. She had done a lot more work with Mike away than when he was around. They had not corresponded. He had called her on New Year's Eve. Collect, because he was at a friend's house and the British would not accept his credit-card charge. She had not asked him about the friend. She did not propose to ask any questions now.

At first it seemed like old times, their sitting before the fire with martinis, Mike on the floor at her feet, his head resting on his arm where it lay across her knees. His hair had begun to thin on the very top of his head. She put her finger to the spot, a cold finger, for she had just put down her glass.

Mike got up and sat in the chair opposite hers, brushing back his hair, something almost tender in the way he stroked the spot.

"I'm wicked, aren't I?" she said, carrying off as best she could what she knew to have been a mistake.

"Tell me about that," he said, purposely obtuse.

"Naughty, I mean."

"Oh, nuts. With the British, every other word is 'naughty.' Aren't I the naughty one?" He mimicked someone's accent. "It's such a faggoty word."

"I guess it is," Amy said.

He fidgeted a moment, as though trying to get comfortable in the chair, then got up and gave one of the logs a kick. "It's not easy—getting reacquainted when so much has happened in between."

"Oh?" In spite of herself.

He looked around at her. "I've been working bloody hard. Five months in Cyprus."

"I know."

"Does nobody in America read history?"

"I suspect the trouble is that nobody listens to those who read history."

"Did you follow my dispatches?"

"Every word, my darling."

Things went a little better. He looked at his glass. "I can't drink martinis like I used to. What kind of vermouth did you use?"

The phone rang and Amy, on her way to answer it, said, "Try putting in more gin."

It was Virginia, of all people. "I won't disturb you except for a minute."

"It's all right. I'm taking a break." She was afraid Mike might put on a record.

"I want to ask a favor of you, Amy. I got myself into a predicament. When Allan called a while ago, I decided I didn't want to talk to him, so I said I was on my way to spend the weekend with you. I don't think he'll call, but in case he does, would you tell him I've gone on a long walk or something like that?"

Amy drew a deep breath and tried to think of something to say that would not expose the extent of her exasperation. The most natural thing in the world would have been: Ginny, the reason I asked you not to come—

"I don't think he will call."

"Okay, Ginny. I'll tell him."

"Get his number and say I'll call him back."

"I'll tell him that," Amy said. It was all a fantasy, and in some way or other Virginia thought she was getting even. If there was an Allan and if these little exchanges did occur, she would then have to call Virginia back and tell her that Allan had telephoned her.

"Was that Virginia?" Mike said.

"Yes."

"Hasn't she hooked herself a man yet?"

"You damn smug—" Amy exploded, possibly because she was annoyed with both Virginia and him. But Virginia, being the more vulnerable and absent, got such loyal defense in the argument that ensued, she would have been stunned. Indeed, it might have changed her whole picture of herself.

Mike and Amy did reach a rapprochement. After all, it was his remembering Amy's complaints about her friend in the old days that had provoked his comment: she should blame herself, not him. After the second martini they were laughing and talking about old intimacies, and how they had used to put the third martini on ice for afterward. Such good memories and the kisses which, if they weren't the same, were better than most, sufficed to get them into the bedroom. There, alas, nothing went the same as it had used to.

"Damn it," Mike kept saying, "this never happens to me."

"It's all right," Amy said over and over again, although well aware he had used the present tense.

Later, watching him stoop to see himself in her dressing-table mirror while he knotted his tie, she said, "Bed isn't everything."

"That's right."

"But it's a lot," she said and threw off the blankets.

By the time she finished in the bathroom, he had gone back to the living room where he stood before the fire and stared into it. A fresh log was catching on, the flames like little tongues darting up the sides. He had not brought the martini pitcher from the kitchen.

"You can't go home again," she said.

"I guess not." He could at least have said that it was fun

trying. But what he said was, "Amy, let's not spoil a beautiful memory."

"Oh, boy. I don't believe you said it. Not Mike Trilling."

"All right. 'You can't go home again' wasn't exactly original either. We aren't going to make it, Amy, so why don't I just take off before we start bickering again? No recriminations, no goodbyes, no tears."

Her throat tight as a corked bottle, she went up the stairs and got his coat and overnight bag.

On the porch they did not even shake hands—a turn and a quickly averted glance lest their eyes get caught, and a little wave before he opened the car door. When he was gone, she remembered the wine. It was as well she had forgotten it. A "thank you" for anything would have humiliated them both.

Returning to the house she felt as sober as the moon and as lonely. There was a whispery sound to the fire, and her aunt's Seth Thomas floor clock ticked with the slow heavy rhythm of a tired heart. Most things break: the phrase from somewhere she could not remember kept running through her mind. The old clock rasped and struck once. Hard though it was to believe, the hour was only half-past eight.

She called Virginia.

Her friend took her time picking up the phone. "I wasn't going to answer. I thought it might be Allan. Did he call me there?"

"Not so far, dear. Ginny, you could make the nine-thirty bus and come on out. The story isn't ready yet. I always start too soon. I'm botching it terribly."

"Thank you, but I don't think I will, Amy. I want to stay home by myself now where I can think things out comfortably. I'm a mess, but since I know it, I ought to be able to do something about it."

"You sound awfully down. Do come and see me."

"Actually, I'm up. Have a nice weekend, Amy."

Have a nice weekend: that was the *coup de grace*. Amy went to the kitchen and got out the martini jug. She closed the refrigerator door on an eight-dollar steak. The cat, her paws tucked out of sight where she sat on the table, opened her eyes and then closed them again at once.

Amy returned to the living room by way of the dining-room door. As she entered, she discovered a man also coming into the room, he by the door to the vestibule. She had not locked up after Mike's departure.

"Hello. I did knock," he said, "but not very loudly. I thought I'd surprise you."

"You have, and now that I'm surprised, get the hell out of here before I call my husband."

"Funny. Ginny didn't tell me about him. In fact, she said you didn't want one."

"You're Allan."

He had stopped. They both had, in their tracks, on seeing one another. They now moved tentatively forward. He was handsome in an odd way: his quick smile and his eyes did not seem to go together. The eyes, she would have sworn, took in everything in the room while not seeming to look directly at anything, even at her when they came face to face.

"Yes, I'm Allan. So Ginny's told you about me? I'm surprised, though come to think of it, I shouldn't be. She's told me a lot about you, too. Where is she?"

Damn Ginny. "She's gone for a walk." She regretted at once having said that. Now it was reasonable for him to expect to wait for her return. "Don't you think, Mr.—" She stopped and waited.

"Just Allan," he said, which she did not like either, the familiarity of it. No. The anonymity: it was more like that.

"Mr. Allan, don't you think if Ginny wanted to see you, she would have arranged it?"

"It takes two to make an arrangement, Amy." His eyes, not really on hers anyway, slipped away to the glass where Mike had left it. Her glass was on the side table near which she stood, the martini pitcher in her hand. He might well have arrived in time to have seen Mike leave.

He then said, "Should I confess something to you, Miss Amy—I guess that's what you'd like me to call you, but it certainly rings strange against the picture Ginny gave me of you—let me tell you the reason I crashed this party. I wanted to see the cottage, and I wasn't sure I'd ever get an invitation, leaving it to Ginny. It's pre-Revolutionary, isn't it?"

"Yes."

"Don't you need an architect?"

That disarmed her—he was a man with humor at least. "Will you have a drink?" She swirled the contents of the pitcher. "A martini?"

"Thank you."

"I'll get a glass."

A few steps took him to the table where Mike's glass sat. "If this was Ginny's glass, I don't mind using it."

No more lies. She hardly knew now which were hers and which were Ginny's. "It wasn't Ginny's glass," she said.

He brought it to her anyway. "Whosever it was, it won't poison me."

All the same, those eyes that just missed hers saw everything that passed through her mind. She wanted to escape them, however briefly, in the time it would take to get a glass from the other room. "That's ridiculous," she said. "Sit down, Allan. That chair is better for your long legs than this one."

His movements were such that she thought him about to take the far chair as she had suggested, but she had no more than stepped into the dining room than he was behind her.

"What a marvelous old room!"

Of all six rooms this was the plainest, with nothing to recommend it except the view of the garden and that was not available at night. One end of it had been chopped off in the nineteen-twenties to provide space for a bathroom. She took a glass from the cupboard.

"May I see the kitchen?" he asked, throwing her a quick, persuasive smile.

"Why not?" This time she stepped aside and let him go on by himself. The kitchen was straight ahead, not to be missed. He had an athlete's build as well as one's lightness of step, she observed as he passed her.

"Puss, puss, puss," he said, seeing the cat. She came wide-awake, stood up, and preened herself for him.

Amy kept trying to tell herself that it was she who was behaving oddly, letting her imagination run wild. She tried to think what he and Ginny would be like together. They were similar in a way she could not put her finger on. Then she had it: Ginny never seemed quite able to hit the nail on the head. God knows, he was direct enough, but his eyes slipped past what he was presumably looking at.

Well, he had made it to the kitchen and if there was something there he wanted—a knife or a hammer—there was no preventing his getting it. She turned into the vestibule, that entrance to it opposite the bathroom, with the purpose of making sure the shotgun was in its place alongside the porch door, more or less concealed by her old Burberry coat and the umbrella stand. She could not see it where she stood, but that did not mean it was not there. For just an instant she thought of making a dash to the front door.

"Amy?"

They very nearly collided, his coming in as she turned back.

"Is the kitchen fireplace a replica of the old one?"

"Probably."

"Afterwards I'll show you where I think the old one was." He caught her hand as though he were an old friend and led her back to the living room. When she tried to remove her hand he gave it a little squeeze before letting go.

She poured the drinks shakily. "I should have got more ice."

"Are you afraid of me?"

"Certainly not," she said.

"I'm harmless enough. You'd have to know that for a fact from Ginny's having anything to do with me."

She laughed, thinking how obviously so that was. If she knew Ginny. Sometimes she felt that she knew Ginny so well she could not possibly know her at all. Maybe there were two Ginnies. "Cheers."

The drink was strong enough, but it was going tepid.

"Would you allow me to get more ice and give these another stir?" he asked.

"I would allow it." She poked up the embers under the half-burned log. The sparks exploded and vanished. Ginny ought to have come even if she didn't believe the story about the story. It was funny how sure she had been that Allan was imaginary. Nor could she remember anything Ginny had ever told her about him. Had she told her anything? Or had Amy simply turned it off, doubting that there was a real live Allan?

He returned with the pitcher and the glasses, having taken them also to the kitchen. They now were white with frost. He poured the drinks, touched her glass with his, and said, "What else would you allow?"

Harmless? She said, trying to strike a pose of propriety without overdoing it: "I'd allow as how—I wouldn't allow much."

He shrugged. "No offense."

"None taken."

He started to shuffle across to the chair she had appointed his, then turned back. "What's much?" Having again amused her, he bent down and kissed her as she was reasonably sure he had never kissed Ginny. "Perfectly harmless," he said and trotted over to the chair while neatly balancing the glass so that he did not spill a drop. "Does she often take long walks at this time of night?"

"As a matter of fact she does."

"And if I'm not mistaken, we're at the full moon." He helped make the lie more credible. Knowingly? "Has Ginny talked about me?"

"Well now," Amy said, avoiding a direct answer, "I almost suggested that she bring you out for the weekend."

"How intuitive of me then to be here."

"I suppose Ginny has given you a complete dossier on me?"

"We do talk a lot," he said in a sly, wistful, almost hopeless way that again amused her. "Have you anything to suggest I do about it?"

She knew exactly what he meant. "A marriage proposal?"

"That's a bit drastic."

"It sounds archaic when you set it off and listen to it by itself—a marriage proposal."

"Or the title to a poem by Amy Lowell," he said. "You weren't by any chance named after her?"

"Good God, no."

"She did like a good cigar, didn't she?" he said, deadpan.

Amy sipped her drink and gave a fleeting thought to Mike,

to the steak in the refrigerator, to the Haut Brion '61. And to the rumpled bed in the room back of the fireplace.

He put his glass on the table and got up with a sudden show of exuberance. "Shall I bring in more wood? I saw the pile of it outside."

"Not yet." Amy put the one log left in the basket onto the fire. While she swept in the bits of bark and ash, he came and stood beside her, bent, studying the fire, but stealing glimpses of her face. He touched his fingers lightly to a wisp of hair that had escaped one of the braids she wore in a circle round her head. "Your hair must be very long and beautiful."

"I've been told so."

"Ginny said it was."

"I wasn't thinking of Ginny."

"I wasn't either. Except in the way you hang onto somebody in the dark."

When they had both straightened up, he waited for her to face him, and then he lifted her chin, touching it only with the backs of his fingers as though to take hold of it might seem too bold. He kissed her. It was a long kiss which, nonetheless, didn't seem to be going anywhere until she herself thrust meaning into it. She had not intended to, but then the situation was not one open to precise calculations. He tasted of licorice as well as gin.

He drew back and looked at her. At that proximity his eyes did not seem to have the disconcerting vagary. He was, despite these little overtures, agonizingly shy: the realization came in a flash. Someone had prescribed—possibly a psychiatrist—certain boldnesses by which he might overcome the affliction. *Miss* Amy: that was closer to his true self.

He said, averting his eyes once more, "Ginny said we'd like one another . . . even though you don't like men."

"What?"

"She thinks you don't care much for men."

"What kind of woman does she think I am then? The kind who gets paid?"

Color rushed to his face. He backed off and turned, starting back to his chair in that shuffling way—a clown's way, really, the "don't look at me but at what I'm doing" routine which reinforced her belief in his shyness.

"I don't want another drink," she said, "but if you do, help yourself. I say what's on my mind, Allan. People who know me get used to it. By the sound of things, Ginny speaks hers too on occasion. I'd never got that picture of her."

"I shouldn't have blabbed that."

"No, you shouldn't." She started from the room, thinking: God save me from middle-aged adolescents.

"Where are you going?"

"To the bathroom for now. Then I'll decide where else."

She had not reached the door when he caught her from behind and lifted her from her feet, holding her close against him, her arms pinned to her sides. He kissed the back of her neck and then with his teeth he removed, one by one, her plastic hairpins and let them drop to the floor. "Please don't be so fierce," he said, his mouth at her ear. She felt the dart of his tongue there, but so tentative, as though he were following a book of instructions.

"Put me down. Your belt buckle's hurting me."

Her feet on the floor, she faced him. "I don't have to be fierce at all," she said and loosened the braids, after which she shook out that abundance of rich brown hair.

He ran his tongue round his lips. "It's just too bad that Ginny's going to be walking in."

"She's not."

"She's not?" he repeated. Something changed in his face, which was certainly natural with that bit of news. "I don't believe you," he said, the smile coming and going.

She motioned to him with one finger as much as to say, wait, and going to the phone she dialed Virginia's number. With each ring Amy felt less sure of herself, less sure of Ginny. Then, after the fourth ring, came the gentle slow-voiced, "Hello."

Amy held the phone out toward Allan. He simply stared, his head slightly to the side. It could not have been more than a second, but it did seem longer before Ginny repeated more clearly, "Hello?"

He was about to take the phone. Amy broke the connection, pressing her finger on the signal, then returning the phone to its cradle.

"I don't get it," he said.

"It was a change of plan. That's all."

"And not anything to do with me?"

"My dear man, I wasn't even sure you were real."

"Maybe I'm not," he said, and smiled tentatively. It seemed flirtatious.

Amy threw her head back. "There's one way to find out."

He gave a funny little shudder, as though a chill had run through him. Or better, something interestingly erotic. He wet a finger and held it up as to the wind. Unerringly he then pointed to the closed door of the bedroom back of the fireplace. He motioned her to move on ahead of him. Had he looked in through, say, a part of the drapes at her and Mike? Or had Virginia told him that Amy slept downstairs? There did not seem to be much Ginny had not told him. With interpretations.

"Don't turn on the lights," he said.

Amy was not surprised. "We can always turn them off again."

"No." And then: "I'm able to see you in the dark."

A good trick. She said nothing. It was beginning to irritate her that Ginny had said she did not like men. Liking sex and liking men deserved a distinction, true. But she did not think it one Ginny was likely to make. And she had loved Mike. She had. Now it was over, ended. Nothing was beginning; nothing was about to be born. Except that you couldn't really tell. That was what was so marvelous about an encounter such as this: you couldn't really tell.

She bent down to remove her slippers. She felt his hand running lightly over her bare shoulder, sweeping the hair before it. A jolting pain struck at the base of her skull. Then came nothingness.

She awoke to the sound of voices and with a headache worse than any she had ever suffered. A woman's voice said that she was coming to. Like hell, she wanted to say; not if she could help it, not with all this pain. There was other pain besides that of her head, and with the awareness of it she began to realize what had happened. She tried to put her hand between her thighs. Someone gently pulled it away.

"Amy?"

She opened her eyes to the familiar ceiling beam with its ancient knot, the eye of the house. She turned her head far enough to see Virginia's round and worried face. "What are you doing here?"

A woman in a white uniform hovered alongside Ginny. She was filling a hypodermic needle from a medicine bottle. When Ginny glanced up at her, she moved away.

"On the phone," Ginny said, "I couldn't hear anything except the clock, but I'd know its tick anywhere. Remember when we were kids: 'take a *bath,* take a bath, take a *bath,* take a bath . . .' I decided I'd better catch the next bus out."

Amy gave her hand a weak squeeze. At the door of the room were two uniformed policemen, one of whom she thought she remembered having once talked out of giving her a speeding ticket. "How did *they* get in on the act?"

"I called the ambulance," Ginny said, and leaning close, she murmured, "You were"—she couldn't bring herself to say the exact word—"molested."

"I guess," Amy said.

One of the policemen said, "When you're strong enough we need the full story, miss. Did you recognize the intruder?"

The intruder. In a way he was, of course. She took a long time in answering. "Is there any way I can be sure he'll get psychiatric attention?"

The cops exchanged glances. "The first thing is to identify him so we can bring him in."

"And then I have to swear out a complaint against him?"

"If you don't, ma'am, some other woman may not get the chance to do it."

"To some extent it was my own fault," she said, not much above a whisper.

The cop made a noise of assent. Neither he nor his partner seemed surprised. "All the same, we better get him in and let the shrinks decide what happens to him. Okay?"

She thought of telling them of the point at which she had

been knocked out and decided against it for the time being. "Okay," she said.

"Can you give us a description? Race, age, height, color of his eyes—"

"Ginny, I'm sorry. It was your friend Allan."

"Oh."

It was a little cry, scarcely more than a whimper.

"Would you give them his name and address? You won't have to do anything else."

"But, Amy, I can't. I mean, actually I've never seen Allan. He calls me and we just talk on the telephone."

A CASE FOR CLARA CATES

by CAROLYN JENSEN WATTS

It ain't that I'm particular because I ain't, but when that rental agent showed us the house and the main bedroom had that dark maroon pile carpet with that orange and brown flowered wallpaper, I about gagged.

I tried to point it out to Cloyd, but he wasn't seeing nothin' except the workshop downstairs and the one-and-a-half-car heated garage. I knew it wasn't any good talkin' to him at all. I'd seen that look in his eyes twice before. Once when we bought this really classy lookin' lemon instead of the station wagon I wanted, and once at Howard's Pizza Shop and Bookstore when I was there with Jimmy Thompson and Cloyd worked there. He kept comin' over to our table to fill our glasses and givin' me that look, and when Mr. Howard would glance over, he'd busy himself near us straightening up the comic books and wiping the mozzarella off the magazines.

Mr. Lane, the agent, had left us alone in the basement to talk things over, and Cloyd was runnin' his hand over the workbench like it was Dresden china.

"This here's where the vise was," he said, showing me some ugly dents. "Looks to me like part of this house has been here since the 1800s, but I think most of it has been renovated, and look here—" he pointed up "—all oak floors, Clara!"

"And do you intend to sleep down here, Cloyd? Have you seen the bedroom?"

He looked at me like I was talking about some faraway island.

"The *bedroom,* Cloyd! You know, upstairs? You ain't just renting a basement and garage, you know."

He plodded up the steps behind me and really saw that bedroom for the first time.

"Oak door frame. That wallpaper *is* unusual."

"Unusual? It's disgusting! You think Mr. Lane would let us repaper?"

Cloyd considered. We are what some people would call thrifty. Hate to throw away stuff and hate to pay good money to replace things just because we're tired of them. So this presented a problem because there wasn't anything whatever wrong with that wallpaper except being ugly as sin and mixing with that maroon carpet like tuna fish on strawberry ice cream. It was nearly new and had that vinyl coating.

"You know what I think?" Cloyd said. "I think whoever done this just bought what he could find on sale."

I thought whoever done it ought to be hung.

But the rest of the house, I had to admit, was very nice. The kitchen was big with plenty of cupboards, and as it had almost an acre of land with some woods and as I didn't want to have Cloyd end up an embittered old man in some nursing home moaning about oak floors and heated garages, we took it.

But from the beginning it was just like what happened with Granny Cates's kitchen floor.

See, they'd bought these chairs at an auction over thirty years ago and one of them was missing a cushion piece on one leg so that every time you scooted up to the table you scratched the floor and sometimes that one leg would stick and the chair would buck. Granny worried Grampa about it from day one, but he didn't do nothin' and pretty soon the linoleum was scratched and gouged every which way. Wasn't until it bucked him one day and he broke his arm that it got fixed—and the floor replaced. Every time after that when they'd have words, she would recall that chair, and when

Cloyd was growing up, she told him that story many times to teach him about fixing things right away. Maybe that's partly why he became an aircraft mechanic.

(By the time I was a member of the family, I had heard that story at least twenty times. I can't imagine how Grampa has suffered all these years.)

Yet I couldn't seem to help it when it came to that wallpaper. From the first night it bothered me and I bothered Cloyd.

"Clara, can't you be still? I have to be at work in four hours!"

I tried—really did—but even in the dark that wallpaper was *there,* and with Molly and Susie in the attic room upstairs and little Roy in the small bedroom down the hall, I had to put my desk in there and writing my children's stories came to a standstill. Seemed to me that wallpaper was more suited to Stephen King than Clara Cates.

Cloyd told me I was obsessed and I said tell me something I didn't know but if I could do anything about it it wouldn't be an obsession, would it?

Some nights I crawled in bed with Molly and Susie, but they complained my feet were cold and I took all the covers and snored. Other nights I slept on the couch and watched Perry Mason reruns.

Cloyd finally got tired of my midnight wanderings, and when we got our income tax check, he promised to call Mr. Lane and ask if we could repaper. I found a nice design with tiny leaves and rosebuds that very day.

I couldn't believe it when he come home that night. Grampa and Granny Cates was there for supper and Cloyd came through that door stomping his feet like it was December instead of the middle of May.

"That stupid Lane! He won't let us repaper!"

I felt my world slipping out from underneath me and sat down. "Did you tell him we'd buy the paper?"

Cloyd nodded.

"And do the work?"

Nod, nod, nod.

"Well, why not?!"

"He says it's Farley Jessup—the banker. He owns this place and wants it left as it is."

"That one's a snake," Grampa declared. "I wouldn't trust him with nothin'."

"I like it," said Granny.

I stared at her. She always did seem a bit crazy.

"It's just like him," Grampa continued. "Gouge the little guy till there's nothin' left."

"But, Grampa," Cloyd pointed out, "this ain't costin' him nothin'! We was gonna do the work and buy the paper!" He snorted. "See if I'm available next time his Cherokee won't start on a Sunday afternoon."

"Cloyd," I pleaded, "are you *sure* Mr. Lane understood everything you said?"

His nostrils flared and I about ducked under the table.

"No, Clara, I ain't sure!" he thundered. "Maybe I was speakin' Chinese! Maybe *you* should call him! If you wasn't so paranoid about that stupid room, wouldn't no one have to call him!" He stomped down to the basement.

Cloyd and I never fight except maybe about money once in a while and the time Molly wanted to join the Boys' Brigade at church. So I was really embarrassed and I think Grampa was, too. Little Roy giggled and clapped his hands and pounded his head on the highchair tray, and Granny just made a clucking noise and started leafing through a newspaper.

I stood up and put the teakettle on. From the basement it sounded like Cloyd was erecting the Eiffel Tower. Rivet gun. I flinched.

Grampa cleared his throat. "Yeah, that Jessup is so crooked he could hide behind a corkscrew. I remember when he was just a smart-mouth kid. Ran off with Carl Jenks's girlfriend and came back in the middle of the Depression. Had a fancy car and money to burn. Said he struck it rich in Mexico or somethin'. Anyway, he bought up all these farms and homes dirt cheap. Just turned people out. Lorded it over everybody like he was king."

"Dirty money, if you ask me," Granny declared. She brightened. "Say, wasn't his wife living here when she died? No one even knew that she'd left him, and then she turns up dead."

"That's right!" Grampa nodded. "Then he turns around and marries some thirty-year-old chippie."

"His wife barely in her grave, too." Granny clucked. "She was in a wheelchair—had that disease, what's it called? Anyway, the one where . . ." Granny went on to describe in great detail some horrible disease that would put you off your food right now. Grampa left the room.

"It still don't make any sense," I mumbled when she was through. "Why would Farley Jessup care if we repapered?"

"Looks new," said Granny. "I bet Mrs. Jessup done it before she died."

"It's probably what killed her," I said, and got up to call the girls for supper.

Cloyd ate in a glowering silence, and I was so flustered I went around the table cutting the kids' spaghetti and cut Granny's, too.

"Clarence!" Granny called to the living room. "You best eat!"

"I tole you I ain't hungry!"

Granny clucked. "Stubborn, that's what he is. Just like when we bought these chairs . . ."

Cloyd and I stared at our plates and slipped into a welcome trance.

It was eleven o'clock that night and Cloyd was still downstairs pounding away. I had tried to sit in the kitchen and work on one of my children's stories, but my heart wasn't in it and the page before me had more doodles than words.

Cloyd had been the one to suggest I write down some of the stories I told the kids and I sold two of them the first year, which was enough to make me addicted to writing like he was to machinery and wood. But when things wasn't right between us, nothin' worked.

I went to check on the kids and found they was just where they was supposed to be and decided I didn't want to fight.

So I went into our bedroom and faced the wall. I'd read all about positive thinking and negative self-talk and decided to try it out.

"You *are* pretty paper," I whispered fiercely. "You are *pretty* paper. I *will* get used to you!"

That paper just grinned in droopy, gaudy flowers of orange and brown and I tasted my spaghetti again and thought how it looked like a shirt from *Hawaii Five-O.*

I went down to the basement then and sat on a cot hugging my knees and watching Cloyd work. We both had already said "hi," like you do in the hall at high school between classes. Cloyd had repaired Susie's wagon, and on the floor was a sheet of metal with rivets in it for no reason at all unless you count getting mad. Now he was planing a slat of wood for a rocker he was making for little Roy for his second birthday. I like to watch him work with wood the best. There's something about sawdust mixing with those little curly-Q things getting stuck in his beard that really gets to me if you understand my meaning. Before long we was both casting glances and knowing looks and half-smiles, and Ellie Hilda had her beginnings on that cot.

In October, Cloyd got a pay raise, which, if you know anything about it, is nearly unheard of in general aviation. But things was looking pretty good at the flying service and the raise was pretty good, too, so we decided to try and buy the house and went to call on Farley Jessup ourselves.

He was a tall, good-looking man with thin sandy hair and about in his mid-seventies. He shook hands a lot, but told us the house wasn't for sale.

"I tell you, Cloyd, my wife Ethel dearly loved that house, and I'm just not ready to let it go. I tell you what, though. I have a house on 314 that I'll let you have for thirty thousand."

That night we went to see that house and there discovered why Mr. Jessup was one of the richest men in town.

In December, Cloyd asked him again if he'd let us repaper, thinkin' to give me a surprise Christmas present. Mr. Jessup got a little angry that time and hinted he might have to ask us to leave as he was thinkin' of tearing the place down. (Which, of course, didn't make no sense at all if he was emotionally attached to it.)

Cloyd decided he was senile, but I thought even then that there was somethin' peculiar about it all.

It was when I was nearin' my due date in February that I made my discovery that people still talk about today.

I don't know about you, but by the beginning of February I am so tired of dull gray days and dirty hard snow I could scream. (I sincerely believe that if we'd all just hibernate in February the world would be a better place.)

The only thing worse than February is being pregnant in February. I don't care what the libbers say. There is a definite difference between a man and a woman emotionally, especially when that woman is pregnant. Maybe none of them never carried four children and every one nearly a month late, or maybe I am high-strung, but toward the end of a pregnancy I begin to get a little more than touchy. I am not always rational, and anyone who comes around best not be, either. I don't mean to say I'm not a good wife and mother and I don't go around and stick pickles in the sock drawer or think I'm Shana of the Jungle or run for Congress, but I am not always myself.

It was on one of them dull cold days when I was big as a buffalo and twice as mean that that wallpaper came down.

Little Roy's Sunday School teacher once told me she thought he was a progressive child with a lot of curiosity. Cloyd says that means he entered the "terrible twos" at one and a half and was still going strong. Little Roy has been to the emergency room three times. Twice for stitches and once for sticking a marble up his nose. (I suppose if you asked anyone who knew him what little Roy was to be when he grew up, they'd say a rock star or a demolition expert.)

That day, all I did was to leave Susie's poster paints on the bed in our room and let little Roy's nature take its course. I watched him wander in there with Boo, his Ohio State stuffed football player, under his arm, and waited fifteen minutes.

Five would have been enough. Besides the walls, he painted the bed and dresser and desk and himself. I was so proud!

I happened to have the materials to remove the wallpaper

on hand, and all that day little Roy and I slopped the paper wet and scraped and giggled. I kept singing about Joshua and the walls that came tumblin' down, and hoped in my heart that Mr. Jessup wouldn't hit a pregnant woman. Roy acted like this was more fun than life could give him.

By three o'clock everything but the closet had been done. I put all the clothes out in the living room, feeling a little guilty about how messy the rest of the house looked, but just a little.

The closet was strange—it was papered just halfway up, like they'd run out or something. It seemed kinda odd to wallpaper a closet at all, but that paper in an enclosed place was truly disgusting. I got it done quick as I could and looked around, satisfied. Every bit of the paper was now garbage. Then I saw it. In the front bottom corner of the closet there was a ragged shred of orange and brown still huggin' that wall. I took the metal scraper and attacked it.

Suddenly there was a creak and the back wall begun to move and I felt dizzy, like you do when you're in a parked car daydreaming and the car beside you starts to back up and you jump to slam on the brake and feel the fool. I grabbed little Roy and jumped back to the bed.

"Wadder?" little Roy pointed.

"Ladder," I nodded.

The whole back wall of the closet had moved over, and there was a ladder hanging in the space.

"Don't this beat all," I stared.

"Wadder, whee!" yelled little Roy and threw Boo down the hole. He looked at me and pointed. "Boo bye-bye," he declared.

I grabbed him up in my arms and made for the phone. Cloyd was out test flying the 210, and I left a message for him to call me right away. There was no answer at Granny and Grampa's and Cloyd's parents were still in Florida (they travel all the time—have a bumper sticker on their trailer that says they're traveling on their kids' inheritance. I don't think that's funny in February, do you?) I waited for about ten minutes, and when I tried the phone again, Mrs. Gaborski was on it and I knew it'd be a long time 'fore the line was open.

So I got a box of animal crackers and set Roy in his crib with them.

"Eh, Boo?" he asked.

"We'll get Boo, honey. You stay, okay?"

"Eh, BOO!" he demanded.

I knelt beside that hole and could see a table with an oil-cloth top, a braided rug, and some chairs. Boo was on the table next to a kerosene lamp. I wished I wasn't so far along because I could've seen a whole lot more laying on my stomach. I checked the front corner then with the flashlight and could see a small white button flush with the wall. I pushed it and the wall closed. I pushed it again and the wall opened.

Roy was laying on his tummy in the crib with his thumb in his mouth and his little butt sticking up in the air. He was hugging Boo's backup, a stuffed frog, and his eyes had that glazed expression like he was about to go to sleep.

I tiptoed down the hall and checked the phone again and wished Mrs. Gaborski had inoperable laryngitis.

When I went back to the closet, I just happened to have a book of matches with me.

There are times I do things that, even as I'm doing them, I know I shouldn't be. This was one of those times.

The ladder was sturdy. Cloyd had made the comment that whoever built this house liked things sturdy and, judging by the wiring and woodwork, had been a craftsman. The air was cold but dry, and as I lit the kerosene lamp, all I could think about was Jacob in the Bible except his ladder went up.

All along the wall across from me there was oak barrels, about twelve of them. There was a sink with a pump, a pot-belly stove, and cupboards, and over to my right a beautiful rolltop desk made of oak. On the wall was a calendar. March, 1932, with a pretty girl and a bottle of Coke.

Then I looked over to the back corner on my left and saw Mr. Tucker. 'Course I didn't know it was Mr. Tucker then. All I saw was this skeleton lying on a cot with his head turned and grinning at me, and his hair and nails grown somethin' fierce, and dressed in a suit. I grabbed onto that ladder like it could whisk me up and out of there, and then the scratching begun and I kept tellin' my legs to move but they wasn't listenin'.

I hadn't considered rats and I closed my eyes tight, expecting to be overrun by a whole herd of them, but when the animal crackers hit me atop the head, I realized it was, oh dear Lord, little Roy.

"Un, foo, free, boom!" he howled and some wallpaper hit me atop the head, too.

I blew out the kerosene lamp and, as well as I could, started scramblin' up that ladder with Boo.

"You, Roy! Back!" I hollered, but already the wall had started closin' and my last look was little Roy waving bye-bye with the metal scraper and all I could think of was being found fifteen hundred years from now. Me and Mr. Tucker and Boo. American Tut.

I hollered some but couldn't hear nothin' from the other side of the wall. It was pitch black and gettin' colder all the time. I knew the girls would be home soon, but I knew little Roy, too, and prayed fervently for his safety, adding the suggestion that perhaps he might think to push that button again.

I lit the kerosene lamp again and determined to examine the body on the cot.

"C'mon, Boo," I said, thinkin' positive.

I had the flashlight and could see a trail of dark stains on the braided rug that led to the cot, so I knew before I got there that this man had been hurt. He had on an old suit like Elliott Ness, with a dark stain at the waist. "Gut shot," I thought, and shuddered. His wallet was in the front pocket of his jacket.

At the table I searched the wallet, and Mr. Tucker and I were properly introduced. There were about twelve cards that said:

WISE JEWELERS
Since 1896 on the Square
in Gamble's Mill
Harlan Tucker, Asst. Mgr.

There was about fifty dollars and a picture of a woman and a pretty little blonde-haired girl. The woman had the kindest eyes and on the back it said, "Hilda and Ellen, Christmas, 1931." There was also two news clippings.

Meanwhile, Cloyd had tried to call and come home to find the house a mess and little Roy enjoying himself by pulling up the bathroom tiles. He worried I'd gone off the edge over that wallpaper.

"Where's Mommy?" he asked little Roy.

Little Roy sadly shook his head and stared hard at his dad. "Gibble fish," he replied, and then started crying for Boo and Cloyd tore up the house more trying to find him. Then the girls came home and Susie started throwing a fit over her poster paints and Molly started crying for me and Granny and Grampa showed up and Granny told Cloyd I always did seem a bit peculiar.

Believe it or not, we are to this day married.

I liked Mr. Tucker. He had a nice smile and his wife had the kindest eyes. The first news clipping was dated February 16th, 1932, and told of the discovery of a jewel theft in Gamble's Mill.

> According to police chief Jerry Bridger, the theft of over one hundred pieces of jewelry, estimated at close to $50,000, took place over a period of months. If it hadn't been for a fluke of fate, the theft might have gone unnoticed for yet another month. Mr. Wise, owner of the store, has been for the past few months traveling in Europe with his wife. He is en route home now and therefore could not be reached for comment. According to Miss Ethel Clowers, a clerk at the store, Mr. Wise had purchased the substantial amount of gems before he left on his long voyage. "All we do is sell the jewelry," she stated. "We had no idea they weren't genuine."
>
> When Mrs. Lance Curliss of Sulphur Springs took an amethyst brooch to a jeweler there for repair of the clasp, she was told that the gem was a clever reproduction. She then reported it to the Gamble's Mill police, and on further investigation the substitution of the other

gems was discovered. All the employees of the store are being questioned.

The second clipping was even more interesting. There was a picture of Mr. Tucker, a dark-haired man with a wide grin that didn't sit well with the caption, "Suspect Harlan Tucker sought in jewel heist."

The story said that several of the genuine pieces of jewelry had been found at the Tucker home. "Mrs. Tucker denied any knowledge of them but promised her husband would explain all when he got home that evening. To date he has not returned, and Mrs. Tucker is unavailable for comment." It was dated March 9th, 1932.

I looked over at Mr. Tucker on the cot and at the calendar on the wall.

"I don't think you stole anything," I said out loud. "But I bet you knew who did."

The air seemed to be getting even colder and I could see a pile of blankets by the stove, so I went over and grabbed the top one and that's when I found the second body.

"Cloyd!" I hollered from the bottom of the ladder, shaking it hard. "Cloyd, you Cloyd!" I stood on one chair and pounded at the ceiling with the other. "Clooyyd!"

I stood there in the middle of the room and tried not to cry. This would be a nice room, present company excepted. I knew I had to keep exploring because I knew if I didn't I'd start blubbering and hiccupping and get red blotches all over my face and look a mess. Then I realized it wouldn't matter if I looked a mess and just almost began to cry anyway.

I went over to the barrels and lifted one of the lids, and a strong smell of moonshine whisky about keeled me over. I promptly dropped Boo in, and when I fished him out, we both smelled like my Uncle Cletus on a Saturday night.

I was half afraid to open the rolltop desk. Probably find a dead midget.

It really was a beautiful piece of furniture. The drawers were locked, but the top was full of books and papers. The books were all technical journals like Cloyd likes. Plumbing, woodworking, electricity, and acoustics. They had the name

"C. Jenks" written in them. Then there was a ledger full of names and numbers like "Ches—12—Skid—2/24"; "Wilt—15—Skid—2/26"; "GM—11—me—3/6." There was a desk calendar with the date March 12th and a note in big block letters: "ETHEL—MUST CALL TODAY." Under that was another scribbled note: "GM—15—Skid." The blotter was interesting in itself. I always thought you could tell a lot about a person by his doodles. These were all sketches and numbers. Pieces of furniture and what looked like carefully drawn lines, and in one corner something real interesting. Pieces of jewelry: brooches, bracelets, necklaces, and rings. Then I found a letter in one of the cubbyholes and understood why it was so important to call Ethel. It was dated March 9th and was on lavender paper with pretty writing.

> Dear Carl,
> You have played me a fool for the last time. I know you went to Millie's Thursday night. Well two can play that game. I want my share now and you can forget all the rest. Or take Millie. Our pigeon knows and since we don't know where he's at, I want out now. So you best call me real soon or you're going to hear me sing.
> Ethel

I sat at the desk tapping a pencil and studying the air. Well, Mr. Tucker must surely be the pigeon and Ethel must be Ethel Clowers, the clerk at Wise Jewelers. Carl, whoever he was, must have been the one to plan the robbery. If these were his books, he was Carl Jenks and this had been his house. But how Mr. Tucker got here and who killed these people and what happened to the jewels I didn't know. Unless it was Ethel? "Hell hath no fury . . ." Something didn't seem right about it.

I sighed and stood and tried to crack my back. I'd eaten all the animal crackers and now, besides being cold and tired, I was hungry as a bear.

The cupboards was full of bottles, some empty, some full. And there were some funnels and hoses. Looked like runnin' shine had been good business. In another cupboard was some canned stuff that looked hard and green and fuzzy, some coffee, and a tin of Prince Albert tobacco. There was a coffeepot, too, but I was afraid to build a fire and burn the house down. I tried the pump but it didn't work, needin' to be primed, and just served to make me thirsty, too. (Uncle Cletus woulda died happy anyway.)

"Well, Boo," I said, givin' him a soggy squeeze, "looks like we're here for the duration." I started to put the tin of tobacco away and heard a clinking sound, so I opened it and dumped the tobacco out on the counter. Somethin' hard hit the sink and fell down around my feet. 'Course I hadn't seen my feet for almost two months now, so I went down on my knees and felt around and then caught my breath.

It was a beautiful diamond ring with pearls surrounding it. I picked it up and tried it on. It was truly gorgeous, catching the light in sparkles of color. I wondered if it was real or fake, and then I saw a note stickin' out of the tin. It read, "Ethel, Have saved the best for you. All my love, Carl."

Carl Jenks seemed paranoid to me. Locks his desk drawers and puts a rock like this in a tin of tobacco. Didn't seem to me he was throwin' Ethel Clowers over for Millie or anyone else.

I tugged at the ring and it wouldn't budge. My fingers, like everything else, was swollen. I tugged and pulled and muttered and then begun to cry, feelin' about as dainty as a beached whale.

Then a thought struck me that made me feel worse because on top of hungry and cold and thirsty and tired and fat, I felt stupid. There had to be a button on this side of the wall, too.

So I started searchin' all around the ladder and the walls. Couldn't find nothin' anywhere. I looked all through the cupboards and under the sink and table and finally pulled up the rug and found the trapdoor.

By this time I was beyond surprise. Little purple men with two heads and six arms could've climbed out of there and I'da said, "How do you do, and have a seat." No ladder—this time it was steps. I got the flashlight and stuck Boo in my blouse and blew out the lamp. It was creepy dark then, and I shivered as I started down.

There were three steps and then I was in a little cave like the hundreds we used to explore in the woods when we was kids. There were about ten cases of whisky there and a tunnel leadin' out. One thing I hate almost as much as February is bats, and I shone my light around on the ground lookin' for their droppings, bein' too scared to shine it up top. I didn't see none and started walkin' down that tunnel.

By this time it was one in the morning and Cloyd was sitting at the kitchen table with Jerry Bridger the third, who was the current chief of police. Granny Cates and Grampa had got the kids to bed and were cleaning up wallpaper and poster paints and floor tiles.

"I told Clara there was a loose corner on one of them tiles," Granny told Grampa. "That's what happens when you let the little things go."

Grampa just growled.

We'd both known Jerry Bridger about all our lives. He even put Cloyd in jail when he was twelve for throwing eggs at cars.

"We've checked all the hospitals, Cloyd. Bet you anything you hear from her tonight or in the morning at the latest."

Cloyd had a stubborn set to his jaw. "I'm tellin' you, Jerry, Clara wouldn't leave little Roy like that. Somebody's made off with her. There's all kinds of nuts out there, you know. There been any jailbreaks?"

"No, there ain't. What d'you think they're gong to do with her, Cloyd? Hold her for ransom? You gonna give them a set of wrenches?"

"Ain't funny, Jerry. You know what they do to defenseless women."

Jerry stared at him a second and then started laughing.

Cloyd jumped up. "You find somethin' funny?" he hollered, and Granny and Grampa rushed in.

"Shush you, Cloyd! Took me three hours to get little Roy to sleep without Boo! Kept runnin' to the closet in what's left of your room, wailin' his heart out for Boo! You want he wakes up again?"

Cloyd sat down. "Sorry." He glared at the police chief, who was wiping his eyes and chuckling.

Jerry Bridger sighed and sat a little straighter in his chair. "I *am* sorry, Cloyd. It's just that Clara never seemed defenseless to me—and don't you see it, man? She's nine months pregnant!"

Cloyd stared at him and then he stared laughing, too, and almost crying at the same time. Then Granny and Grampa started, even though they didn't know what they was laughin' at, and it was like no one could stop.

Was then that I walked by the kitchen window and saw them all. I slammed through the back door grimy and hungry and cold with that old blanket wrapped around me and Boo peeking out from the top of my blouse.

"You havin' a good time, Cloyd?" I bellowed. "You want I should go get hit by a truck so's you can have a party?"

Well, of course then everyone was full of comfort and cheer, getting me dry clothes and food and hot tea and asking a million questions like where had I been and who kidnapped me and was I drunk.

"Just let me get dry and fed. And, Jerry, don't you leave. I think I got an idea on a robbery happened over fifty years ago."

The tunnel I took had had cases of whisky stacked all the way through it and every once in a while a name and a date scratched in the wall, like "Ernest Hatten—1858," "Louisa Simpson—1860," and one that caught my attention: "Samuel Jenks—The Truth Doth Set Them Free—1858." Was that inscription and Granny and Grampa's memories put it all together.

The five of us sat at the table. I had checked on the kids, wanting like all the world to wake them, but Boo was in the wash and I had to find some things out.

"Granny, I got one question for you," I started as they all looked at me.

"Lord amighty!" she cried. "Where'd you get that ring?"

"I'll come to that. I just gotta know one thing. Who was it Farley Jessup ran off with?"

"Carl Jenks's girlfriend," said Granny.

"Ethel Clowers," said Grampa. "She was quite a looker, remember, Molly?"

"Hmph!"

"But wild," Grampa hurried on. "Real wild."

"And she lived here afore she died, right?"

They nodded and Granny clucked. "Poor woman in a wheelchair, y'know, had that disease . . ."

"I knew it!" I interrupted, and hit at the air with my fists. "I knew that wallpaper was ugly for a reason!"

They stared. "Clara, you sure you ain't been drinkin'?" Cloyd asked.

"This," I said holding out my hand, "is from a robbery at Wise Jewelers in 1932."

"I remember that," said Grampa. "Was that fella Tucker."

"Was not," I shook my head. "Was Ethel Clowers and Carl Jenks."

"Jenks?" Jerry Bridger stared at me. "But they found some of the jewelry at Tucker's! I remember my dad was surprised at him."

"We all was," nodded Granny. "Harlan Tucker seemed to be a good man. Made it awful hard on his wife and girl . . ."

I waved my hand. "That jewelry was planted by Ethel Clowers. Tucker was framed by her and Jenks."

"I recollect Jenks," said Grampa. "Big gruff man with never a how-de-do. He was an electrician."

"And he disappeared the same time as Tucker, right?"

"Right." Jerry nodded. "Went after his girl and Jessup, everybody thought. They were all looking for Tucker. Why? You seen Jenks?"

"In a manner of speakin'."

"You seen Tucker?"

"Just today."

"What's he say?"

"Nothin' much." I studied the ring on my finger.

Cloyd leaned back on the chair. "Clara, you best quit fooling around. I know that look. Just tell us."

"Better I show you."

Needless to say, they was all impressed with the wall and the room. Jerry jimmied the drawers of the desk open and found drawings of some of the jewelry and a couple of addresses of some people in Chicago, and then we all gasped when he opened the bottom drawer and found a whole case filled with jewels.

"Bet those are fake," I said. "More substitutions they couldn't use once they was found out."

"So it was Jenks, Wonder why?" Cloyd was lookin' through the technical books, ignoring the jewelry.

"Greed," I said. "And this was 1932. Prohibition was about to end. Jenks was more bootleg than electrician. You should see all the cases of shine in that tunnel."

"I seen enough already," said Grampa, looking at the two skeletons. "I'll be upstairs."

Granny studied Mr. Tucker. "Seems to me if he's here, he had somethin' to do with it."

"Well, I got another question. Did Farley Jessup have a nickname?"

Granny considered. "Seems he did. He was a rouster. Flashy. Worked part time at the Mercantile but always seemed he had lotsa money. Had a car he liked to race around town, too. Asked me out once."

"He did?" I stared, a little too surprised for my own future good.

"Clarence and I had had a fallin' out. Clarence never could make up his mind about nothin'—still can't. Anyway, I give him back his ring and there was Farley Jessup. He was about eighteen, four years younger than me. I went for a ride in his car out by Clarence's. Next day Clarence brought back my ring and said we was to be married the next week."

"And what happened to Jessup?"

"Oh, of course Jessup tried what he could," she picked daintily at her blouse, "but I put him in his place, all right. Skid. That's what it was—Skid Jessup."

"I knew it! Jerry, you got to arrest Farley Jessup."

"For what?"

"Murder. Don't you see? He was never in Mexico. He killed Carl Jenks and Harlan Tucker and run off with Ethel Clowers and the jewels."

Jerry sat down. "You know what, Clara? Nothing would

suit me better than to arrest Jessup. He kicked my uncle off his farm. But we don't got any real proof."

Cloyd had been studyin' over by the desk and clapped his hands. "Clara! Right here is the plan for the wall on the paper stuck in this here book!" He came over to the table and moved the kerosene lamp. Right there, nice as you please, was a button. He pushed it and the wall closed. I looked at the scribble on the piece of paper and stared at Cloyd. "You are truly amazin'," I said.

Jerry had been looking at the newspaper clippings. "So you think Harlan Tucker suspected Ethel and followed her here?"

"Yes, and Jessup was already here. Mighta already shot Jenks. Way I see it, Jessup had turned Ethel against Jenks by telling her he was seein' another woman, and at the same time he started movin' in on her himself. Her letter talks about two of them playin' at that game."

"But how do you figure Jessup in the robbery?"

"Well, I ain't sure about this part. I think he started out just trying to steal Ethel, but then she told him about the jewels and he saw his chance to strike it big. He robbed the robber and then shot him in the back. That musta been the night Tucker followed them from the cave in the woods to this room—so Jessup shot him, too, gut shot, and left him here to die, the rat."

"If that's true, why didn't he get rid of the bodies when he came back?"

"Look here." I showed them the ledger. "See here, 'Ches' is Chesterville; '12,' I figure, is twelve cases of shine; 'Skid' is Jessup; and '2/24' is the date. And if you look at the desk calendar, Jenks was expecting Jessup that night. Jessup was a shine runner for Jenks. But I don't think he ever saw any entrance but the tunnel. He knew there was one from the house, but he didn't know where. Granny, Jessup come back in 1934, right?"

"I ain't rightly sure. It was at least two years."

"Well, that cave comes out right beside Willowbrook. Do you remember what that was?"

(Willowbrook didn't have willow or brook—just a bunch of pre-fab houses.)

Granny brightened. "The CCC! They was clearin' and cuttin' the forest and replanting some parts!"

I grinned. "When Farley Jessup came back, there was a CCC camp in the area of the cave entrance. After that, with all the work they done, he couldn't find it because it was all changed."

"And," Cloyd added, excited, "Jessup probably never seen the cave except at night, because of runnin' shine."

"Right!"

"It still ain't enough," said Jerry. "We need proof. This letter ain't enough, and it's gonna be mighty hard to prove Jessup's movements fifty years ago."

Granny clucked. "It don't make sense. Why didn't Ethel tell Jessup where the secret wall was?"

"Well, in the first place, I don't think she expected him to kill Jenks, and in the second place, she might not have known how to open the wall, even though she knew where it was. Besides, that was the only thing she could hold over Jessup. Remember, he'd already killed two people."

"No wonder she started drinkin'." Granny clucked again.

"And if Farley looked for it," I continued, "he couldn't find it, but that's why he didn't want us to mess with anything in the house. I think Ethel chose that awful paper on purpose, hoping someone would find the place. And she did the closet herself; the paper only goes halfway up, her being in a wheelchair."

"Why didn't she go to the police?" asked Jerry.

"I don't think she could face the shame." I stretched, somewhere between a yawn and a sigh. "I really do feel sorry for her. She was runnin' most of her life, scared of the police and scared of Jessup. I think it was when he started runnin' around with that younger woman she decided to move in here and hope someone would find the room."

"How do you know," Cloyd considered, "that it was Jessup that killed them and not Ethel?"

I'd been afraid someone would ask that. "Well," I answered, feelin' a little embarrassed, "the only suspicion I got is that ugly wallpaper. You gotta agree it brings attention to the room. Either Ethel killed them and the guilt was eatin' at her, or Jessup killed them and she wanted it known. Whichever, I think she wanted this room found. You're right, Jerry. I ain't got proof. But listen. I do got a plan."

They sat quiet as I told them my idea, and when I was finished, Cloyd took my hand and kissed it.

"Clara, *you* are truly amazin'," he said.

Ellen Tucker looked a lot like her mama. She was about sixty-three, with soft blonde hair and kind eyes. She was a history professor at the college over in Richfield, and when Cloyd and I called on her, I liked her right away. Her house looked like a small town library.

"Have you read all these?" I looked at her in amazement.

"Most of them, I'm afraid. That's why I'm single." She laughed.

"We thank you for seein' us . . ." Cloyd began.

"Well, I must admit, I was quite intrigued by your note. You have word of my father?"

Suddenly I wished we hadn't come, and handed her the photo.

She caught her breath and her eyes filled with tears. "I remember when this was taken," she whispered. "I was ten and got a pair of ice skates that Christmas. Papa used to call us his Norwegian beauties. My mother was an immigrant. . . ." She wiped her eyes. "I'm sorry. Where did you get this?"

I stopped a second, feeling all choked up.

"Well, Miss Tucker . . ." I stopped.

"Please. Call me Ellen. I know my father's dead, Mrs. Ca . . . Clara. I've known that since I was twelve. Papa would never have let us go through what we did. And I know something else. He didn't do it."

By now I was blubberin' a little and Cloyd was standin' there bitin' his lip and rubbing my shoulder.

"You know—" her eyes filled again. "A lot of people in Gamble's Mill thought this ruined my mother. But it didn't, really. She never lost faith in my father. And when the other children laughed behind my back—or came right out and said my papa was a thief—it was her faith that carried me through. And pretty soon I had that faith, too—'what was meant for evil was turned to good,' you know? It really made me a stronger and better person in the end."

Now we was all cryin' a little, and Ellen got us all a cup of tea and we talked about the weather while it brewed. Then the time came I was able to begin.

"We moved into this house and our bedroom had this awful wallpaper . . ."

February was over, but my pregnancy wasn't. It was on one of them early thaw-slushy days in March that Miss Ellen Tucker went to see Mr. Farley Jessup.

He shook her hand. "Miss Tucker? I'm pleased to meet you. My secretary says you wish to discuss a financial arrangement with me?"

"That is correct."

"Retirement fund? Bonds?"

"No."

"Well, then, a will perhaps?"

"No, Mr. Jessup. I want to know I will be financially secure for the rest of my days."

He laughed.

"Don't we all! What did you have in mind?"

"I have in my possession a letter from your wife."

(I guess ol' Farley turned white as a sheet.)

"My wife Louise?"

"No. Your wife Ethel. Guilt does strange things, Mr. Jessup. Perhaps you knew my father, Harlan Tucker? Your wife had some information about him."

Jessup stood and paced a little.

"My wife was very ill for a number of years before she died. She was not altogether rational."

"Let us understand each other, sir. I know my father's dead. I can't bring that back. I would like my last years to be secure."

"How secure?"

"To travel. See the world. I have heard it said you were in Mexico?"

"Many years ago. What did Ethel tell you?"

"She told me about a secret room in a house. Once used for hiding slaves, it was transformed into a warehouse for bootleg whisky. She told me about a man named Jenks and a young rouster named Skid."

"Where is this letter?"

"Safe. Ethel warned me of your tricks."

"You can't prove a thing!" Jessup spat it out viciously. Then, quieter, "How much?"

"Forty thousand dollars."

"Impossible."

Ellen stood, raising her voice a little. "Then I shall give this letter to the papers and you will know what it is like to live with a clouded reputation. You, sir, are a greedy, unscrupulous man!"

Jessup sucked through his teeth. "Don't you talk to me about scruples, lady! You're trading off on your father! I killed those two men when I was young and foolish and ambitious, but you! You are calculating and crass, for all your fine talk!"

Ellen sat down. "I had to hear you say that," she answered, and bowing her head began to cry.

Farley Jessup stared as the office door opened and Jerry Bridger, Cloyd, and I walked in. (You shoulda seen his face. It was a sight.)

"I was glad to hear you say that, too," said Jerry.

"You won't be needin' your Cherokee for a while," added Cloyd.

"I just had to get rid of that disgustin' wallpaper," I declared.

Ellen Hilda Cates was born on March 14th, weighing seven pounds and exactly two weeks late. Cloyd was actin' silly counting her fingers and toes.

"What do you think of this?" I asked him, waving my notebook in the air. "The Case of the Pregnant Detective."

"Huh! Ellie will probably grow up to be a coal miner."

"Archeologist, maybe. You know, Cloyd, my worst fear was that I would go into labor right there in that tunnel."

"A week early? And ruin your record?"

"I ain't kiddin'. All I could think of was them newspapers at the grocery checkout with great big headlines—BABY BORN TO WOMAN BURIED ALIVE!"

"Well, it didn't happen. Hey, I got the room down there all fixed up for you. That guy Jenks may have been a nut, but he was somethin' when it came to woodworking and wiring."

"Is that whisky all gone?"

"Yeah. Busted open in the woods."

He bent over and snuggled at my neck. "There'll be a lot of drunk chipmunks for a very long time."

"I'm glad we met Ellen."

"Me, too. She acts like it ain't important that she's a college professor and I'm a grubby mech."

"It ain't. Sometimes I think we kinda shut out whole groups of people because we think we ain't their type. It ain't that they think they're better. It's that we think they think they're better."

Cloyd scratched his head. "You wanna go through that again?"

"Never mind." I hugged his arm. "Did Granny get the paper?"

Cloyd hesitated. "Well, Granny thought she could get somethin' almost like it at Herick's cheaper. Then she found this bargain . . ."

"Cloyd, you shut up!"

"It has big blue frogs with shiny red tongues and green flies and purple squirrels . . ."

At the hospital they have this rubber ring you can sit on after you have a baby. I grabbed it and whacked him upside the head.

That's how me and Cloyd got into the detective business, and if you know anything about it, it ain't a bad idea when you're in general aviation. (By the way, we got a reward for the diamond ring. It made a good down payment on the Jenks homestead.)

GUILT FEELINGS

by CELIA FREMLIN

The muted rustlings, the gentle inconsequential murmur of the public library on these precious Wednesday afternoons were like a benediction, and for the first few minutes Sarah would simply sit, her book unopened in front of her, and savor the peace of it, the lovely impersonal peace. Better even than solitude was this audience of hushed and shuffling strangers, not one of whom was entitled to come up to her and say, "Can't we go home now?" or "What's for tea?" or "But you said you'd be here by two." No demands. No deadlines. Nobody knowing her from Eve.

Peace. Delicious, incomparable peace. But, of course, peace, like any other commodity, has to be paid for, and in Sarah's case this blissful two hours, from two to four each Wednesday, had to be paid for by sensations of enormous guilt. Or rather—Sarah strove to be honest with herself—enormous fear of being found out. The risk was small, certainly—she hadn't been so foolish as to elect to spend her hours of truancy in her own local library—but all the same there was just the chance that a neighbor or acquaintance might drop in, might catch sight of her, and then might easily—albeit innocently—happen to mention this fact in front of one or another of the various people Sarah was deceiving.

The list of these people was long—and growing longer. People were very kind, and, having heard that Sarah's mother-in-law had had to be moved into a Home, they were willing enough to take turns babysitting for her on Wednesday afternoons so that she could go and visit the old lady.

And, to start with, that was exactly what she had dutifully done. Rain or shine, she had caught a bus, and then another bus, to the red brick-building, whose entrance hall, shining with polish and desperate with flower-arrangements, formed an antechamber to realms of such variegated pains and distresses as were hard to comprehend. Down the pale, shining corridors Sarah would make her way; her heels clicking obtrusively, unnervingly on the pale, shining floors until she reached the door behind which Mrs. Kinglake spent her empty and yet laborious days, furiously battling her way through the recalcitrant minutes that blocked the passage between one small happening and the next.

"It's gone quarter-to!" would be the old woman's greeting to her daughter-in-law, and she would brandish her watch—her last remaining weapon against the four corners of the world—under Sarah's contrite eyes. "I've been sitting here waiting for you ever since dinner! You said you'd be here by two!" And Sarah would have to explain—gently, of course, but over and over again—that it was the *babysitter* who came at two—she, Sarah, still had to fit in the journey, the two buses, the waits at the bus stops. And all the while she was speaking so brightly, so soothingly, she would be watching the glazed resentment filming, like cataract, the old eyes. Mrs. Kinglake wasn't listening to a word, not one word. She was simply waiting for Sarah to finish speaking so that she could continue with her grievance just where she had left off.

"Two o'clock!" she would resume as soon as Sarah's excuses had faltered to an end. "Since two o'clock I've been sitting here! I've missed my nap waiting for you, expecting you every minute! I'll be feeling ill all the rest of the day now, missing my nap like this—I'll be worn out!"

"Oh, but, Mother, there's no need!" Sarah would protest, week after week, "I've told you. You must have your nap as usual and if you *are* still asleep when I get here, why, I can always wake you up, can't I?" This with a little laugh, to make it sound like a cozy little joke between them.

At this, the old eyes would brighten for a moment, as they always did at the sighting of a new grievance glimmering out of the greyness of the days.

"Wake me up? You don't catch me that way twice! I don't trust you. Nor Graham, either. *I* know what you do when you find me asleep—you tiptoe away again! Yes, you do, don't lie to me!"

It wasn't Sarah who had done this, actually, it was Graham, on one of his Sunday visits to his mother.

"You looked so peaceful, it seemed a shame to wake you," he'd guiltily tried to explain away his defection, but he'd never heard the last of it, and neither had Sarah. It had become one of the staple subjects of conversation during that fairly short stretch of time after Mrs. Kinglake had finished complaining about Sarah's late arrival and before she started complaining about her early departure.

"Can't wait to get away, can you?" she would challenge. "I can't think why you bother to come, I'm sure!" And then, answering her own question: "It's the money, that's what it is! Buttering me up so's I'll leave you all my money, that's what you and Graham are after, isn't it? But don't you be too sure, my girl! I could leave it all to June if I wanted. Yes, I could! She may be only my stepdaughter, but Junie's the one who loves me! Such a lovely girl—never a cross word!"

Easy, thought Sarah, when you lived in New Zealand and only ever sent Christmas and birthday cards with printed greetings—which, true enough, never included any cross words. Well, they wouldn't, would they? Where would be the market for such a card?

"It's all a lot of nonsense, she hasn't *got* a lot of money," Graham had airily assured his wife when she'd reported one of these conversations. "She just likes to pretend she has—it gives her a feeling of power. Well, poor dear, with all her real powers gone, you can understand it, can't you?"

And Sarah could understand it; but it didn't help. To understand all may be to forgive all, but it does nothing to alleviate boredom, or to hold off rain at bus stops, or to render enjoyable an hour of unremitting reproaches and accusations.

At first, Sarah had tried to brighten the old woman's darkening and bitter days by telling her bits of family news—amusing little anecdotes about the children, and so forth. But Mrs. Kinglake's resistance to having her days brightened was absolute. She hated hearing about other people, grandchildren or not, and she also hated being told anything she didn't already know. Really, it was all very difficult.

Still, duty is duty, and all that winter Sarah had slogged back and forth on Wednesdays, organizing this or that neighbor to babysit with Tamsin and Lucy. Tedious though it was, it did seem vaguely worthwhile, if only because it helped to allay Graham's sense of guilt when—as not infrequently happened—he missed one of his own Sunday visits to his mother.

But as the months passed, even this vestige of a reason for the visits began to disappear. The old lady's memory had been deteriorating fast of late, and the time came when she simply didn't remember afterwards that Sarah had come at all.

"That wife of yours, she let me down again this week," she would complain to Graham on the following Sunday. And though Graham did his best to convince her that Sarah had indeed come, and to jog her memory about the visit, it was never any good.

"Hasn't been near me for weeks!" the old woman would sullenly insist. "Got no time for me, that's what it is! Bone selfish, that's her trouble! Now, my Junie—!"

And in the end, all Graham could do was to shrug and let the matter drop, later apologizing to Sarah on his mother's behalf.

Really, there was nothing else he *could* do—Sarah could see that. But all the same, as the weeks went by and the pointless, unappreciated visits came and went, Sarah found it impossible not to begin asking herself *why?* What am I doing it for? If all I get is accusations of hardheartedness and neglect, I could get those far more easily without any trouble or effort at all.

Sarah could hardly say outright to her husband, "I'm not visiting your mother any more, there's no point." It would be too hurtful. But on the other hand, the babysitting rota was nicely established now and going smoothly. So why not, just for once—that was the way it started—why not simply take the afternoon off and give herself a break? No very heinous degree of lying was called for, either to Graham or to the babysitter, because it was long indeed since there had been any news to relate of these grimly monotonous visits. ("How did you get on?" "All right. Not much change, I'm afraid" would be the extent of the exchanges incurred, and it didn't seem too wicked just to say these things yet again.)

At first she'd meant only to do it the once. She'd headed for the library that day simply because it was raining and she couldn't think where else to go. But peace and leisure are addictive and she found herself on the following Wednesday playing truant yet again. And then—

And then? Give a man a treat three times, they say, and you have created a need. And thus it was with Sarah. This little oasis of free time, of quiet uninterrupted reading, had become a need, and the attendant guilt feelings had, by habituation, begun to diminish.

After all, what harm am I doing? she asked herself. Not, of course, expecting an answer.

Who does, when they ask themselves this question?

"Mummy! Mummy! Guess who's here!"

Tamsin, with three-year-old Lucy stumbling bemusedly in her wake, rushed to meet Sarah at the front door.

"Guess—just guess!" And dragging her mother by the hand across the hall, she banged open the sitting-room door and, with the air of a conjurer successfully overruling the laws of Nature to produce a five of diamonds, she exhibited her prize.

"Auntie June—see? This is our Auntie June, she's flown here all the way in an airplane! All the way from New Zealand! In an airplane!"

For a moment Sarah would not have recognized in this svelte and stylish figure, ash-blonde, elegant in black linen, the mousy, ill-kempt young woman who had been introduced to her as her new sister-in-law some twelve years ago.

"Oh, June! How lovely!" she managed to say. But before

she could get any further, June's arms were around her and drifts of expensive scent were in her nostrils. Such an embrace seemed just a trifle overeffusive, seeing that they had met only once before, all those years ago.

"A lovely surprise!" she resumed. "But—my dear—why didn't you let us know? I do hope everything's—?"

But by now the children were clamoring for further attention.

"All the way from *New Zealand!"* Tamsin was reiterating. *"New Zealand,* where—"

"Where all the peoples walks upside-down!" Lucy contributed, awestruck. "Auntie June says—"

"No, she doesn't! Don't be silly!" interjected Tamsin scornfully. *"Of course* they don't walk upside down, how could they? It's just—just that—" Here Tamsin herself seemed momentarily at a loss. Then: "It's because the world is so *big,"* she hazarded. "That's why everywhere on it comes right way up. Isn't that right, Auntie June?"

There was a note of anxiety in her voice—because how small would the world have to be for this *not* to be the case? Suppose the globe of Earth was only as big as—well, as a very big field. *Then* would the people on the bottom side of it be upside down? The confidence with which Tamsin turned to her brand-new aunt for reassurance on this tricky question was really quite touching. And after only one afternoon's acquaintance, too. June must certainly have a way with children.

"Quite right, sweetie," June was beginning—but now Lucy, desperate to prevent the brand-new aunt's attention slipping beyond her grasp into something obviously incomprehensible, interrupted.

"Tell us anuvver story, Auntie June!"

"The one about the bad, bad Hijack man," ordered Tamsin, leaning confidingly against the tailored black linen, entranced by the clack and tinkle of the silver earrings that dangled so fascinatingly above her head.

"No, no!" Lucy was desperate to compete. "Not the hijack man, I want the one about the camel who felt cold and they knitted him a hump-cozy."

"Silly! You couldn't knit a hump-cozy, could you, Auntie June? You'd have to crochet it, because it's a round-and-round thing."

Clearly, Auntie June was being a big success—and when later in the evening Graham arrived home, the welcome she received from him was scarcely less enthusiastic. Brother and sister hugged each other, and soon a long-hoarded bottle of champagne was being uncorked in honor of the occasion.

"To the success of whatever the hell you're up to, Junie!" Graham toasted his sister, and then: "Incidentally, what *are* you up to? What's brought you here all of a sudden, after all these years? An unprovoked but uncontrollable yearning for your long-lost brother?"

"Fancy yourself, don't you!" June laughed. "Just like old times!" Then, twirling her glass between her fingers and staring down at the glittering curve of the liquid: "Actually, it was Mother, really. Sort of. I mean, your last letter—sorry I didn't answer it, but you know what I am—from your last letter it sounded, well, you know, as if she—I got the feeling that if I didn't come now, right away, I might never—it might be too late."

Graham nodded sadly. "Yes," he said, "I'm afraid you're probably right. The way she's been of late—" He turned to Sarah. "How did you find her, Sal, this afternoon? Any better at all?"

A tiny gasp from June almost threw Sarah off balance. It was bad enough answering this sort of question, anyway. With a third party listening it was going to be worse still. Carefully, Sarah tried to choose her words so as not to be actually lying. "I'm afraid she doesn't improve at all," she said. "I don't think we can expect it now. So far as I can judge, she was pretty much the same today as she was last Wednesday."

"How do you mean, 'pretty much the same?' " June's voice, sharp with anxiety, startled Sarah out of her carefully rehearsed composure. She was used to answering only one question on these Wednesday evenings, to telling, at most, only one lie.

"Do you mean you *talked* to her?" June persisted, with

irritating intensity of concern. Sarah could see that she was going to be dragged into a web of detailed lying such as she had managed skillfully to avoid all these weeks.

"Well, yes—I always do, naturally, when I go. I do my best. I tell her things about the children—Tamsin's dancing class, Lucy's play group. Though I never know if she's listening, if she takes any of it in."

Graham was listening placidly enough to this familiar recital. But June was staring, open-mouthed, as if listening to a voice from the grave. Was the news of her mother's condition a shock to her, then? Had she not expected the situation to be much like this?

"Of course," Sarah amended, trying to soothe her sister-in-law, "she's not *always* as bad as I've made it sound. There are moments when she—"

And just then, mercifully, before she sank any deeper into this morass of deceit, the phone went, and Graham hurried out to the hall to answer it.

From inside the room, they couldn't hear what he was saying, but from the deepening gravity of his tone, and from the long, listening pauses in between, both women knew exactly what the news would be long before he came slowly back into the room.

Yes, Mother had died. Yes, very suddenly. This morning, they'd said, but of course that must be a mistake, because Sarah had visited her this afternoon. "I told them you'd found her pretty much as usual," Graham said, turning to his wife. "They were surprised. Apparently the doctor said she'd been dead for some hours when he came—but of course they can't always be certain, it must vary a lot. They want to talk to you, Sal, about exactly how you found her this afternoon—whether you noticed anything different from usual in her behavior, that sort of thing. They're going to send someone around right now. That's okay, isn't it? You don't feel too—you know, the shock?"

The appallingness of the shock was something he must never know. "Of course it's okay," she said—and if her voice shook a little, well, why shouldn't it? Natural enough, surely, when you've just had news of a death in the family.

* * *

It was only when the "someone" they sent around turned out to be a policeman that the truth of the matter began to dawn. This was no natural and expectable death from one of the ordinary hazards of old age—heart attack, stroke, or the like. This was a murder case. And so of course Sarah's evidence, to the effect that the old lady had been alive and well (that is, no worse than usual) between two and four in the afternoon was a vital clue, an all-important guide to the direction and scope of the inquiry.

Had Sarah realized right from the start exactly what was at stake she might have retracted her false statement. But what with the policeman being so kind, and breaking the thing to her so gently, and with so many euphemisms, she had not fully grasped what had happened or the significance of what she was doing until it was too late. She had made her statement and she had signed it—it wasn't until later in the evening when the policeman had gone, accompanied by Graham to go through the formalities of identifying his mother's body, that she found herself face to face with the full consequences of what she had done.

"Sarah," cried June as soon as they were alone together, "oh, darling, darling Sal! You're a heroine! I'll never forget it to my dying day! I never *dreamed* you'd stand up for me like that—and at the risk of drawing suspicion on yourself, too! So brave! So noble! I'll never, never be able to thank you enough—oh, Sal, *darling! darling!*"

Utterly bewildered, Sarah extricated herself from the unexpected embrace and stared at her sister-in-law. "Thank me for what? What on earth have I done?"

"Done? Why, you've saved my life! Let me off the hook! By swearing blind that Mother was still alive this afternoon, you've put them off the scent! Because of course I've got an absolute alibi for this afternoon—being your babysitter, for one. So *clever* of you, Sal, to see exactly what to do—and how brave, how marvelous of you to do it!"

"June!" Sarah stepped back, aghast. "You mean it was *you?"*

"But you *know* it was! Why else did you tell all those lies to save me? Oh, you were wonderful, I'll never be able to repay you! Though of course when I get all that money—"

The barrage of gratitude seemed unstoppable, but gradually, under Sarah's questioning, the main outlines of the story became clear.

Death had been instantaneous, June assured her. A blow on the head from behind with a heavy vase. The poor old soul couldn't have felt a thing, and now she was out of her misery—wasn't that a blessing?

And, well, no, it hadn't been a mercy-killing, not really. June had had this letter some little while ago in which her mother said she had changed her will and was leaving everything to her, June. "And so I thought, wow, let's make sure of this before she changes her mind. So I packed in my job, sublet my flat, and popped over by the first plane I could get and conked her one.

"It was just before midday and they were all running around doing things about lunch, so I thought no one would see me. Unfortunately, I ran into two of the old hags on my way out and I've been terrified that they might tell. They were probably both potty and won't remember anything, but you never know. I've been worried as hell all afternoon, so you can imagine how grateful—how *superlatively* grateful—I felt when I heard you telling those lies for me! It was like an answer to a prayer, you sticking to your story that the old girl was alive in the afternoon. So now it doesn't matter *who* saw me or *what* those two old hags may choose to say because nothing that happened that early is of any relevance. Oh, Sarah, isn't it marvelous? And you *did* do it for my sake, I *know* you did, whatever you may say. Well, after all, I *am* your husband's sister, aren't I, it would be quite natural for you to protect me, blood being thicker than water. Blood-in-law, I suppose I should say."

And so on. Afterward, Sarah couldn't remember exactly what she had said in reply to this terrible confession, recited as it was in such a strangely casual and offhand manner. She remembered the night, though—the long, silent hours, with Graham sleeping unaware beside her while her thoughts tilted this way and that, ever and again slopping over the edge of consciousness, like water carried no matter how carefully in a shallow tray.

"Of *course* I must go to the police and admit that I lied" slopped over on the one side, to be followed almost at once by a massive shifting of weight to the other, where a whole medley of rival thoughts slopped over. What about Graham? What about the children? What about family loyalty? Besides, will the police even believe me? By changing my story, I shall have become a lying witness in a murder case and automatically under suspicion myself.

It could ruin Graham's career. It could darken the children's lives for years to come. A mother—or even an aunt—on trial for murder, and then in prison for probably the whole of their childhood and schooldays!

Besides, Sarah told herself as dawn began to brighten outside the window, besides, it's *done* now. The old lady is dead. She can't be brought back to life—to her miserable life—even if anyone were cruel enough to wish to do such a thing.

"Auntie June! Auntie June! It's *my* turn now!"

"Look, Auntie June, look at me! I'm being a flapping bird! Look! Look!"

Sarah must have slept in the end, because here she was being startled awake by the joyous squeals from across the landing. Tamsin and Lucy had evidently scuttled across into their enchanting new aunt's bedroom, all agog with the joys of early morning, and enticed her into a glorious game of romps. Soon the trio appeared at the door of the parents' room, the little girls, flushed with excitement, clutching one on each side the skirts of the scarlet-and-gold housecoat that swung in exotic splendor from Auntie June's shoulders.

"Mummy, Mummy, get up! Auntie June says that after breakfast she'll take us to see—"

"Mummy, look what Auntie June's gived me! A *real* feather from a *real* peacock! Isn't it, Auntie June?"

And so it went on. Auntie June was marvelous with the children—and, incidentally, a marvelous help to Sarah, taking them off her hands at this busy time—busy, of course, with arrangements for the funeral (much delayed by the necessity for an inquest) and with the complex and exhausting business of sorting out the old lady's belongings, getting them removed from the Home, and all the rest of the wearisome chores incident on a death. So busy was she, indeed, that Sarah found herself at times almost losing sight of the nagging burden on her conscience, still not wholly resolved.

June was such a delightful person, that was the problem; and the children adored her so. Graham, too, delighted in his sister's company, after their long separation. How could Sarah bring herself to destroy, forever, all these life-enhancing relationships? Knowingly, deliberately to put in their place a grim and inescapable tragedy, to hang as a black cloud over the whole family, forever?

On the other hand, June was a murderess, self-confessed.

But, of course, she wasn't *only* a murderess, any more than a postman is only a postman. He is also a husband, a darts-player, a breeder of canaries—hundreds of things. Similarly, June was not *only* a murderess, she was also a loving aunt, an amusing companion, a clever cook, an affectionate sister, a marvelous story-teller—generous to a fault, and with such a gift for happiness.

Irresistible qualities: and with every passing day of her enlivening presence, the fact of the murder seemed to become more and more remote, fading ever further into the past.

Except that, now and again, something would happen disconcertingly to recall it. A further interview with the police, perhaps, who of course were still painstakingly pursuing the false trail on which Sarah had launched them. And then, of course, there were June's reiterated and disconcerting expressions of gratitude towards Sarah, which seemed unstoppable and which made Sarah squirm with discomfort. There had been a bad moment, too, when June had remarked on her own foresight in wearing a really good black suit for the plane journey—"Because of course I knew I was coming for a funeral!" she'd laughed.

It was this sort of levity, almost as much as the murder itself, which upset Sarah at times, and filled her with distaste and unease. At other times, though, she would find herself wondering if it was not this very lack of guilt feelings, this very absence of conscience, which was the real secret of June's charm, especially for the children. Here was an adult traveling light as a bird through life, unencumbered by any of the burdens which weigh the normal adult down.

The days turned into weeks, the funeral was long over, and the whole affair had faded from the papers before the next thing happened.

It was nearly two months after the event, and June had become an established member of the household, when Sarah, looking through the local paper, came upon the item which, deep in her heart, she had been dreading from the very beginning. They had caught the Sunset Home murderer, it was claimed—a teenage layabout with a couple of minor burglaries to his name had been seen loitering around the Home soon after four o'clock on the fatal day. Two women had already come forward to identify him, and on top of this his fingerprints had been found on and around one of the windowsills by which he could have gained entrance. It appeared to be an open-and-shut case.

Sarah was aware of a shadow falling over the print as she sat, numbed with horror. The familiar expensive scent wafted across her consciousness. Over her shoulder, June was leaning down reading the report.

"But how marvelous!" she cried joyously. "Now we're *really* in the clear! Oh, Sarah, darling, isn't it *wonderful!*" and it was as her sister-in-law's arms came around her in delighted congratulations that Sarah at last came to her decision.

A LITTLE MORE RESEARCH

by JOAN HESS

Bart Bellicose realized time was running out. In the distance, he could hear the whine of sirens, and he knew the police cars were closing in on him like a swarm of killer bees. He stepped back, then threw his two hundred forty pounds of bulk against the flimsy door. It gave way with a shriek of pain, and Bellicose stumbled into the apartment.

There on the carpet lay the mortal remains of his client. Even in death, the semi-nude body was as undulating as the ocean, as smooth as the inner petals of a rose. He could see that his client was as dead as the proverbial doornail, one of which had ripped his arms in an angry slash of

"Terry, honey, when are you gonna be finished? I'm getting hungry, and it's almost too late to make reservations."

"I've asked you not to interrupt me. The deadline's tomorrow morning at nine o'clock, for pete's sake, and my editor's about to have an apoplectic fit. I can't concentrate when you come in here every five minutes."

"I'm sorry. It's just that I get all lonesome out there by myself. Maybe it would help if I rubbed your neck . . . ?"

"It would not. I'm on the last chapter and I need to get it done tonight. Please don't interrupt me any more."

"Okay, I'll be a good little guest and wait in the living room. All by myself."

"Thank you so very much. And shut the door, will you?"

grinning blood. It was obvious to anyone who'd ever eyed a fresh corpse that the

"Don't let me disturb you, but how about if I make reservations for later just in case you get done with your story?"

"I'm not going to get done if you don't leave me alone. I told you when you insisted on coming over tonight that I absolutely must have peace and quiet in order to concentrate."

"I happen to be speaking very quietly, my dear Hot Shot Writer."

"You also happen to be standing in the doorway, which means I'm looking at you rather than at the word processor. Go ahead and make reservations any place you want. I really don't care."

"Well, maybe I'll just do that."

It was obvious that . . . It was obviously murder. Bart could see that as he stared at the Bart frowned at the gaping Bart gasped as he spotted the hilt of the dagger protruding from the contoured chest

"Honey, telephone."

"I'm not home. Take a message and I'll call back tomorrow."

There was something about the dagger that touched a raw nerve. He'd seen it

"It's your editor, and he sounds real mad."

"Tell him I'm not here, and close the door on your way out."

"But I already told him you were home and working real hard on the story. He says he wants to talk to you right this minute."

"All right, damn it."

before. Sorry, Bart. Back in a minute. Try to remember, huh?

"Yo, Terry baby, how's it going?"

"It was going quite well until you called and interrupted me, Irwin. You do realize every time I'm interrupted I lose my train of thought?"

"Right, right. I wanted to remind you that we go into production tomorrow, with or without the last chapter. The book's gonna look pretty funny with a bunch of blank pages at the end. You promised me this manuscript. We paid a fat advance, and then waited patiently while you missed not one but two deadlines. You're in the catalogue. I've held the production people back till the bitter end, but the bottom line is that's where we are."

"And I'm not in my office finishing the book. *Au contraire,* I'm standing in the kitchen chitchatting with you. Goodbye, Irwin. I'll be in your office at nine o'clock."

"You and Bellicose, I presume."

"At this very moment Bellicose is standing over a body, and he'd like to investigate in the immediate future."

"So you finally got the plot straightened out?"

"Yes, I finally got the plot straightened out. Tomorrow at nine, okay? We can celebrate with Danishes."

"I'll get a dozen of them. Just make sure you show up for the party."

"I'm hanging up now, Irwin. Next time you get lonely, call your ex-wife."

He'd seen the dagger somewhere. Great.

Forget the dagger.

Bart stared at the bullet hole in the forehead. It was a third eye, as unseeing as the deep blue pools he'd

"Are you off the telephone?"

"No, I had the receiver implanted in my head and I'm listening to the time and weather as we speak. What is it?"

"I was trying to catch you before you started writing again to ask if you think Chinese sounds good. Or Japanese, I suppose, but not squid or tofu or anything creepy like that."

"I don't care. Do you mind? I mean, do you really mind giving me more than three minutes undisturbed?"

"I was just asking. You're acting like you've forgotten about last night. You didn't object to my company then."

"When I get this story done, maybe I'll remember. Please?"

"I'll sit in the living room and be as quiet as a mouse."

Deep blue pools of squid ink. On tofu.

Deadline. Deadline. Deadlineeeeee.

Bart recognized from the size of the wound that the bullet was of a low caliber. Could it have involved the swarthy woman with the mustache who'd come to his office yesterday, the one who'd cried and begged him to help her save her missing dauuuuuu

"What was that, damn it?"

"Don't pay any attention, Terry. I'll clean it up. After all, I don't have anything else to do."

"Clean what up?"

"Don't worry about it. It's no big deal."

"How can you say it was no big deal? It sounded like a friggin' nuclear explosion."

"I don't remember seeing you at Hiroshima. Just go back to work and stop yelling at me like I was some kind of kid or something. I said I'd clean it up."

"Was it the plate glass window?"

"Go back to work."

"The television? My new state-of-the-art television that I have three years to pay on?"

"No, and leave me alone so I can clean it up. I thought you had a deadline tomorrow . . ."

ghter. Bart stared around the room, which looked as if a nuclear bomb had gone off minutes before. The plate glass window was a spiderweb of cracks, and the television, a particularly expensive model with remote, built-in video cassette recorder, quadraphonic stereo, and one hundred thirty-seven channel capacity, was nothing more than a smoldering ruin of useless wires and busted tubes and would still suck up thirty-five more monthly payments.

But Bart warned himself not to dwell on the devastation and bent over the body. The flesh was still warm, and a ribbon of blood flowed from one corner of the mouth, which was twisted into a faint smile of surprise. So the victim had known the perp, Bart decided as he reached into his pocket and took out a pack of

"Did you take my cigarettes?"

"What?"

"I said, did you come into my office and take the pack of cigarettes I keep in the bottom left drawer for emergencies?"

"It was an emergency. I was out."

"Well, so am I. Bring that pack back."

"I smoked all of them this afternoon while I was watching this really great old movie about this debutante that falls in love with her sister's—"

"I'll read the newspaper if I want a review. Go down to the deli and get me another pack. You know I can't write when I'm out of cigarettes."

"No way. It's already late and I'm not about to get myself mugged just because you want a pack of cigarettes. It's your crummy neighborhood, not mine. If you're so desperate, go get them yourself."

Bart realized there was no time for a cigarette, not with the police moving in like a pack of vicious, slobbering wolves. Despite the sense of panic that could be appeased only by a cigarette, by a long deep satisfying lungful of carbon monoxide flavored with nicotine, he reluctantly turned back to the body, keenly aware that the evidence before him would lead to the identity of the murderer.

The clue was there before his eyes. He could almost see it, almost touch it, almost smell it, that acrid redolence of smoldering

"I smell smoke. What the hell's burning?"

"Nothing, Terry."

"Don't give me that. I smell smoke. I smell cigarette smoke, damn it! I thought you said the pack was empty."

"Don't short out your pacemaker over it. There was one cigarette left in the pack, that's all."

"The pack that you stole from my office? Is that the pack we're talking about? I cannot believe you would not only steal the pack from my desk, but then lie and say it was empty while sneaking the last cigarette!"

"If you keeping huffing and puffing like that, you're gonna blow the door down. I am sitting in here on the sofa holding my breath so I won't disturb you, and it seems to me you're the one bellowing and snorting and carrying on like a baby who wants a lollipop. It's like you've got some kind of oral fixation or something."

"First you steal my emergency pack, then you—"

"This is very childish. Perhaps you might worry a little less about me and a little more about the deadline tomorrow morning?"

The lingering smoke meant nothing, Bart thought with a snarl. No, the clue, the goddamn clue

No, now he could see what must have happened in the seedy apartment. The jagged corner of yellow paper beside the body was the exact same shade as the scrap he'd found at the nightclub. And that explained it. Yes! Yes!!! It was the link to the woman who'd lost a daughter, and it was the link to the strange fellow in the fedora who'd been following Bart for all those long days while he'd been on the case. It was as if the sun had finally broken the horizon after so many long weeks of arctic winter.

Bart smiled as the police stormed the room, their revolvers aimed at his heart. He knew he could explain

"Terry, I made reservations at that Thai restaurant everybody talks about all the time. We need to leave pretty soon if we're going to get there on time."

"Screw the Thai restaurant."

Bart held up the scrap of paper and said

"They're always packed, and the only reason we got the reservation is because a bunch of Shriners got drunk in the bar and refused to eat."

"Screw the Shriners."

Bart said screw the shriners oh hell come on bart you know who did it and who that fedora dude is and the scrap of yellow paper come on bart bellicose don't forget you can remember you had it a minute ago and it was good bart it was good and it was tight and it was right up there with brilliant and

it is gone finito ciao adios arrivederci

"Is everything okay, Terry? You're making an awfully funny noise in there."

"Don't worry about me. See, here I am in the kitchen and I'm just fine. As soon as I find a certain something in the drawer, I'm coming in the living room. Why don't you fix us a nice drink?"

Bart Bellicose left the police station, trying not to strut as he remembered how deftly he'd wrapped up the case in a pink bow to hand over to the detectives. They had listened in awe as he'd explained how his client, an errant husband with a fondness for exotic dancers, had blackmailed the sultry, smoky-eyed postal carrier who moonlighted at the Turkish Bizarre. The chump had opened the door to sign the yellow slip for a registered letter. Now his coffin and the case were closed.

There would be another case tomorrow, another chance to outwit the police. But for the moment, Bart savored this victory. If you wanted a case solved—and you wanted it solved right—then you called Bart Bellicose, by damn.

The end.

Yahoooooooooo.

"Yo, Terry, what time is it? Lemme get the light. Jeez, it's after midnight and I got to face the production guys in the morning."

"Stop at the bakery on your way to work, Irwin. Bart Bellicose has pulled it off again."

"It's done? You got it done? Lordy, I was sweating in my sleep for you. I'm not kidding; my pajamas are sticking to my armpits. All those glitches in the plot, those false starts and stops . . . I can't believe it."

"I'll admit I was having trouble with it. I just couldn't get a handle on the corpse sprawled on the living room floor. I couldn't see him, if you know what I mean. I couldn't touch his body, smell his blood, analyze his expression of surprise and fear."

"But you figured something out, huh?"

"With a little help from a friend."

"Well, I'm glad to hear it. Hey, I've got a bottle of twelve-year-old scotch I've been saving for my son's wedding. Now he says he wants to be a priest. Hop a cab and come on over to celebrate. Bring your friend."

"A fine idea, Irwin, although I'm afraid my friend's not up to a small party. I'll stop at the deli for a pack of cigarettes and be over shortly."

"Then be careful. You may write the hardest boiled private eye series in the industry, but you look more like a genteel lady librarian from Phoenix. Too bad Bart can't come along as your bodyguard. So tell me the truth—how'd you pull it off so quickly?"

"I realized that all I needed to do was a little more research. That's what it took—a little more research."

THE UPSTAIRS FLAT

by ELIZABETH A. DALTON

The instant I knew the sound of thunder directly overhead wasn't an act of God but a free-for-all or worse, I sky-rocketed off the rollaway and landed smack-dab on my cast-encased foot.

While I stood writhing in pain, trying to regain my senses, Mother sat not ten feet away serenely watching the soundless black-and-white TV, completely oblivious to the racket up-stairs, a vision of contentment with her silver braid swirled around her head like a halo.

I took one long deep breath, hopped over, planted myself between her and the late movie, pointed upward, and shouted, "Mother, what's that god-awful commotion?"

She looked up, smiled, and touched her hearing aid, un-concerned.

"The ceiling's caving in!"

"Oh, Charlotte," she soothed, "it's only the new tenants and their youngsters settling into the flat upstairs."

I shook my head. "Nobody's moving furniture this time of night—and that isn't the pitter-patter of little feet. Not unless the whole kit and caboodle's related to the mastodon family!"

She gave me one of her infamous know-nothing looks, waved me aside, and tuned out again. I got the message. Pretend nothing's wrong.

After I swallowed two Excedrins and eased back into bed, I

hoisted my cast back over the top of two pillows and muffled my ears with the patchwork quilt.

Perhaps she's right, I thought. Pretending would be so much easier. Where did meddling get me, anyway? Besides a fractured ankle, that is. And if I wasn't so clumsy at the art of intervention, I wouldn't be occupying Mother's lumpy rollaway, recovering from a nasty spill at the supermarket.

When I hobbled into the breakfast nook the next morning, Mother was waiting. "Charlotte, you look ghastly," she said, reaffirming my own sentiments after an earlier peek in the mirror.

"It's my ankle."

"It's the new tenants," she corrected me. "I pray, Charlotte, that you forget about the business upstairs. I know how you get once an idea weasels its way into your head. It's like your storytelling. You let ideas grow and grow until you're wild with them. You don't stop. As if the incident at the market wasn't enough, now you're zeroing in on the new people upstairs. Believe me, you're just suffering from an overworked imagination. It's purely coincidental."

"There are no coincidences," I said, poking air holes in my egg yolk with a fork, thinking how much she sounded like Uncle Emil.

Uncle Emil had picked me up at the street entrance to St. Mary's emergency room the afternoon my ankle had been X-rayed, wrapped, and set. After he buckled me into his Volvo, he glared at me over the top of his black-rimmed trifocals and said, "My God, Charlotte, look at you! You look as bad as that time when your father was still alive—"

That was old news. Father was gone. I stared straight ahead and concentrated on the present. I was in excruciating pain. What I needed now was a sympathetic ear. Instead, as we drove to the westbound expressway, Uncle Emil continued, "Only a nut, a crazy nut at that, runs interference for a lady in the supermarket after her old man's just backhanded her a good one. It could've been more than your ankle that got broken if you hadn't slipped on those grapes, you know."

I'd nodded my aching head for Uncle Emil then just like I

nodded for Mother now. An acquiescent agreement to their well founded message.

"Live and let live." Mother poured a spray of hot water over the teabag in my cup. "That business upstairs is none of your concern."

I looked down and studied the listing teabag. Its gauzelike keel heaved a final, gallant huff of strength, succumbed, and sank.

"Please listen," Mother was saying. "You must stop this foolishness of concerning yourself with certain affairs you can't change. Even after my hearing was gone I held my head high. I stuck by your father, may he rest in peace, even when I knew certain things would never be different." She puckered her thin lips a moment before continuing. "You've always been too high-strung for your own good. You must relax. Rest. Bones can't heal unless they have rest. Didn't you sleep well last night?"

"Could you? If you'd heard that poor soul crying her heart out upstairs all night—"

Mother gave me another look, turned down her hearing aid, and left the table.

I went outdoors and lay down on a dew-covered chaise. While I elevated my throbbing foot and cleansed my lungs of the stagnant air in Mother's flat, the door latch to the upstairs deck snapped open. I hauled myself out of the chaise and up on my crutches. When I'd shuffled clear of the overhead deck and was on safe footing in the communal courtyard I called out, "Hello up there!"

A young woman—pretty, but a bit on the thin side—with a toddler astraddle each hip stepped timidly to the wood railing.

"I'm Charlotte Pennington, your downstairs neighbor," I told her. "Temporarily, that is. I'm convalescing with my mother until I'm back on both feet."

"Are the children bothering you?" she asked.

I shook my head. "Never. Children are my biggest audience. I'm a traveling storyteller. Usually spinning tales of my own making. Libraries, schools—wherever I'm needed. I love making up new stories and planting little seeds of wisdom in their heads. Children harvest ideas and never forget. They're intuitive.

"Your two are beautiful," I told her. The wide-eyed babies looked as if they hadn't been bathed in a week. "I wouldn't mind looking after them for you after I've conquered the stairs. I wouldn't be a reliable sitter before then. But I could give you a breather now and then while the children are napping. You could go shopping, get your hair done—"

At that the woman hugged the babies to her and quickly backed away.

I heard the door shut behind her.

Mother's face was like a stone mask when I repeated the incident to her. "Of course the poor girl was frightened," she said. "You, a stranger, offering to take care of her children! It was nothing more than that."

Mother and I tacitly agreed to a truce and made believe the matter upstairs didn't exist. Our days became routine. She camped in front of the television watching soaps and I lay off in the corner on the rollaway, my foot up, pretending to be absorbed in a new bestseller. But my mind was still on the situation upstairs.

And I found myself remembering how it was when Father was alive. Days upon days of bone-chilling silence, my instincts always on red alert. Waiting. Waiting for the other shoe to drop.

Then, as if Father were directing the script, the scene overhead warmed up again. He terrorized. She whimpered.

My heart was in my mouth and a plan began to take shape in my mind.

Despite my condition, I managed to hop away from the flat, along the hallway, and up the outside stairs like a wounded jackrabbit. I was red-faced and breathless by the time I rang the buzzer.

She cracked the door.

"May I come in?" I wheezed.

I believe it was my pitiful condition, rather than a welcoming gesture, that prompted her to open the door.

The place was a pigsty. Dirty dishes. Clutter everywhere. A three-legged chair in the corner. His doings, I suspected. And she, like the box-sized flat, looked battered, her anemic pallor and pencil-thin arms a colorful shield of bruises.

No use beating around the bush. "I know you're in trouble up here," I said boldly.

She stared at her feet. Ashamed.

"I want to help," I said kindly.

"There's nothing—"

"The police?"

She shook her head.

"There's always hope," I said. "You could leave, go to a shelter for women. They'd put you up."

"I left once—but he came around. Me and the kids are all he got."

"It's your affair, of course," I said, hating myself for sounding like Mother.

Only when I stood like dead weight in her doorway and repeatedly swore that my intentions were truly neighborly did she finally agree to allow me to visit.

And so I did, arriving daily about noon when he wasn't at home to raise the roof. Sometimes I'd bring fresh fruit as an offering and the four of us chatted outdoors on the deck. I'd offer a strawberry to each of the babies and say, "Chew them up real good. The juice will put red in your cheeks." They squealed with delight and chewed.

Because she was a horrid housekeeper, I warned her to be careful to clean up the fruit after I left. "If you step on squashed fruit, it's like skating on a sheet of ice. I'm speaking from experience," I reminded her, looking with mock woe at my cast.

Sometimes I played indoors with the toddlers and made up little stories. Mostly about daddies who went away to the moon and how the mothers and children stayed behind and lived happily ever after.

The night before my cast was scheduled to be removed, I was awakened from a dream in which I danced barefoot across a field of daisies, free as a bird. Suddenly I found myself sitting upright and listening.

The racket upstairs was so loud it seemed as if the flat would come down on our heads. Then there was a terrible crash from the porch.

I pulled on my pink-chenille robe, limped to the patio, and flipped on the floodlight.

It was him, the man from upstairs, spreadeagled on the ground, his hands still clinging to a shattered section of the upstairs railing. His head was twisted and blood came from it. I knew he was dead.

When I saw his shoes, I wasn't surprised. She was truly a horrid housekeeper. The soles of his shoes were slick with grapes. I woke Mother before calling the police. It wouldn't do for her to awaken unprepared. Soon there would be dozens of people milling around and investigating his fall before they sent the man away to the moon.

THE TAKAMOKU JOSEKI

by SARA PARETSKY

Mr. and Mrs. Takamoku were a quiet, hardworking couple. Although they had lived in Chicago since the 1940's, when they were relocated from an Arizona detention camp, they spoke only halting English. Occasionally I ran into Mrs. Takamoku in the foyer of the old three-flat we both lived in on Belmont, or at the corner grocery store. We would exchange a few stilted sentences. She knew I lived alone in my third floor apartment, and she worried about it, although her manners were too perfect for her to come right out and tell me to get myself a husband.

As time passed, I learned about her son Akira and her daughter Yoshio, both professionals living on the West Coast. I always inquired after them, which pleased her.

With great difficulty I got her to understand that I was a private detective. This troubled her; she often wanted to know if I were doing something dangerous, and would shake her head and frown as she asked. I didn't see Mr. Takamoku often. He worked for a printer and usually left long before me in the morning.

Unlike the De Paul students who form an ever-changing collage on the second floor, the Takamokus did little entertaining, or at least little noisy entertaining. Every Sunday afternoon a procession of Orientals came to their apartment, spent a quiet afternoon, and left. One or more Occidentals would join them, incongruous by their height and color. After a while, I recognized the regulars, a tall, bearded white man, and six or seven Japanese and Koreans.

One Sunday evening in late November I was eating sushi and drinking sake in a storefront restaurant on Halsted. The Takamokus came in as I was finishing my first little pot of sake. I smiled and waved at them, and watched with idle amusement as they conferred earnestly, darting glances at me. While they argued, a waitress brought them bowls of noodles and a plate of sushi; they were clearly regular customers with regular tastes.

At last, Mr. Takamoku came over to my table. I invited him and his wife to join me.

"Thank you, thank you," he said in an agony of embarrassment. "We only have question for you, not to disturb you."

"You're not disturbing me. What do you want to know?"

"You are familiar with American customs." That was a statement, not a question. I nodded, wondering what was coming.

"When a guest behaves badly in the house, what does an American do?"

I gave him my full attention. I had no idea what he was asking, but he would never have brought it up just to be frivolous.

"It depends," I said carefully. "Did they break up your sofa or spill tea?"

Mr. Takamoku looked at me steadily, fishing for a cigarette. Then he shook his head, slowly. "Not as much as breaking furniture. Not as little as tea on sofa. In between."

"I'd give him a second chance."

A slight crease erased itself from Mr. Takamoku's forehead. "A second chance. A very good idea. A second chance."

He went back to his wife and ate his noodles with the noisy appreciation that showed good Japanese manners. I had another pot of sake and finished about the same time as the Takamokus; we left the restaurant together. I topped them by a good five inches, so I slowed my pace to a crawl to keep step with them.

Mrs. Takamoku smiled. "You are familiar with Go?" she asked, giggling nervously.

"I'm not sure," I said cautiously, wondering if they wanted me to conjugate an intransitive irregular verb.

"It's a game. You have time to stop and see?"

"Sure," I agreed, just as Mr. Takamoku broke in with vigorous objections.

I couldn't tell whether he didn't want to inconvenience me or didn't want me intruding. However, Mrs. Takamoku insisted, so I stopped at the first floor and went into the apartment with her.

The living room was almost bare. The lack of furniture drew the eye to a beautiful Japanese doll on a stand in one corner with a bowl of dried flowers in front of her. The only other furnishing was a row of six little tables. They were quite thick and stood low on carved wooden legs. Their tops, about eighteen inches square, were crisscrossed with black lines that formed dozens of little squares. Two covered wooden bowls stood on each table.

"Go-ban," Mrs. Takamoku said, pointing to one of the tables.

I shook my head in incomprehension.

Mr. Takamoku picked up a covered bowl. It was filled with smooth white disks, the size of nickels but much thicker. I held one up and saw beautiful shades and shadows in it.

"Clam shell," Mr. Takamoku said. "They cut, then polish." He picked up a second bowl, filled with black disks. "Shale."

He knelt on a cushion in front of one of the tables and rapidly placed black and white disks on intersections of the lines. A pattern emerged.

"This is Go. Black plays, then white, then black, then white. Each tries to make territory, to make eyes." He showed me an "eye"—a clear space surrounded by black stones. "White cannot play here. Black is safe. Now white must play someplace else."

"I see." I didn't really, but I didn't think it mattered.

"This afternoon, someone knock stones from table, turn upside down, and scrape with knife."

"This table?" I asked, tapping the one he was playing on.

"Yes." He swept the stones off swiftly but carefully, and put them in their little pots. He turned the board over. In the middle was a hole, carved and sanded. The wood was very thick—I suppose the hole gave it resonance.

I knelt beside him and looked. I was probably thirty years younger, but I couldn't tuck my knees under me with his grace and ease: I sat crosslegged. A faint scratch marred the sanded bottom.

"Was he American?"

Mr. and Mrs. Takamoku exchanged a look. "Japanese, but born in America," she said. "Like Akira and Yoshio."

I shook my head. "I don't understand. It's not an American custom." I climbed awkwardly back to my feet. Mr. Takamoku stood with one easy movement. He and Mrs. Takamoku thanked me profusely. I assured them it was nothing and went to bed.

The next Sunday was a cold, gray day with a hint of snow. I sat in my living room in front of the television drinking coffee, dividing my attention between November's income and watching the Bears. Both were equally feeble. I was trying to decide on something friendlier to do when a knock sounded on my door. The outside buzzer hadn't rung. I got up, stacking loose papers on one arm of the chair and balancing the coffee cup on the other.

Through the peephole I could see Mrs. Takamoku. I opened the door. Her wrinkled ivory face was agitated, her eyes dilated. "Oh, good, good, you are here. You must come." She tugged at my hand.

I pulled her gently into the apartment. "What's wrong? Let me get you a drink."

"No, no." She wrung her hands in agitation, repeating that I must come, I must come.

I collected my keys and went down the worn, uncarpeted stairs with her. Her living room was filled with cigarette smoke and a crowd of anxious men. Mr. Takamoku detached himself from the group and hurried over to his wife and me. He clasped my hand and pumped it up and down.

"Good. Good you came. You are a detective, yes? You will see the police do not arrest Naoe and me."

"What's wrong, Mr. Takamoku?"

"He's dead. He's killed. Naoe and I were in camp during World War. They will arrest us."

"Who's dead?"

He shrugged helplessly. "I don't know name."

I pushed through the group. A white man lay sprawled on the floor. It was hard, given his position, to guess his age. His fair hair was thick and unmarked with gray; he must have been relatively young.

A small dribble of vomit trailed from his clenched teeth. I sniffed at it cautiously. Probably hydrocyanic acid. Not far from his body lay a teacup, a Japanese cup without handles. The contents sprayed out from it like a Rorschach. Without touching it, I sniffed again. The fumes were still discernible.

I got up. "Has anyone left since this happened?"

The tall, bearded Caucasian I'd noticed on previous Sundays looked around and said "no" in an authoritative voice.

"And have you called the police?"

Mrs. Takamoku gave an agitated cry. "No police. No. You are detective. You find murderer yourself."

I shook my head and took her gently by the hand. "If we don't call the police, they will put us all in jail for concealing a murder. You must tell them."

The bearded man said, "I'll do that."

"Who are you?"

"I'm Charles Welland. I'm a physicist at the University of Chicago, but on Sundays I'm a Go player."

"I see . . . I'm V. I. Warshawski. I live upstairs: I'm a private investigator. The police look very dimly on all citizens who don't report murders, but especially on P.I.'s."

Welland went into the dining room, where the Takamokus kept their phone. I told the Takamokus and their guests that no one could leave before the police gave them permission, then followed Welland to make sure he didn't call anyone besides the police, or take the opportunity to get rid of a vial of poison.

The Go players seemed resigned, albeit very nervous. All

of them smoked ferociously; the thick air grew bluer. They split into small groups, five Japanese together, four Koreans in another clump. A lone Chinese fiddled with the stones on one of the Go-bans.

None of them spoke English well enough to give a clear account of how the young man died. When Welland came back, I asked him for a detailed report.

The physicist claimed not to know his name. The dead man had only been coming to the Go club the last month or two.

"Did someone bring him? Or did he just show up one day?"

Welland shrugged. "He just showed up. Word gets around among Go players. I'm sure he told me his name—it just didn't stick. I think he worked for Hansen Electronic, the big computer firm."

I asked if everyone there were regular players. Welland knew all of them by sight, if not by name. They didn't all come every Sunday, but none of the others was a newcomer.

"I see. Okay. What happened today?"

Welland scratched his beard. He had bushy, arched eyebrows that jumped up to punctuate his stronger statements. I thought that was pretty sexy. I pulled my mind back to what he was saying.

"I got here around one thirty. I think three games were in progress. This guy"—he jerked his thumb toward the dead man—"arrived a bit later. He and I played a game. Then Mr. Hito arrived and the two of them had a game. Dr. Han showed up and he and I were playing when the whole thing happened. Mrs. Takamoku sets out tea and snacks. We all wander around and help ourselves. About four, this guy took a swallow of tea, gave a terrible cry, and died."

"Is there anything important about the game they were playing?"

Welland looked at the board. A handful of black and white stones stood on the corner points. He shook his head. "They'd just started. It looks like our dead friend was trying the Takamoku joseki. That's a complicated one—I've never seen it used in actual play before."

"What's that? Anything to do with Mr. Takamoku?"

"The joseki are the beginning moves in the corners. Takamoku is this one"—he pointed at the far side—"where black plays on the five-four point—the point where the fourth and fifth lines intersect. It wasn't named for our host. That's just coincidence."

Sergeant McGonnigal didn't find out much more than I had. A thickset young detective, he has had a lot of experience and treated his frightened audience gently. He was a little less kind to me, demanding roughly why I was there, what my connection with the dead man was, who my client was. It didn't cheer him up any to hear that I was working for the Takamokus, but he let me stay with them while he questioned them. He sent for a young Korean officer to interrogate the Koreans in the group. Welland, who spoke fluent Japanese, translated the Japanese interviews. Dr. Han, the lone Chinese, struggled along on his own.

McGonnigal learned that the dead man's name was Peter Folger. He learned that people were milling around all the time watching each other play. He also learned that no one paid attention to anything but the game they were playing, or watching.

"The Japanese say the Go player forgets his father's funeral," Welland explained. "It's a game of tremendous concentration."

No one admitted knowing Folger outside the Go club. No one knew how he found out that the Takamokus hosted Go every Sunday.

My clients hovered tensely in the background, convinced that McGonnigal would arrest them at any minute. But they could add nothing to the story. Anyone who wanted to play was welcome at their apartment on Sunday afternoon. Why should he show a credential? If he knew how to play, that was the proof.

McGonnigal pounced on that. Was Folger a good player? Everyone looked around and nodded: Yes, not the best—that was clearly Dr. Han or Mr. Kim, one of the Koreans—but quite good enough. Perhaps first kyu, whatever that was.

After two hours of this, McGonnigal decided he was getting nowhere. Someone in the room must have had a connection with Folger, but we weren't going to find it by questioning the group. We'd have to dig into their backgrounds.

A uniformed man started collecting addresses while McGonnigal went to his car to radio for plainclothes reinforcements. He wanted everyone in the room tailed and wanted to call from a private phone. A useless precaution, I thought: the innocent wouldn't know they were being followed and the guilty would expect it.

McGonnigal returned shortly, his face angry. He had a bland-faced, square-jawed man in tow, Derek Hatfield of the F.B.I. He did computer fraud for them. Our paths had crossed a few times on white-collar crime. I'd found him smart and knowledgeable, but also humorless and overbearing.

"Hello, Derek," I said, without getting up from the cushion I was sitting on. "What brings you here?"

"He had the place under surveillance," McGonnigal said, biting off the words. "He won't tell me who he was looking for."

Derek walked over to Folger's body, covered now with a sheet which he pulled back. He looked at Folger's face and nodded. "I'm going to have to phone my office for instructions."

"Just a minute," McGonnigal said. "You know the guy, right? You tell me what you were watching him for."

Derek raised his eyebrows haughtily. "I'll have to make a call first."

"Don't be an ass, Hatfield," I said. "You think you're impressing us with how mysterious the F.B.I. is, but you're not, really. You know your boss will tell you to cooperate with the city if it's murder. And we might be able to clear this thing up right now, glory for everyone. We knew Folger worked for Hansen Electronic. He wasn't one of your guys working undercover, was he?"

Hatfield glared at me. "I can't answer that."

"Look," I said reasonably. "Either he worked for you and was investigating problems at Hansen, or he worked for them and you suspected he was involved in some kind of fraud. I know there's a lot of talk about Hansen's new Series J computer—was he passing secrets?"

Hatfield put his hands in his pockets and scowled in thought. At last he said to McGonnigal, "Is there someplace we can talk?"

I asked Mrs. Takamoku if we could use her kitchen for a few minutes. Her lips moved nervously, but she took Hatfield and me down the hall. Her apartment was laid out like mine and the kitchens were similar, at least in appliances. Hers was spotless; mine has that lived-in look.

McGonnigal told the uniformed man not to let anyone leave or make any phone calls and followed us.

Hatfield leaned against the back door. I perched on a bar stool next to a high wooden table. McGonnigal stood in the doorway leading down the hall.

"You got someone here named Miyake?" Hatfield asked.

McGonnigal looked through the sheaf of notes in his hand and shook his head.

"Anyone here work for Kawamoto?"

Kawamoto is a big Japanese electronics firm, one of Mitsubishi's peers and a strong rival of Hansen in the mega-computer market.

"Hatfield. Are you trying to tell us that Folger was passing Series J secrets to someone from Kawamoto over the Go boards here?"

Hatfield shifted uncomfortably. "We only got onto it three weeks ago. Folger was just a go-between. We offered him immunity if he would finger the guy from Kawamoto. He couldn't describe him well enough for us to make a pickup. He was going to shake hands with him or touch him in some way as they left the building."

"The Judas trick," I remarked.

"Huh?" Hatfield looked puzzled.

McGonnigal smiled for the first time that afternoon. "The man I kiss is the one you want. You should've gone to Catholic school, Hatfield."

"Yeah. Anyway, Folger must've told this guy Miyake we were closing in." Hatfield shook his head disgustedly. "Miyake must be part of that group out there, just using an assumed name. We got a tail put on all of them." He straightened up and started back towards the hall.

"How was Folger passing the information?" I asked.

"It was on microdots."

"Stay where you are. I might be able to tell you which one is Miyake without leaving the building."

Of course, both Hatfield and McGonnigal started yelling at me at once. Why was I suppressing evidence, what did I know, they'd have me arrested. "Calm down, boys," I said. "I don't have any evidence. But now that I know the crime, I think I know how the information was passed. I just need to talk to my clients."

Mr. and Mrs. Takamoku looked at me anxiously when I came back to the living room. I got them to follow me into the hall. "They're not going to arrest you," I assured them. "But I need to know who turned over the Go board last week. Is he here today?"

They talked briefly in Japanese, then Mr. Takamoku said, "We should not betray guest. But murder is much worse. Man in orange shirt, named Hamai."

Hamai, or Miyake, as Hatfield called him, resisted valiantly. When the police started to put handcuffs on him, he popped another gelatin capsule into his mouth. He was dead almost before they realized what he had done.

Hatfield, impersonal as always, searched his body for the microdot. Hamai had stuck it to his upper lip, where it looked like a mole against his dark skin.

"How did you know?" McGonnigal grumbled, after the bodies had been carted off, and the Takamokus' efforts to turn their life savings over to me successfully averted.

"He turned over a Go board here last week. That troubled my clients enough that they asked me about it. Once I knew we were looking for the transfer of information, it was obvious that Folger had stuck the dot in the hole under the board. Hamai couldn't get at it, so he had to turn the whole board over. Today, Folger must have put it in a more accessible spot."

Hatfield left to make his top-secret report. McGonnigal followed his uniformed men out of the apartment. Welland held the door for me.

"Was his name Hamai or Miyake?" he asked.

"Oh, I think his real name was Hamai—that's what all his identification said. He must have used a false name with Folger. After all, he knew you guys never pay attention to each other's names—you probably wouldn't even notice what Folger called him. If you could figure out who Folger was."

Welland smiled; his bushy eyebrows danced. "How about a drink? I'd like to salute a lady clever enough to solve the Takamoku joseki unaided."

I looked at my watch. Three hours ago I'd been trying to think of something friendlier to do than watch the Bears get pummeled. This sounded like a good bet. I slipped my hand through his arm and went outside with him.

DIGBY'S FIRST CASE

by ANNE PERRY

Freddie Dagliesh sat in bed propped up by pillows while the gas lamp hissed gently in its bracket on the wall. It was essential he stay awake—one could not make an assignation with a woman one liked as much as he liked Daisy Beech, then fail to keep it because one had fallen asleep.

But it was also of the utmost importance he wait until the last of his guests had gone to their rooms and closed the doors for the final time, and the ladies' maids had completed their duties and retired to their own quarters. There were proprieties to be observed. This might be 1894 and all London aswirl with the wit of Oscar Wilde, the antics of the Prince of Wales, and the beauty of Lily Langtry, but only four years ago Charles Stewart Parnell had wrecked his political aspirations on the scandal of his affair with Mrs. O'Shea.

And this was a highly political weekend: within the next few days a decision would be made as to which of three men present would receive an excellent appointment to the Foreign Office—one which could lead to the cabinet, possibly even to Downing Street.

Would it be Andrew Delamain, with his brilliant mind and too frequently unguarded tongue, his wit and his large appetites? He would be a good choice; his wife Lucy was elegant, accomplished, and well connected. There was something faintly brittle about her that worried Freddie, but perhaps that was merely a matter of taste; he preferred more comfortable women, solid, frank, with quiet humor—like Daisy.

The minister might choose Evan Marshall, volatile, charming, so hard to predict. He was not from quite the ideal background, but of the three of them he probably had the greatest flair for the art of politics, he understood all manner of people, he had instinctive knowledge of both weaknesses and strengths. Pity he was unmarried, but that was something he could remedy any day he chose, probably to a duke's daughter if he wished.

And of course there was Anthony Beech, suave, well-bred, and so very distinguished with his dark hair greying in stylish wings at the temples. He was a decent enough man, and if he were not married to Daisy, Freddie might well have found him agreeable—but he had liked Daisy too long and with too deep an emotion to be fair. Beech was ten years younger than she, barely into his forties, and immeasurably better looking—the kindest one could say of Daisy was that she was "interesting"—but it was Daisy who had the money.

This party needed a hostess, so Freddie had done as he usually did and asked his widowed sister Pamela Selden to stay. Beautiful Pamela—she did it so very well. This time she had brought her daughter with her. Poor Sophie was smitten with Anthony Beech, but perhaps that was natural enough at eighteen, and no doubt it would pass.

And of course there were the Puseys, the archdeacon and his wife. Personally Freddie found them pompous and exceedingly tiresome, but since Mrs. Pusey was the minister's sister, they could hardly be refused hospitality this week, dearly as he would have liked to.

Surely they must all be in their rooms by now? He could hear nothing except the hissing of the gas, no footsteps, no murmured voices. Was it safe?

Somewhere in the house a clock struck midnight. Better not go yet—it was too soon. Leave it another half hour at least. If Daisy were asleep, it could be very pleasant waking her. He had been surprised to discover that weekend at the Walsinghams' what a delicious sense of humor she had. Not that she had much occasion to indulge it, Anthony was such a stuffy beggar, and vain, always admiring himself in mirrors. And ambitious—one could almost taste it when he spoke. He was so careful in his courtship of those who mattered it made Freddie ache to watch him.

But Daisy was different. He drifted into a pleasant contemplation. She was generous, she was wise, and she had the ability to laugh at the world's eccentricities without unkindness.

Half past midnight. Time to go.

He got up, straightened the sheets a little, then crept to the door and opened it. The corridor was empty, just the faint glow of the night lamps burning. Third room on the right, she had said. First room, linen cupboard, second room—third! He felt a delightful tingle of excitement. Softly he turned the handle and pushed the door open. Silence. He slipped inside and pulled it to. The curtains were drawn; only a thin bar of moonlight showed him the wide, canopied bed.

She must be asleep.

His smile broadened. This would be fun. He took a deep breath and undid the sash of his dressing robe, letting it fall open. It was about three yards to the bed. He made it with a great leap, shouting, "Tally ho!" with a whoop of delight.

"Hell fire!"

Freddie was transfixed. It was a man's voice.

There were tangles of limbs and bodies underneath him. He moved his hand and felt an enormous bosom, a loose blancmange of flesh. Unwittingly his fingers closed on it in a spasm of horror.

"How dare you!" Mrs. Pusey's voice throbbed through the darkness with outrage.

Freddie snatched his hand away. The archdeacon's round belly was under his knees, there seemed to be legs everywhere. A sweat of horror broke out all over his body.

If he said nothing, perhaps they would never know who he was? He would lie—say he had not even woken all night. Please God? He must get out, find the door and escape. This was worse than the worst nightmare imaginable.

He made a mighty heave and fell onto the floor on the far side of the bed next to the window, dragging the counterpane with him, suffocating and entangling. There was a shriek from the bed. In blind panic he fought the counterpane, kicking and thrashing. His foot struck the chamber pot with a clang. At last he was free. On hands and knees he scrambled round the end of the bed and across the floor. He reached up for the door knob, and a moment later was outside in the corridor, gasping for breath, shaking like an aspen.

He could not stay here. The archdeacon would be out at any moment to look for him. It would be unbearable. No excuse in the world would do. And when the minister heard of it, it would be disaster.

He straightened up and walked smartly back the way he had come, past the table and the flowers; one door, two, the linen cupboard, his own room . . . thank heaven! Once he was inside he would be safe. The archdeacon, like everyone else, thought this was Pamela's room; he would never presume to waken her.

He pulled on the handle, swung it open, and slid into sanctuary, a prayer of relief on his lips.

He needed a drink. Ridgeway was a pompous blighter, but he was an immaculate butler, he would have seen to it that a tray was left—a tot of brandy might help and it could not hurt. Turn the gas up—see what he was doing.

It took only a moment, then the soft glow filled the room. Where was that tray? He turned to look.

It was incredible! There was Daisy in the bed, waiting for him, her hair spread out on the pillow. How could they have misunderstood each other so disastrously?

He dimmed the light, slipped off his robe, and climbed back into the bed. He reached out to take hold of her. Her body was warm and firm, just as he remembered it. He held her closely, gently; but she did not respond.

"Daisy!" She could not possibly be asleep so soon. "Daisy!"

Still she did not move. He sat up and pulled her sharply. Her head fell back, her eyes closed.

"Daisy!" Suddenly there was panic in him. It was impossible—wasn't it? "Daisy!" He shook her, then again violently.

She was unconscious. What in heaven's name was he going to do?

He could not leave her here, nor could he manage to carry her back to her own room—he did not even know which one it was. The memory of Mrs. Pusey brought the sweat out on his skin again. He could feel hysteria beating its way up inside him, ready to explode.

He must call someone. If Daisy were ill he must get her help, quickly. But who? Who was there who would not go off into a barrage of idiotic questions rather than dealing with the problem?

Dealing with it! He had another man's wife lying unconscious in his bed! How could anyone deal with that?

"Oh God!" he howled desperately. "Oh God, help me!" He covered his face with his hands. He was ready to weep. Perhaps he had had too much brandy after dinner and this was all an abominable hallucination? Please—please, that was it!

No. He looked through his fingers and she was still there, her face mottled red. She had not moved at all.

He was shaking all over as if he were in an icy wind, but it was a hot summer night.

This was useless. He must help her.

Pamela—Pamela would come! She would help Daisy first —if she wanted to lecture him on his wits or his morals, she would do it after. At least he was sure where Pamela was—in his room in the west wing.

He went out again and almost ran along the corridor. He knocked very sharply and, when there was no immediate answer, rattled the knob.

A moment later Pamela appeared, dressing robe thrown around her shoulders.

"Freddie! What's happened? Is the house on fire?"

He realized suddenly that he had been banging on the door almost as if he would force it, and that he still had nothing on but his nightshirt.

"Something awful has happened!" he gasped. "You've got to help me. Daisy Beech is ill—in a coma—I can't rouse her—"

Pamela's eyebrows shot up. "You can't rouse her?" she repeated incredulously.

Freddie felt sick with misery. "Pamela, for God's sake help me. She's ill—in my bed."

"Oh Freddie, for—" Then her outrage dissolved as she recognized the fear in his voice even though she could not see his face against the light. "Of course. You'd better stay here. I'll get Digby." She went back into the room, turned up the gas and lit it, then rang the maid's bell. Freddie followed her in and sat down sharply in the dressing chair, his legs weak.

Five minutes later Pamela was outside on the landing with her lady's maid, a middle-aged, stocky woman of immense common sense.

"Digby, we have a problem," Pamela said frankly. She trusted Digby more than anyone else in the world. "Lady Beech has been taken ill—in Mr. Dagliesh's bed."

Digby's wispy eyebrows rose over her round grey eyes, but her Yorkshire voice remained perfectly calm. "Indeed, ma'am, then we had better help the poor lady."

Pamela led the way, tiptoeing along the passage. At the bedroom door she pushed it open gently, beckoned Digby in, closed it, and turned the key. Inside, the gas lamps still burned dimly, winking in the brandy decanter and the glass. Daisy Beech was lying motionless and red-faced between the rumpled sheets.

Pamela walked over to the bed. She looked at Daisy, then put the backs of her fingers gently on the vein in her neck and waited for a moment.

"Is there a mirror on the dresser, Digby?" she asked.

"No, ma'am," Digby answered. "I'll get the brandy glass." She picked it up and polished it before passing it.

Pamela put the smooth barrel of the glass in front of Daisy's mouth, then held it up and examined it. There was no shadow of breath clouding it.

"She's dead," Pamela said very softly, her mouth dry. She turned to look at Digby. "She must have had a stroke or something."

"Then there is nothing more we can do for the poor creature," Digby replied with a little shake of her head.

"Except keep her reputation." Pamela looked where Daisy was lying, one arm spread wide, her silk nightgown open at the neck, embroidered in white thread. It was beautiful, but hardly modest. "And Freddie's," she added. "We'll have to get her back to her own room. Can you take her feet if I take her shoulders?"

Digby let out her breath in a sharp little sigh, but she did not argue. She had been in service to the Quality since she was fourteen, and she had seen many unusual events, although this was unique even for her. Obediently she retied the sash of her robe a little more firmly and moved up to the bed. "I think we had better take her in the sheet, ma'am," she suggested practically. "For decency's sake." As she spoke she folded Daisy's arms gently and pulled the linen over her and round, covering her face and shoulders.

"Just a moment!" Pamela whispered fiercely. "I'm going out to turn off the lamps in the corridors. I'd far rather risk stumbling in the dark than meeting anyone and trying to explain this to them."

"Who would we meet?" Digby hissed back.

"I don't know. Anyone. Someone else might be—visiting. Or have heard us." She slipped out of the door, and a moment later the passageway outside dimmed, and then went totally dark. She came back into the room and hurried over to the bed. Together, very awkwardly because Daisy was a big woman, they eased her off the bed, carefully wound in the sheet, then onto the floor, and with intense effort, gradually, step by step, catching their feet in the trailing drapes, they moved across the room, out into the corridor. Breathing heavily, whispering warnings and imprecations at each other and the night in general, they made their way along the passage. Once Pamela stood on the sheet and all but pitched over. Digby stifled a squeal of horror.

At the corner they bumped into a wall and nearly collapsed. Daisy was incredibly awkward; she seemed to have a passion to fold up in the middle and sit down. Digby's arms ached with the effort of holding her, and Pamela was groaning as she struggled to hang onto Daisy's shoulders.

Only a few yards more to go.

Then they froze. Horror prickled on Digby's scalp and she felt all her hair rise. There was someone else in the corridor, someone creeping.

Pamela's breath came out in a sigh close to her ear.

They waited. Seconds ticked by. Pamela pulled at Digby's sleeve. They must move before the other person found the light on the wall at the corner and re-lit it.

Slowly they began again: a yard, another yard. Pamela caught her feet in the trailing sheet, swayed, stubbed her toe on a table leg—and bit her lip to prevent herself from swearing.

Then just as the corridor lamp burned up, Digby closed the door and they were alone in Daisy's room. They staggered over to the bed and heaved her onto it; then Pamela drew the covers over her and they both sank to their knees on the floor.

"Now what?" Pamela said hopelessly. "What on earth are we going to tell Anthony Beech?"

There was silence for a moment. Indeed the question was not as easy as either of them had assumed.

"That poor Lady Beech is dead," Digby replied at last. "Although how we account for the fact that we discovered her, I cannot imagine."

"We have to tell him," Pamela said reluctantly. "We can't just leave her here."

Digby's plain, northern common sense asserted itself. "We'll have to do that, ma'am. There's nothing we can do for her except keep our discretion. It won't be Sir Anthony who finds her, it'll be Croft, her maid who came with her, bringing in her tea in the morning."

"Couldn't you?" Pamela asked hopefully. "It would be—"

"I dare say I can find a way—" Digby could not promise. She climbed to her feet slowly, legs shaking. "But we'd better take that sheet back."

"What? Oh!" Pamela gazed at the extra sheet, still half under Daisy. "Damnation! That would have taken some explaining."

With another awkward effort they managed to extricate the sheet and laid Daisy in a fairly natural position, covered by the quilt, then turned the light out and crept back, feeling their way along the wall this time, to Freddie's room to replace the sheet, and finally back to their own beds; Digby to the servants' quarters, Pamela to the west wing where Freddie was waiting, ashen-faced.

"I'm awfully sorry, Freddie—I'm afraid she's dead. We put her back in her own room," she said, sitting down wearily. "We'll get the doctor in the morning, but there's nothing he can do."

"We can't get the doctor till Tuesday," Freddie replied. "He's gone away for the weekend."

"How did it happen?" She looked up at him. "Was it a stroke?"

"I don't know, I—" He stared at her, his eyes hot and unhappy, but still not a shred of color in his face. "I came back and found her like that."

"You what?"

"I—I went to her room—and—and somehow we missed each other. When I got back to my own room, Daisy was there—like that."

"Oh." Pamela stood up. "Well, you'd better go back to bed, and in the morning just pretend you know nothing about it. It's the kindest thing you can do for Daisy now."

"I'd rather—" he looked wretched· "—I'd rather not go back—"

She touched him gently. She had not realized he was so truly fond of Daisy Beech. "Then go to the library and sleep on the couch. I'll see you in the morning."

"Thank you, Pamela." He touched her gently, briefly.

Pamela slept little and was already awake when Digby came in at half past seven with a hot cup of tea. She put it down on the bedside table and drew the curtains before saying rather self-consciously, "I'm extremely sorry to tell you, ma'am, that Lady Beech passed away during the night. I have told her maid, Croft, but I thought perhaps you would prefer to tell Sir Anthony yourself. I'm afraid Mr. Dagliesh is not at all well this morning."

"Thank you, Digby." Pamela met her eyes and smiled

weakly. She took the tea and sipped it, and began to feel as if perhaps she could cope.

Digby's face was anxious, but there was a familiarity about it that was reassuring.

"Yes," Pamela agreed. "I'll tell Sir Anthony. You'd better get out something black—or grey at least."

"Yes, ma'am, I already did, the grey silk. You won't be wanting a bath this morning?"

"No, thank you, there isn't time."

Pamela was barely dressed and Digby was putting up her hair when there was a knock on the door and Sophie came in. She was just seventeen, slender and pretty, but her charm lay in her coloring and her expression; she would never be the beauty her mother was.

"Good morning, Mama," she said cheerfully. "Is it all right if I go for a carriage ride this morning? I thought I should like to call on the Misses Burridge at the Grange."

"No—no, I'm afraid not." Pamela handed hairpins to Digby. "Lady Beech passed away during the night."

"Oh!" Sophie sat down suddenly on the bed. "Oh, how awful! Poor Sir Anthony! I—"

Pamela turned round, looking at her daughter more closely. She was perfectly aware that for some time past Sophie had cherished a yearning admiration for Anthony Beech, but she had hoped it would run its course and be replaced by something more suitable. Now Daisy's death made Beech an even more romantic figure, and she could see it already in Sophie's young face and wide eyes.

"I think you should respect his privacy this morning," Pamela said. "It is not kind to intrude upon people's moments of grief, especially a man's. He will want to present a dignified appearance, particularly now when he is seeking high office. Give him time to compose himself, my dear."

"Oh." Sophie looked crestfallen. She had been about to rush forward with gentleness and sympathy, but she realized the wisdom of Pamela's guidance. "Yes, I suppose so. How terrible—I didn't even know she was ill, although of course we all knew she was so much older than he—"

"She was only fifty-three," Pamela said tartly. "Now go and change into something plain."

Sophie went out, and, now that her hair was finished, Pamela thanked Digby and prepared herself to tell Anthony Beech his wife was dead.

She found him in his room, standing in front of the mirror adjusting his tie.

"Good morning, Mrs. Selden," he said, raising his eyebrows a little, but he was too well-mannered, too careful, to show outright surprise.

She closed the door. "I am afraid it isn't a good morning, Anthony. I have some very bad news for you—I am extremely sorry—Daisy passed away during the night."

"What?" He stood uncomprehendingly, blank-faced.

"Daisy passed away during the night," she repeated. "I think it may have been a stroke—" She wanted to say something about its being sudden, but he would wonder how she knew that and explanation was impossible. "I'm so sorry. I expect you'd like to be alone for a while—I'll send Ridgeway with tea or a brandy, if you'd prefer. I'll see that everything is done to help, and please ask for anything you wish."

"Daisy—gone?" He was very pale. He looked elegant, polished—and empty. "Dear God, how awful! She can't—"

"I am afraid there is no doubt."

He sat down slowly and put his head in his hands, closing her out. There was nothing for Pamela to do but retreat quietly and seek Ridgeway to tell him of affairs and send him to do what he could. The rest of the household would have to get on by itself.

Breakfast was ghastly. Andrew Delamain was the first one down and was busy at the sideboard helping himself to deviled kidneys, bacon, sausages, and eggs when Pamela came into the dining room. His first reaction was one of pleasure. His eyes lit up and he was about to speak when he saw the pallor of her face, the shadows and the tensions around her throat. His concern was immediate and genuine.

"Are you all right?"

"Yes, thank you, but I'm afraid Daisy Beech died during the night." She did not use any euphemism. Delamain was one of the few people with whom pretense was unnecessary; it was the quality in him she liked most.

"I'm sorry." He looked shocked. He put his hand out and clasped her arm in an instinctive gesture of compassion.

The door opened again and Lucy Delamain came in, fair, elegant, and fragile. Instantly her eyes flew to Delamain's hand, and her face tightened with the memory of other glances, laughter shared, and hot, bright moments observed and cut off. "Good morning, Mrs. Selden," she said icily, her voice thick with emotion. "You don't look well."

"Daisy Beech died in the night," Delamain said abruptly.

Lucy winced at the uncouthness of expression. One did not die, one passed away, or was taken. "I'm sorry," she said aloud. "Poor Anthony must be very distressed."

"Naturally," Pamela replied. "So are we."

The dining room door swung open and Archdeacon Pusey stood in the entrance, red-cheeked, his hair in grey, startled tufts round his ears, his eyes glaring.

"Mrs. Selden!" he said with quivering voice. "I do not know where Mr. Dagliesh is—he appears not to have arisen yet—so I must make my complaint to you. I apologize for the gross indelicacy, but I am left no choice. Mrs. Pusey and I have been unpardonably insulted. Only my duty to the minister, and to my country, compels me to remain under your roof an hour longer. But you may be sure it will not be forgotten."

Pamela was bewildered, and found the whole thing both ridiculous and irrelevant. Daisy Beech was dead; what could an ill-chosen or tasteless remark matter? She tried to find something soothing to say, but nothing came.

Delamain's hand tightened on her arm, steadying her.

"Lady Beech passed away in the night," he said crisply. "I think you would be more use comforting Sir Anthony than cherishing your grievances, whatever they may be."

The archdeacon's face blanched first with outrage at being spoken to in such a manner, then with shock as the comprehension of death reached him.

Evan Marshall appeared in the doorway behind him, his mercurial face full of sympathy.

"Did you say Lady Beech passed away in the night?" he asked quietly. "I'm extremely sorry, she was a charming woman—we shall all miss her."

Upstairs Digby offered her help to Croft, Daisy Beech's maid. Laying out the dead was a grim business, and natural compassion for a woman obviously badly shaken and frightened for her own now uncertain future prompted her to offer her assistance.

They were halfway through the sad but necessary offices when suddenly Croft stopped, her body motionless, her face even more pallid than usual. Digby was afraid she was going to faint.

"Sit down!" she commanded. "Sit down and put your head forward—I'll finish."

But Croft did not move. "You don't understand," she said hoarsely. She held up Daisy's dead hand.

Digby stared at it; it was smooth and soft, fingers tapered, by far the loveliest feature of an otherwise plain woman, except that today there were three fingernails torn off, leaving rough, ugly edges.

"They weren't like that last night," Croft said almost under her breath. "I'll swear to that. I buffed them and filed them for her. And she'd never have gone to bed with them all tore like that, even if she'd had an accident—she'd have called me—or even done them herself."

"Well, they *are* torn," Digby said.

"Then someone else did it." Croft would not be moved. Her face was set hard, and as white as whey. "She fought with someone."

Digby opened her mouth to say "Nonsense!" but the word died on her lips. "Well, let's see if we can find the torn nails," she said instead. She was certainly not going to tell Croft that Daisy had died somewhere else. She looked more closely at the hand, then at the other. There was dried blood thick under two of the nails.

Together they searched all the bedding and round the floor, but found no torn nails.

"I think you had better have a hot cup of tea," Digby suggested, her mind racing. "Who on earth would want to—to fight with Lady Beech?"

"Whoever killed her," Croft said breathlessly. "Oh, Gawd help us!"

"Sit down," Digby ordered. "I'll get you the tea—and we'll think about this, and what's to be done."

Outside in the corridor she was overwhelmed. Murder! The scandal would be appalling. They would never recover. The very first thing she must do was stop Croft spreading it all over the place or the whole house would be in an uproar. She would put a good stiff dose of laudanum in her tea; that should take care of this morning at least.

But by the time she had got back to Daisy's bedroom, the upstairs maid had been in, and even though she managed to persuade Croft to take to her bed and remain there, the damage was begun.

Could it be true? She must be sure. She went back to the room where Pamela had called her in the middle of the night. It was empty, Freddie had refused to come back to it. Inside she closed the door and walked over to the bed. It took her five minutes before she found two of the ragged nails. Then, breathless, her heart beating in her ears, she stood up and pushed her hair with a shaking hand. She looked at the bed. Daisy Beech had been murdered here sometime last night, between Freddie Dagliesh's leaving it and his coming back. By whom? And why?

She stared at it. There was something wrong with the bed apart from the top sheet's being in a tangle where Pamela had thrown it—but what? It was not as a bed should be . . . pillows! That was it—there was a pillow missing! Was it torn where Daisy had scrabbled at it as it lay pressed over her face? Was there blood on it? There must be something—some reason why the murderer had removed it rather than simply leaving it where it belonged.

This was too much to manage alone. She must find an ally.

Without any very clear idea, she went downstairs to the kitchen, locking the bedroom door behind her.

In the main kitchen two scullery maids were struggling

with piles of vegetables, the pastry cook was waving her hands in the air, scattering flour all over the place, another maid wept, a fourth slopped around with a wet mop regardless of them all. And Mrs. Jenkins, the cook, sleeves rolled up, was shouting at anyone and everyone.

Ridgeway appeared in the doorway at the far side of the room, magnificent in regal black, his cravat tied immaculately, his face wearing an expression of monumentally affronted dignity.

"May I ask what the trouble is, Mrs. Jenkins?" he said in a pained voice.

"Trouble?" she shrieked, flinging her hands up and inadvertently hurling half a dozen slices of cucumber into the air.

"If the garden produce is unsatisfactory, I suggest you inform the outside staff and send for more," Ridgeway said coldly. "I am sure there will be another cucumber ready in the glass house, if you ask the appropriate person."

Her mouth fell open; then, with a mighty effort, she collected her wits.

"There's been a terrible death in the house an' I've got maids sniffling around in 'ere," she said furiously, "scared half senseless by stupid talk. Rosie took to her bed with the grippe, a houseparty upstairs is expecting to be fed like royalty, and somebody's talking about murder! Murder, indeed! And me with a headache like a tin bucket. And you standing there as if you've nothing to do in the world but ask me fool questions 'bout a cucumber! That's what's the matter, Mr. Ridgeway."

"You threw the cucumber before I mentioned it, Mrs. Jenkins," he pointed out stiffly. "I shall attend to the housemaids; however, the kitchen staff are your concern. I suggest you find sufficient work to occupy them so they have no time left over to speculate on the affairs of their betters."

He looked at the pastry cook with an icy eye. "And, madam, you are spreading flour over half the kitchen, which I can hardly believe is constructive in the preparation of luncheon. If you have nothing of your own to attend to, I am sure something can be found."

Mrs. Jenkins swelled up in indignation. "As you remarked,

Mr. Ridgeway, the kitchen staff are my concern. I will thank you to leave their discipline to me and get back to your own responsibilities. What do you want in my kitchen anyway?"

"A glass of milk and a raw egg," he said. "I might suggest the same thing for your own headache."

One of the girls giggled and scurried away with a pan in her hands, head bent to hide her face.

Mrs. Jenkins snorted. The pastry cook took herself off, and Ridgeway began to prepare his egg and milk and put it on a tray to take up to Freddie.

Digby was in a turmoil. There was something even more urgent in her mind than preventing a ruinous scandal. Since Daisy Beech had been murdered in the dark, while lying in Pamela's bed, it was a hideous but quite possible fact that the murderer may have mistaken his victim and that it was Pamela he had intended. And might still intend.

She went to Pamela's room. There were duties which still had to be done, and it gave her the opportunity to be alone to think. Beginning to tidy up, she came upon a copy of the *Strand* magazine. She knew from a previous comment that Pamela had borrowed it from Ridgeway. It fell open where it had last been read—to a story by Conan Doyle about a highly peculiar person by the name of Sherlock Holmes, a private detective. She sat on the bed in the sun for a full twenty minutes reading it. It was a most unsuitable subject for a lady —but it really was most absorbing! What a remarkably brilliant man, such perception, and such courage. Of course Dr. Watson was not nearly so clever but he was totally loyal.

Then quite suddenly she had an idea, indeed a stroke that was so dazzling it quite stunned her. She folded the magazine, took a final glance round the room to make sure it was satisfactory, and hurried downstairs.

Ridgeway was in his pantry. She closed the door behind her and stood with her back to it.

"Mr. Ridgeway, I have something which I believe I should return to you, and perhaps I might seek a moment or two of your time. There is a concern upon which you might advise me, it is most serious—"

"Certainly, Miss Digby. How may I be of assistance?" He indicated a chair, then parted his coattails and sat down himself, his face courteously expectant.

She held out the magazine. "I believe this may be yours, Mr. Ridgeway."

"Indeed." He took it with a faint touch of pink in his cheeks. He thought to deny it, then caught Digby's eye and discarded the idea.

Digby looked back at him. There was no time for personal feelings now; there was most pressing business to be done. Briefly and simply she told him everything that had happened from the time Pamela had rung for her in the night, right up to her one dreadful conclusion that there had been murder done—and might yet be done again.

"Mr. Ridgeway, it seems to me that the methods employed by Mr. Holmes and Dr. Watson invariably produce success. I regret that beyond question a reasonable person must conclude that there has been a murder in this house, and whoever is responsible is still here. I believe it is our duty to discover who this person is before there is a scandal which will ruin Mr. Dagliesh and may even lead to another death."

"Miss Digby!" He was almost bereft of speech. His face had lost all its color and remained ash-white for an instant; then, as his mind grasped the enormity of what she had said—and that they should bend their minds to solving it—he blushed cherry red.

"Miss Digby! You are a woman of—of great perception. I can see that you are perfectly right. We must assemble our facts and use our deductive powers. I have read every story of Mr. Sherlock Holmes to date—I believe I am familiar with his methods. If you will be so good, you may be my Watson." He was conferring an immeasurable privilege upon her—a mere woman.

She had no intention of being his Watson; she intended to be Holmes, and he to be her Watson. But it would be impolitic to say so.

"Thank you," she forced herself to reply demurely. "Now we had better put in order all the facts we know—those which are indubitable. Have you a piece of paper?"

Ridgeway fished for a notebook out of his pocket, and a pen. Digby began immediately.

"We may imagine that whoever it was did not stop to light the gas, so the crime was committed by whatever little moonlight came through the curtains."

"Is that important?" Ridgeway did not write it down.

"Yes, of course it is!" Digby said impatiently. "Since it was Mrs. Selden's room, and as far as I know, no one knew of the change except Mrs. Selden herself, Mr. Dagliesh, and, we must presume, Lady Beech." She colored faintly pink at the necessity of discussing such a thing, but circumstances left her no alternative. Her mother had always said that curiosity was a characteristic of the vulgar, but how else could one detect?

Ridgeway wrote something in a meticulous hand. "Do we know that beyond doubt?" he asked. "If we do, then we must assume—" he stopped and cleared his throat "—we must assume the impossible."

"Impossible?" Digby raised her eyebrows. "Mr. Sherlock Holmes says—"

"I know what he says," Ridgeway interrupted quickly. "When we have eliminated the impossible, whatever is left, however unlikely, must be the truth. So either Mrs. Selden was the intended victim, or someone else knew of the change." He smiled with some satisfaction at Digby's puzzled look. "We cannot believe that Mr. Dagliesh killed Lady Beech in his own bed. Or that Mrs. Selden did, in her brother's bed, and chose to help conceal it in such a way. And certainly not that Lady Beech killed herself."

Digby was furious with herself for not having followed through the logic of it—it was not a promising beginning. It made her sound exactly like Dr. Watson at his most typical.

"Indeed," she said dryly. "So someone else knew, either beforehand or else saw Lady Beech in the corridor and followed her to take his chance."

"Precisely. We have no evidence as to opportunity." Ridgeway wrote it down. "The means appears, from what you say, to have been a pillow, which we have not yet found. You might instigate a search for it, Miss Digby. Speak to the upstairs maids. It might be helpful if we were to discover where it is, although of course it may have been deliberately left somewhere to lay a false trail."

"We are left with motive," Digby finished the summary for him. "We must consider crimes of gain, or fear, or—" she hesitated and cleared her throat "—or passion."

Ridgeway kept his eyes on his pencil. "Only Miss Sophie would gain from Mrs. Selden's death, and that is something we do not need to consider. Lady Beech's death, however, is quite a different matter. It is commonly known that she was a lady of considerable wealth; indeed the unkind have suggested—" He did not complete the thought, the implication was obvious.

Digby was less squeamish. "But Sir Anthony had the use of it," she pointed out. "He always has had; his style of living is witness of that."

"Perhaps he had debts that Lady Beech would not settle for him," Ridgeway suggested. "Gentlemen sometimes gamble, or even—" He looked up at Digby's round eyes and homely face. "They have even been known to run establishments for other women, which may be a considerable expense. Lady Beech would certainly not have countenanced that—especially when Sir Anthony is in strong contention for such an important position."

Digby shook her head. "He is a most ambitious man," she said with conviction. "I don't believe it is in his character to keep a mistress at such a time—it is far too great a risk. But I suppose it is possible he may have fallen in love and wished to marry someone else, which would not be possible with Lady Beech alive."

"And he would inherit Lady Beech's money," Ridgeway added. "They have no living children. But we must consider all the possibilities. One of the other gentlemen may have had a motive we do not yet know of." He stared at the paper. "A jealous passion seems unlikely."

"If there were such a thing, it would make far more sense to kill Sir Anthony," Digby pointed out.

Ridgeway thought for a moment. "I doubt we are looking

for sense, Miss Digby. If a man felt a woman had betrayed him, he might act quite irrationally."

"We would appear to be back to Sir Anthony again," Digby said with irrefutable logic. "He does not seem to me to be a man of such passion."

"It is not merely passion, Miss Digby. There is much in man's nature that is complex and obscure. A man may feel intense possessiveness for something he does not particularly value, simply because it is his—and regard any man who trespasses as having violated his dignity unforgivably. I believe it is an adequate motive."

"Possibly." Digby was reluctant. "I think Sir Anthony a colder person than that. Mr. Marshall or Mr. Delamain I would believe it of."

Ridgeway's eyebrows rose. "You have had remarkable opportunities for observation, Miss Digby," he observed with a mixture of envy and incredulity.

She would not lower her gaze in the slightest. "I have overheard the ladies talking," she replied with a blush; it did not do to repeat what one overheard—not ever! But these circumstances were unique, and of very pressing danger to the people in question. She plunged on. "If the killer thought it was Mrs. Selden, then it may very well have been Mrs. Delamain—I am afraid Mr. Delamain's admiration for Mrs. Selden is very deep, and of a somewhat . . . passionate nature. It has not gone unremarked."

"Jealousy." Ridgeway wrote it down. Then suddenly he looked up and met Digby's eyes over the paper. They both had the same dreadful thought at the same moment. They had seen Sophie's longing looks at Anthony Beech, had seen her gaze following his figure, marked the hesitant conversations, the quick blushes.

"Certainly not," Digby said without the certainty she had intended. "But we must prove it."

"We will." Ridgeway stood up. "Miss Digby, you must begin your detection by offering your services to Sir Anthony to pack Lady Beech's effects. If we apply our intelligence and deductive reasoning, we should be able to discover the truth, and prove it beyond dispute. There must be something which will lead us to an inevitable conclusion."

With another dose of laudanum for Croft, and plenty of sympathy, Digby had no difficulty in finding herself alone in Daisy Beech's room with the task of packing her belongings for Sir Anthony to take home with him when he left. Daisy herself was laid in the small family chapel in the east wing.

It was a sad duty, but Digby steeled herself to do it not only as a skilled ladies' maid, but as a detective at least the equal of Ridgeway.

The clothes yielded nothing, except that they were not only of excellent quality but of a taste that Digby could only admire for its mixture of dignity and panache. All the underlinen was immaculate. The hats and gowns were expensive; she imagined Daisy's own money had probably purchased far more of them than Sir Anthony's. How much had that disturbed him? Was he aching to have the mastery of that money himself? What would he do with it? Pay debts? Keep a mistress? Marry some other woman, younger, prettier than Daisy?

The toiletry articles were what she would have expected, the arts and artifices of retaining what charms of youth were possible, richness of the hair, softness and bloom of the skin, a little color, a delightful perfume, the rustle of taffeta when one moved, the glimpse of lace.

Subconsciously she had put off the most distasteful task until last, but her sense also told her it would be the most likely to yield anything of use. Normally she would have packed a letter case without opening it, simply making sure that everything was cleaned out of any desk, pigeonhole, and drawer. Now she had to remind herself how much was at stake, and open and read every sheet of paper. Not that there was a great deal, it was only a stay of some six or seven days. There were a couple of business letters, which were surprising in themselves—Digby would have expected financial affairs to have been dealt with by Sir Anthony, even if the money were actually Daisy's—but it seemed she also made the serious decisions, at least about the proposed purchase of a house in Bath. Judging from a letter addressed to her, the agent in the matter was answering some highly pertinent questions she had asked, and with care; it was no flattery of a woman who could be fooled.

Digby turned to the personal letters. The first was from a duchess and thanked Daisy for some past guidance, at the same time inviting her and Sir Anthony to visit them in the country for a weekend in the near future. The second came from a junior cabinet minister, and was couched in terms of both friendship, and, more curiously, a considerable regard for her counsel. He thanked her for past advice and told her how well it had resulted, and begged her suggestions in a further matter. Daisy's reply was already half written. It was of outstanding clarity, and she neither flattered him nor withheld her opinions yet the whole was well-expressed and courteous.

Digby stood in the center of the room with an extraordinary feeling of amazement and dawning wonder. It would seem Daisy Beech was far from the rather pedestrian, middle-aged figure of some pity she appeared to Sophie and her like—in fact she was both highly intelligent and wise enough to be discreet about it.

Digby had often heard Pamela Selden say that much of the real political business of the nation was conducted not in Whitehall but in the homes of the mighty and the salons where the powerful met. The right wife, wise, discreet, with enough wit to amuse and enough charm to please, might be one of a diplomat's greatest assets.

Had Anthony Beech known that? Was that Daisy's true worth to him, far above her money?

Or had he perhaps not known it, and imagined his success was his own? Perhaps it had never occurred to him that without her he was of little value. Or maybe he believed she was simply a stepping stone for him, and had survived her usefulness.

These were ideas that altered all measures of motive.

Digby was still standing in the middle of the room. Everything was neatly packed in trunks and suitcases, the wardrobe and drawers empty and ready to be relined. She looked at the pile again. Perched on top were the hat boxes, the writing case, and the leather jewel case. She had kept the key to give to Sir Anthony. She had not looked through that, it would do little beyond establish Daisy Beech's wealth and her taste, which was already known.

But thoroughness was important; Sherlock Holmes would not have overlooked it, no matter how distasteful or purposeless it seemed—or how dangerous. What explanation could she give for rooting through Daisy Beech's jewel case? She might easily be suspected of vulgar inquisitiveness at best, at worst of intent to steal.

Better lock the door first.

With the doorkey turned, she opened the jewel case and cast an experienced eye over necklaces, bracelets, earrings, brooches, and rings. There was a movable tray, which she lifted out. Underneath it were three stickpins of very moderate value, a silver frame with a lock of baby hair, memory of a life too brief, and under a cameo without a pin, a gold-plated locket with the chain missing. Feeling ashamed and intrusive, Digby opened it and stared at the picture inside. It was a young man, dark-haired with brilliant eyes, the sort of face that demands attention. It was familiar, yet for several minutes she could not place it. She had seen those eyes before, and recently, yet the hairline and the mouth seemed different—

Then as the upstairs maid's footsteps scurried in the passage outside it came to her—Evan Marshall! Evan Marshall twenty-five or thirty years ago. She snapped the locket closed, dropped it in the bottom of the case, replaced the tray, and fastened the lock.

Someone tried the door handle. Digby replaced the jewel case and locked it.

Knuckles rapped smartly on the door.

"Coming!" Digby called, turned the key, and found the upstairs maid pink and flustered, hair wisping out of her cap, standing outside.

"Oh! Miss Digby!"

"You may do the room now," Digby said with as much composure as she could. "I have packed everything. It is all complete. Just leave it where it is." And she swept past to find Ridgeway and give him the latest evidence.

Ridgeway received it with great interest, but Digby could not judge from his expression how much importance he attached to it. He spoke about logic and deduction and methods of reasoning until the library bell summoned him.

The evening was sad and subdued. No one felt like eating and conversation was stilted, more of an embarrassment than an ease. Anthony Beech had decided to remain; Daisy would not be helped by his abandoning his professional ambitions, the position she had helped him so much to build.

But under the sober exchange of minor politenesses the emotions were still there. Delamain and Evan Marshall subtly crossed swords, Sophie gazed at Anthony Beech with aching sympathy, and some time after the port had been passed, she at last found her opportunity to talk with him alone.

Freddie did his duty as host, but it was a shadow of his old art. The sense of loss seemed to have touched him more deeply than anyone else.

Delamain was subdued, compared with his normal wit, but not even death could spoil his admiration for Pamela, nor hide it sufficiently from Lucy for her to miss the look in his eyes and the lift in his voice.

The following day was Sunday and everyone went to church in the village, the ladies wearing their most sombre clothes even in the sharp sun, looking like moths against the pastels and scarlets of the flowers.

In the afternoon Digby found Sophie sitting alone in the library staring through the french windows at the garden. She looked round as Digby came in. "Don't bother to iron my lilac dress for dinner, Digby," she said with a shadowy smile. "The pale grey will do—but thank you."

The lilac was far more flattering, and Digby knew it. "Don't you feel well, Miss Sophie?" she said with concern.

Sophie turned back to the window, the long lawn and the Albertine rose swamping the wall of the kitchen garden with a mass of coral blooms. "I'm quite well, thank you."

"You must give him time to grieve," Digby said. "In a few months it will be different."

"I doubt it," Sophie said bleakly, her voice hopeless.

Digby spoke from instinct, not detection. "Why not? Whatever has been said now is on the spur of shock and natural distress. You mustn't take it to heart."

Sophie turned round, tears in her eyes. "Time will not make any difference, Digby. I thought I was in love with him—he was so—so wise and dignified. I thought he had such earnestness—not like the shallow young men I know. But when you talk to him properly, I mean alone, he isn't like that at all." She sniffed hard and blushed. "Digby, he's—terribly ordinary—in fact he's rather a bore."

At first Digby was overwhelmingly relieved for her. The last thing Sophie needed, whatever she thought, was an alliance with a man twice her age, destined for political office that would require her to forfeit all the levity of youth and to assume onerous responsibilities from the day of her engagement.

Then the other implications of what Sophie had said came to her. A bore! Terribly ordinary when you talked to him alone. So it had been Daisy—her skill, her judgment, her charm—not only at the beginning, but even now—he was lost without her!

The question was—who knew it?

Digby found Ridgeway in his pantry decanting brandy. She went in quickly and closed the door. Ridgeway stopped, bottle in mid-air, his eyebrows raised. He was highly irritated that he had discovered very little of interest himself, but determined that his superior logic would interpret the facts she brought as Holmes interpreted the facts the loyal Watson delivered to him. He knew from Digby's face that there was something new.

"Well?" he inquired. "What have you observed?"

"It is far more than an observation, Mr. Ridgeway, it is a fact."

"Indeed?" He did not entirely hide his skepticism. "Facts may have many meanings. We must apply our intelligence to it." He began very carefully to pour from the bottle again. "Well—what is it?"

Digby felt a trifle dampened. Put like that it did not sound as revelatory as she had thought it at the time. "Sir Anthony is dull—in fact something of a bore."

Ridgeway looked at her over the top of the bottle. He might have been addressing an underfootman with grubby shoes. "A fact, Miss Digby?"

The color burned up her face. "Yes, Mr. Ridgeway," she said indignantly. "When one spends time alone with him and speaks to him socially he is most disappointing."

"That is the loosest of opinions," he said critically. "Lots of gentlemen are not especially witty or entertaining in conversation. It does not make them murderers."

"And it very seldom makes them diplomats either!" Digby snapped back.

Slowly Ridgeway put the bottle down and stared at her, comprehension spreading across his face.

"Are you sure? How do you know? Whose opinion is that, Mrs. Selden's?"

"No." Digby dismissed that; he was quite right, she might well be biased. "No, it is Miss Sophie's."

"Miss Sophie? But I thought she—"

"She did! Until she had time to speak with him alone and at some length. She is most painfully disillusioned. In company and at some little distance he is glamorous; closer to, I am afraid he is very uninspiring."

"Ah!" Ridgeway let out his breath slowly. "So it would appear Lady Beech was the key to his success, not her money but her charm and judgment. But, Miss Digby, we must ask ourselves the question upon which all hangs. Who knew that? First of all, did Sir Anthony know it himself? If he did, we may exclude him from our list of suspects."

"I imagine he may suspect it," Digby began.

"Imagining is not fact, Miss Digby. It is not enough. We must do much better than that."

Digby drew breath to retaliate, then decided to play him at his own game. "Indeed," she said crisply. "We will work on eliminating the impossible. And it would seem we cannot eliminate Mr. Marshall. Since it is obvious from the photograph in the locket that he and Lady Beech were closely acquainted in their youth, he must have known that she was highly intelligent." She frowned as the thought occurred to her. "In fact, one is led to wonder why, if he was a suitor, she did not choose him instead of Sir Anthony."

"Perhaps she did not have the opportunity," Ridgeway suggested. "Her father may have preferred the Beech family, in spite of their lack of money. They are considerably better thought of than the Marshalls—whoever they are! But we may never know that, and it does not concern us now. I think we may safely assume that Mr. Marshall was aware of Lady Beech's qualities, and quite possibly of Sir Anthony's limitations."

"So it would be greatly to his advantage if Lady Beech were dead," Digby finished for him. "His chances of obtaining the position in the Foreign Office are increased in proportion—especially since Mrs. Delamain has been behaving so—unreliably—with regard to Mrs. Selden. Jealousy, however well founded, is something a lady should never allow herself to show."

"Indubitably, my dear Miss Digby," Ridgeway said with aplomb. "Mr. Marshall had a motive—Sir Anthony may have, although one doubts it. Now how about Mr. Delamain? We cannot discount him. To prove the possible is not enough—we must also disprove the impossible."

Digby sat down. "Mr. Ridgeway, if Mr. Marshall murdered poor Lady Beech in order to incapacitate Sir Anthony for the position at the Foreign Office, he must have known that Lady Beech was an essential asset to him."

"We have already concluded that," Ridgeway frowned. "I thought we were agreed."

"We are," Digby answered. "But would it not also be necessary, in order for Mr. Marshall's plan to work, for the minister who is to do the selecting also to know of Lady Beech's importance? Otherwise Sir Anthony might be chosen anyway, and he would have killed her for nothing."

"Oh!" Ridgeway sat down also. For several seconds he remained silent; then he lifted his head, gave a very slight sniff, and straightened his back. "Then, Miss Digby, we must use our ingenuity to discover whether the minister did indeed appreciate Lady Beech's value—or not, as the case may be. And further to that, we will discover whether Mr. Marshall knew that the minister knew—if you follow me?" He raised his eyebrows questioningly. "And of course, whether Mr. Delamain knew. You will begin with Mrs. Selden, if you will be so good. I shall begin with Archdeacon Pusey. I understand Mrs. Pusey is the minister's sister. The archdeacon may be party to much that we need to know." He stood up, readjusting his jacket to hang even more elegantly, and opened the door for Digby. "Come, Miss Digby, we have much to do if we are to obtain justice and prevent further tragedy."

Digby learned nothing of use from Pamela, but she did serve the other primary function of protecting her, as well as she could. After all, if they were wrong in their deductions so far, and it was not Daisy Beech who was the intended victim but Pamela, there must still be an intense danger present.

Ridgeway decided to be most solicitous for the archdeacon's welfare, to do all he could, personally, to make up for the shocking—and unnamed—insult that he and Mrs. Pusey had suffered in his master's house.

He knocked on the library door after having ascertained that the archdeacon was alone there, nursing his grievance—since he had no idea who was the culprit—by avoiding everyone.

"Good evening, sir," Ridgeway said graciously, closing the door behind him. "I wondered if you would care for a glass of Madeira before dinner? I have taken the liberty of bringing up the best the cellar has, sir; also a bottle of a most agreeable light sherry wine."

"Ah!" the archdeacon grunted, but his eyes lit up. He was fond of a good Madeira, and personal service always pleased him. "Yes—yes, I think I will."

"Very good, sir." Ridgeway put the tray down. He poured a little into the glass and offered it to him. "Is that to your taste, sir?"

The archdeacon swallowed it all. "Yes, it is, thank you." He passed it back and Ridgeway filled it again and put both the tray and the bottle within the archdeacon's reach.

"A most difficult time, sir," Ridgeway remarked, moving a cushion here and there as if he had some reason to linger. "I am sure everyone appreciates your generosity in remaining. You must be a great comfort to poor Sir Anthony."

The archdeacon looked slightly surprised, but he was not a man to turn down a compliment.

Ridgeway sighed earnestly. "The fruits of victory will have little savor now, with such bereavement."

"Victory?" The archdeacon took another long swig at the Madeira, and looked confused.

"The appointment to the Foreign Office, sir—if Sir Anthony should be the man the minister chooses to fill it."

"He won't," the archdeacon said with conviction.

"Do you think not, sir?" Ridgeway's voice was heavy with doubt. "Surely he is a most excellent candidate? Fine family, such dignity, presence—"

"Rubbish!" the archdeacon snorted, then realized he had spoken with less than discretion and changed it into a sneeze.

"Shall I close the window, sir?" Ridgeway offered.

The archdeacon glared at him. "No, thank you. Lovely evening!"

"More Madeira, sir?"

The archdeacon held up his glass and Ridgeway filled it yet again.

"So you don't believe the minister will choose Sir Anthony?" Ridgeway pursued it in a most uncharacteristic way. It was ill-mannered, and not a butler's place, and it hurt him acutely. But if he were to solve the murder of Daisy Beech, he must have information. "Lady Beech was, of course, a great asset to him," he pressed on.

"Very great!" the archdeacon agreed with a wry face.

"Does the minister appreciate that, sir?" Ridgeway lifted his voice as if he were surprised.

"Of course he does, man! He's not a fool!"

"Indeed, sir, of course not! I'm sure Mr. Marshall will be most happy when he learns that—"

"Knows it already," the archdeacon said sharply. "Ambitious man, but not out of the top drawer—not at all."

"No, sir. Then I expect it will be Mr. Delamain," Ridgeway would not give up yet. "He will be pleasantly surprised to discover that without Lady Beech, Sir Anthony is so much less suitable."

The archdeacon looked at him curiously. "I wouldn't know about that," he said with disapproval. "Thank you for the Madeira. That will be all."

"Yes, sir," Ridgeway bowed very slightly and withdrew.

"We have the facts." Digby and Ridgeway were alone downstairs in the silent kitchen. The last of the other servants had gone upstairs and the house was silent. It was quarter to midnight.

"It isn't enough," Ridgeway continued. "It is indicative, but it is not proof."

"It is not proof at all," Digby agreed. "There is a perfect case against Mr. Marshall. We know beyond dispute that he had the motive—he desires the position, and knows that Sir Anthony may well be considered more suitable, as long as Lady Beech is alive, and he knows the minister is aware of this. But Mr. Delamain might have known the same."

"We have no proof that he did." Ridgeway put the tips of his fingers together. "But your logic is irrefutable, Miss Digby," he sounded slightly surprised. "On the other hand, of course, we have no proof that he did not. And it is always possible that Sir Anthony himself was not aware of his own limitations."

Digby looked very worried. "And there is still the dreadful possibility that it was Mrs. Selden the murderer intended to kill—and that may mean Mrs. Delamain."

Ridgeway thought hard. "We must devise a trap—that is definitely what Mr. Sherlock Holmes would do. It will be dangerous—" He looked at Digby. "Have you the courage, Miss Digby?"

"Of course I have, Mr. Ridgeway."

"Excellent. Then this is what I propose . . ."

* * *

Dinner the following evening was elaborate, exquisitely appointed, and set on a table white as snow and glittering with ranks of glasses and polished silver. Under the lightest veneer of civility the emotions showed raw every now and again. Freddie was subdued, still pale with loss; Anthony Beech spoke little and what he said was trite; Evan Marshall exercised his usual wit and amusing knowledge on all manner of subjects; Andrew Delamain did not or could not hide his intense attraction towards Pamela—so much so that by the time dessert was served, Lucy Delamain was white-faced, except for two scarlet spots on her cheeks, and her eyes were hectically bright. It was not helped by Evan Marshall's referring to her situation a number of times with both wit and sympathy.

Ridgeway, flitting in and out to supervise, observed it and was not surprised. It was profoundly in Marshall's interest that Lucy Delamain should disgrace herself by an outburst of uncontrolled jealousy. Either Delamain himself was unaware of the danger, or else he was so obsessed he could not help himself.

By the time the gentlemen rejoined the ladies after brandy, the atmosphere was as brittle as spun glass, waiting to fracture at a touch. Shortly after ten the party broke up and Ridgeway had the opportunity to drop the explosive information he and Digby had devised. Separately and privately he told each of them, as if it were a small but happy incident, that after a decent interval Anthony Beech would marry Pamela—and was it not most fortunate, because then he would still have a wife of charm, beauty, and marked political skill.

He could not help trying to gauge their reactions, and the result was disappointing. Delamain was startled, but he hid his chagrin more smoothly than Ridgeway would have credited, and Evan Marshall instantly closed his expression so that nothing showed except a heat in his dark eyes. It could easily have been no more than a natural dashing of his hopes.

The minister would arrive the following day.

There was nothing more to do now but retire—and wait. Digby and Ridgeway had played their last card.

Out of sheer necessity Digby had been forced to tell Pamela of her alliance with Ridgeway, and of their deductions and the steps they had taken to prove the truth.

At midnight Pamela was lying awake in her bed, but the lamps on the wall had been turned down and there was no light in the room except a filmy glow from the moon, enough to see a figure by. Digby was sitting in the dressing chair deep in the shadow behind the tallboy, and Ridgeway, tense, excited, and highly self-conscious, stood pressed against the wall on the far side of the wardrobe.

The seconds ticked by. Pamela lay between the white sheets with her hair spread on the pillow, her eyes closed, and her heart thumping so violently the pulse of it beat in her throat.

Somewhere in the house a clock chimed the half hour. Digby was getting stiff. She shifted her weight. Was this ridiculous? Had they been too obvious, laying a trap any fool would see—and avoid? Maybe no one had believed for a moment that Pamela would marry Anthony Beech. They had nothing in common . . . but then neither had many married people. Who could account for love or physical passion—or ambition?

Ridgeway moved his feet restlessly.

Quarter to one.

Pamela turned over, still wide awake.

Digby glanced at the bedroom door. It was open! She had not even heard the latch. Someone was coming in. The black figure was outlined for an instant against the white lintel, then softened and faded into the darker pattern of the wallpaper.

Digby sat so still her breath faltered on her lips. Ridgeway would not have seen him yet—he could not till the figure was level with the bed. Digby strained her eyes, but all she could see was a thickness in the gloom, a form, anonymous, menacing in its utter silence.

It was coming closer. Pamela's eyes were still closed.

Please heaven she did not lose her nerve and open them or she would frighten him and he might even now escape.

He was level with the bed. Ridgeway froze.

The figure stood motionless, staring down at Pamela. The moonlight was plain on his face now; it was Evan Marshall, his eyes black, his mouth hard and sad, but there was no irresolution in it, regret, but not pity. He reached for the extra pillow, picked it up in both hands, and leaned over with a powerful, quick movement, pressing it over Pamela's face.

Ridgeway lunged forward, banging the wardrobe with his elbow, and landed almost on top of Marshall. He was a powerful man and heavy. Marshall had no chance against him. In moments it was all over, Digby had turned up the lights, Marshall was senseless on the floor, Pamela was ashen-faced, bruised, but otherwise all right, and Ridgeway was rumpled, hair wild, dignity to the winds, and totally, magnificently victorious. "Congratulations, Miss Digby," he said with extreme graciousness.

"Thank you, Mr. Ridgeway," she replied breathlessly. "Not quite elementary, I think—but most satisfactory—wouldn't you say?"

NIGHT VISION

by B. K. STEVENS

"Your academic preparation is adequate," Iphigenia Woodhouse said. She was one of the biggest women I'd ever met—almost six feet tall, broad-shouldered, and lean. Her hair was black and a little bit gray, sort of frizzy but sort of nice, except that it was pulled back from her face too hard, caught at the nape of her neck with a thick blue rubber band. She frowned at my transcript again before flipping back to my resume. "What else have you got? A black belt, a marksmanship certificate—not very relevant, except as indications of a commendable but naive enthusiasm. Our caseload is numbingly nonviolent. The secretarial experience, on the other hand, is extremely relevant. Now. One more thing." She took off her glasses and stared at me, managing to look both intense and, at the same time, almost bored. "Are you nice, Miss Russo?"

I blinked. "Nice? What do you mean, nice?"

She sighed impatiently. "Nice. You know. Kind. Considerate. Pleasant. That sort of nice. I had to fire my last five assistants for insufficient niceness. So. How nice are you?"

Back in Cleveland, I'd paid two hundred dollars for a Power Interviewing seminar. It hadn't prepared me for this. "I don't know," I managed. "I try to be nice."

"Trying isn't good enough." She stuck her glasses back on her face. "This job requires a high, consistent level of niceness. Specifically, it requires extreme niceness toward Mother." She pointed to a mahogany rocking chair outfitted with red cushions. It was set against a bay window, ten feet from Miss Woodhouse's desk, and next to it was a card table spread with brushes and oils and a large paint-by-number canvas of a lighthouse ringed by stormy seas. "Mother's upstairs napping now, but normally she sits there. If you get this job, you will always be nice to Mother. You will always treat her, and speak to her, with great respect. If she asks you for any sort of assistance—*any* sort of assistance —you will provide it promptly and cheerfully. You will not chew gum in front of Mother. You will not smoke in front of Mother. You will not use foul language in front of Mother."

"But I never smoke or use foul language," I protested.

She scowled and lit a cigarette. I could see I hadn't won any points by saying I didn't smoke. "I don't give a hot damn about what you 'never' do. My sole concern is with what you do, and do not do, in the presence of Mother. Oh, yes. Clothing. No low-cut blouses, no short skirts, no tight slacks, no high heels. Mother doesn't approve."

When I'd come here, I'd felt just about desperate to get this job. I'd run through five cities and all my savings without advancing one inch toward my dream of an apprenticeship at an East Coast detective agency. Annapolis had felt like my last chance, and Woodhouse Investigations had seemed, at first, ideal. Now I wasn't so sure. What sort of private detective kept a well-cushioned mother rocking in the front office, painting by number and imposing a dress code? Would Philip Marlowe have stubbed out his cigarettes and censored his language in deference to Mother? Visions of the Bates Motel flashed through my mind, and I felt more than a little uneasy.

"Is your mother a detective?" I asked cautiously. "Your partner?"

She took a long, fretful drag on her cigarette. "No. Mother is my most trusted advisor, but she takes no professional interest in investigation work. She is a professor of classical languages and literatures—or rather, she was, until medical developments forced her premature retirement from academia, some sixteen years ago. I might as well tell you now, Miss Russo, that some people would consider my mother somewhat eccentric. I can assure you, however, that she is an acute observer of human events, and that her insights have been of incalculable value to me on countless occasions."

"I see," I said, and began to feel that I really did. I'd done some background research on Iphigenia Woodhouse—one of my Power Interviewing strategies—and had learned that, until sixteen years ago, she'd been a successful, ambitious police detective: a lieutenant by thirty, rising fast, regarded as likely to be the first woman to head the homicide division. Then, abruptly, she'd left the force, broken off an engagement to a fellow detective, and founded Woodhouse Investigations. Now I thought I understood why. "Is it Alzheimer's?" I asked gently.

She ground out her cigarette, so emphatically that tiny sparks scattered onto her desk blotter and sizzled out harmlessly. "I'll thank you not to be in such a hurry to slap labels onto my mother. No, it is not Alzheimer's. She had a breakdown—the doctors don't know why—and in some respects she has never completely recovered—the doctors can't explain that, either. At the moment, however, our focus is on you, not on the failures of the medical profession. Tell me why you want to become an investigator—or perhaps I can guess. It was the public library, wasn't it? You got bored with being a secretary, you started reading detective novels, and you decided you want to be exactly like Philip Marlowe and Sam Spade."

"Not exactly like them," I said, blushing because she'd come so close to the truth, and because it sounded so silly. "I wouldn't want to sleep around that much, or kill that many people."

At least it made her smile—the first smile I'd seen since the interview started. "You might do after all, Miss Russo. You and Mother might get along just fine. Now. As to your duties. There'd be a lot of typing and filing and answering the telephone, and you'd also handle most of the legwork. Mother doesn't like me to go out if I can avoid it. Anything requiring tact or real intelligence I would of course handle myself."

It occurred to me that she should maybe consider reassigning the tact work, but I held back. "I'd like to do as much legwork as possible," I said. "I'm eager for field experience."

"Yes, I'm sure you are. Well, let's give you a trial assignment." She opened a desk drawer, rummaged efficiently for a moment, and pulled out a manila folder. "This," she said, tapping the folder with her index finger, "is the simplest of all possible assignments. Mere babysitting. If you can't handle this, you can't handle anything. The client is Christopher Sinclair, director of the Bay Club."

"Is that a country club?" I asked.

"Yes, an extremely exclusive one. Mr. Sinclair has a seventeen-year-old daughter, Jennifer. When Jennifer was three, Mr. Sinclair divorced her mother and quite cheerfully surrendered custody. The mother moved to California, and Mr. Sinclair evidently gave not another thought to his daughter's existence until about a year ago. Then the mother died in a plane crash, and custody bounced back to Mr. Sinclair."

"And he wasn't exactly delighted to receive it?" I guessed.

She shrugged. "Jennifer is not the sort of daughter best calculated to inspire delight. You know the type—long orange hair with a bright green streak, tight skirts and thick thighs, lots of mascara, lots of acne, late nights, loud music, lousy grades. Plus the usual miniature messes at school. He was appalled, but he was stuck. So he assigned her a back bedroom and was remarkably successful at continuing to ignore her.

"Then, one month ago, she cut her hair and dyed it brown. She started wearing baggy clothes, she stayed home every night, she stopped getting in trouble at school, and her grades shot up. Her father thinks she must be on drugs."

"Drugs?" I echoed incredulously. "Now? Why would he think that now?"

She waved her hand in contempt. "He read a pamphlet. 'Watch for sudden changes in your teenager's behavior. Changes in appearance, in social habits, in academic performance—these can be the warning signs that all add up to drug abuse.' The standard wisdom on the subject."

"But that doesn't seem likely in this case, does it?"

"Not likely at all. I told Mr. Sinclair that, the first time he came here, but he insisted it must be drugs. My guess is that he's hoping it's drugs, so he'll have an excuse to slap her into one of those residential rehabilitation programs and forget about her for a few months or a few years. Even without the orange hair, she's a dumpy, pimply embarrassment to him."

"He sounds like a horrible person," I said. I couldn't help it.

"He's a charmer," she agreed, "but he pays his bills. At any rate, he wants Jennifer watched." She glanced at the clock. "She gets out of school in half an hour. All you have to do is follow her while she walks home—about six blocks. You don't have to worry too much about being spotted because she never takes her eyes off the sidewalk. And you definitely don't have to worry about anything dramatic happening. I've been following her every day for a month, and she never goes any place racier than the orthodontist's office. Generally, she just walks straight home. Once she gets there, Attila the Housekeeper takes over, and your job is done. Mr. Sinclair doesn't want a full-scale investigation—too much risk of scandal, he says. So you're not to speak to Jennifer or to attempt to question her friends. Understand?"

"Yes," I said, sorry that the job sounded so easy and unimpressive.

"Good." She started writing rapidly on an index card. "This may be our last day on the case. I called Mr. Sinclair again yesterday and told him he's wasting his money, that if he wants to know what's going on in his daughter's life, he might consider the heretofore untried technique of talking to her. He said he'd think about it."

"I hope he does," I said, and looked up at her slowly. "Why do you think she *did* change so suddenly, Miss Woodhouse?"

"At that age, who knows? Chances are she fell in love with the president of the Young Republicans Club and decided to change her image. Or she got tired of being a junior delinquent, or she got religion, or she just plain grew up. Here." She handed me the index card and a photograph. "The address of the high school, and a picture of her. I took it last month, from my car window. In the most recent photo her father had, she was in diapers."

"Thanks." I put the things into my purse. "You said this was a trial assignment. If I do all right, do I get the job?"

She sat back in her chair and looked at me skeptically. "Well, if you botch something this simple, you definitely don't get the job. I have a policy against hiring hopeless incompetents. If you don't disgrace yourself, you may meet Mother. And then Mother will decide about the job."

If you've ever seen pictures of Annapolis, you've probably seen the city dock, or the state house, or narrow streets crowded with tiny, elegant houses and artsy shops and seafood restaurants. Well, all that quaintness is packed into about two square miles, called the historic district. After that, there's the business district, nice enough but nothing special, and then you cross the bridge, and it's just malls and discount stores and endless stretches of bland, expensive suburbs. Annapolis calls itself a tourist center, but if you come, plan on a short tour. You can visit every spot that has even a shred of interest without using up half a tank of gas.

Woodhouse Investigations occupies the bottom floor of one of those tiny, elegant houses in the historic district, almost within sight of the dock; Miss Woodhouse and her mother live on the top floor. I was parked on one of those narrow streets, across from the gracefully crumbling Calvert High School, waiting for the students to make their daily escape. I took out the picture of Jennifer Sinclair and studied it again, to make sure I'd recognize her. She looked so drab and sad—short, chunky, mud-brown hair chopped off in a thick fringe, a black skirt that drooped several inches below her knees, a bulky gray sweater. She was hunched over the stack of books she carried, her eyes riveted on the ground. I had no way of knowing, of course, but I'd guess she had looked better with the mascara and the orange hair—no prettier, maybe, but cheerfuler. I propped the picture up on my dashboard, and wondered why any seventeen-year-old would do this to herself.

I heard the hollow echo of a bell, and the school began to

empty. It wasn't hard to spot Jennifer. She was one of the last ones out, hanging back, not talking to anybody. She looked exactly as she did in the picture—the graveyard outfit, the back stooped, the head down, the books hugged to her chest like a shield, or like a security blanket. When she reached the sidewalk, her head popped up for a quick look in all directions, and then it snapped down again and she took off down the block, plowing through the ambling, laughing crowd of students like a determined, slightly demented bulldozer. I eased into the flow of cars, anonymous among all the mothers and girlfriends and boyfriends converging on the school to pick up passengers. Even if Jennifer had been looking for me—and she wasn't looking for me, she wasn't looking for anybody, she was studying the sidewalk—she probably wouldn't have spotted me. This job was an obvious cinch.

At the corner, though, she turned left, and that made me perk up. Miss Woodhouse had said Jennifer always turned right here. Chances were, she was just making a detour to return an overdue library book or grab a quick midafternoon pizza. Then again, maybe she was finally on her way to make a drug buy. Maybe this assignment would turn into a chance to prove myself after all. I kept my eyes tight on her as she took one unpredictable turn after another, straight into the heart of the historic district. She was walking faster, she never looked up once, she tunneled down Duke of Gloucester Street, and then suddenly, before I realized what was happening, she shot up a cobblestone walkway and disappeared into St. Michael's Church.

A church. Nothing Miss Woodhouse had said had prepared me for a church. Still, what could be more innocent? And this kid had Troubled Teen written all over her. Probably she was meeting sweet old Father Somebody for a counseling session. I searched frantically for a parking space, settled for one in a loading zone half a block away, and tried to figure out my next move. Should I follow her like a ninny and lose the chance to see sweet old Father Somebody pass her a dime bag? What would Travis McGee do? I chewed my lip, and tugged at my hair, and couldn't decide.

At least I was bright enough to keep an eye on the rear

view mirror, so I saw the silver Cadillac pull into a handicapped spot right in front of the church, saw the man climb out, scan the street quickly, and start up the cobblestone path. He didn't look handicapped, and he didn't look like sweet old Father Somebody. He looked like a pimp. He was maybe forty, short and wiry, lavender suit, black shirt, white tie, blond hair slicked back tight across his skull, designer sunglasses. Oh, my God, I thought. White slavery, and the world's least suspicious-looking pickup spot. I jumped out of my car and raced down the street to rescue Jennifer.

He made it into the church maybe a minute before I did. I tried to fling open the oversized oak door, found it too heavy to be flung, struggled to pull it back, and scrambled inside. The adjustment from sunshine to semidarkness cost me another few moments. I was at the back of the sanctuary, and Jennifer was in a front pew, already struggling with the man in the lavender suit. He had her by the left arm, he was pulling her toward the aisle, he had something in his right hand. Her right hand was reaching for something inside her baggy sweater.

All this registered in about a second. Then there was a shot —just one, very loud. He lurched back a few inches, his hand still on her arm, his face stretched with astonishment. He fell, and she screamed.

I didn't think at all. I just felt sick. "Oh, no!" I cried. "Jennifer!"

Her head jerked back in shock—obviously, she hadn't noticed me before. But she noticed me then. I'd never seen such pure terror in a human face.

She screamed again, and then she must have stepped over the body, or jumped over the body. Within seconds, she was charging up the aisle at me, howling—a deep, wild, hopeless howl. Whatever happened next, it was a disgrace to all my years at Mr. Lee's Aerobic Kung Fu Studio. I don't think I even went into a stance. She ran straight at me, she smacked the side of my head with her gun, and then I think she must have just run over me. I have a vague memory of falling down, of hitting my head on the carefully preserved eighteenth century stone floor, and of feeling stupid.

* * *

"Your first name is Harriet, isn't it?"

I opened my eyes slowly. I was lying in a crisp, narrow bed, and for a second I thought the woman sitting next to me was Iphigenia Woodhouse. The gray eyes were right, and the thick, almost archless eyebrows, and the large-lean frame, and the your-opinion-doesn't-matter-much voice. But this woman's hair was white, gathered into a fat, neat braid that descended almost to her waist, and her face was saggy and spotted. And would Iphigenia Woodhouse be holding an eight-inch square metal loom on her lap, or be busily engaged in weaving a pink and green potholder?

"My daughter told me all about you," the woman said, frowning as she threaded a polyester loop through the haphazard maze she'd constructed. "She didn't want me to come along—she never wants to take me anywhere. But I wasn't about to let her go to a hospital without me. It would be such a perfect chance for her, wouldn't it, to talk to the doctors and make her plans. She wants to put me in an asylum, you know. She wants them to lock me away and feed me on bread and water, and then she can run straight to That Man and stay out as late as she likes and eat greasy food and smoke cigarettes. Well, I was too quick for her. 'You take me to that hospital with you, Iphigenia,' I said, 'or it's no allowance for the rest of the month.' And, as you might imagine, she didn't have much to say to *that.*"

I'm not usually a lucky person. But on this one occasion I said the perfect word, and it must have been luck that led me to it—I certainly wasn't thinking very clearly, and even at my clearest I wouldn't have been sharp enough to know what she most wanted to hear.

"Are you Professor Woodhouse?" I asked.

Groggy as I was, I could see the thrill shoot through her when she heard the word "professor." The shoulders straightened, the old gray eyes danced, and the thick braid twitched with pleasure.

"Why, yes, I am," she said. "I am Professor Woodhouse. And you are Harriet Russo—poor, sweet Harriet, who's had such a nasty bump on the head. Iphigenia said some very nasty things when she heard about it—she's always been a nasty girl, you know—but don't worry. I'll make her be nice to you."

She walked to the door and looked down the hall. "Iphigenia," she called. "Put out that smelly, awful cigarette and come here this minute. Little Harriet's awake now." She squeezed my hand and winked at me before sitting down again.

Iphigenia Woodhouse walked into the room, stood at the foot of my bed, crossed her arms across her chest, and scowled. The galloping pain in my head got a lot worse.

"Well," she said. "How do you feel?"

"Not too bad," I lied. "What happened?"

She scowled again. "You may well ask. Let's review your progress on your first case, shall we? You were given the difficult assignment of following a teenage girl as she walked home from school. During the seven or eight minutes you had her under your surveillance, she killed a man in a church, assaulted you, fired three wild shots at a policeman who tried to stop her as she ran down the street, and disappeared. Thanks to you, I had to call my client and tell him that his daughter, who had never before been convicted of anything more serious than smoking in the girls' room, is now a fugitive from justice, wanted for murder and a fistful of other felonies. How would you rate your performance, Miss Russo?"

Professor Woodhouse reached for her potholder loom. "Don't you dare blame poor, sweet Harriet, you nasty girl," she said severely. "This entire fiasco is your fault. You shouldn't have given her such a dangerous assignment on her very first day."

Iphigenia Woodhouse's eyebrows popped up, and you could see her scrambling to adjust to the fact that I had become, in her mother's eyes, "poor, sweet Harriet." When she spoke again, her voice was so much gentler and more tentative that you'd have thought it was a different person. "I'm very sorry, Mother," she said. "I didn't mean to upset you. And you're right: I shouldn't have given Miss Russo the assignment. But I didn't think it would be dangerous. Jennifer didn't seem at all violent, or—"

"She'd smoked in the girls' room," Professor Woodhouse cut in. "That should have told you what sort of person she is. It's just the sort of mess you always used to get into yourself, you nasty girl. What were you thinking of, exposing dear little Harriet to someone who had smoked in the girls' room?"

Iphigenia Woodhouse sank into a chair. "Yes, she'd smoked in the girls' room," she said wearily. "And now she's killed a man."

"Six of one, half a dozen of the other," Professor Woodhouse said, continuing placidly with her weaving. "If anything, she's taken a step up. There's absolutely no legitimate excuse for indulging in such a filthy, unhealthful habit, especially not on school property. There are, on the other hand, any number of legitimate reasons for killing a man."

Iphigenia Woodhouse lifted her head slowly, a look of wonder transforming her face. "You're absolutely right, Mother," she said.

"He *did* seem to be attacking her," I offered cautiously. "He was dragging on her arm, and she looked awful scared."

"You see?" Professor Woodhouse demanded. "When I finish this potholder, dear little Harriet, I will give it to you. Indeed, I will make you a set of three matching potholders, and that will be very nice. Iphigenia, have the police identified the nasty man who was shot in the church?"

"Edward Fox," Miss Woodhouse said glumly. "A fence, from Baltimore. The police figure Jennifer was planning to sell him something she'd stolen from her father, to get money for drugs. Then something went wrong, and she shot him—with a gun also, presumably, stolen from her father."

"The police seem to be making a number of unwarranted assumptions," Professor Woodhouse observed. "I'm sorry to see you guilty of the same mistake, Iphigenia. Thank goodness you have sweet little Harriet with you now, to keep you from making similar mistakes in the future. Now, you get some good rest tonight, little Harriet, and in the morning you can go with Iphigenia when she offers her apologies to Mr. Sinclair."

Miss Woodhouse nodded meekly, and it was settled. Impossible as it seemed, I apparently still had a chance at this job.

I'd figured Mr. Sinclair would stay home the next day, to pace by the phone and hope for news about his daughter. But no, he went to work. We found him in the Bay Club's restaurant, a big, sunshiny room with huge picture windows overlooking a quiet stretch of the Severn River. There were round tables with pastel linen tablecloths, and pale wooden chairs with slender backs, and in the middle of each table there was a bunch of flowers—real flowers, but so bright and glossy and flawless you'd have sworn they were fake. It was elegant. Mr. Sinclair was elegant, too, slim and silver-haired and dressed just so. I sure wouldn't have picked him as Jennifer's father. He was standing near the hostess's station, talking to a very stylish, very thin, very blonde woman who looked maybe thirty from across the room, maybe forty-five close up. She was flipping through some pages attached to a clipboard, taking notes once in a while and nodding a lot.

"Lillian Dexter complained about the salmon again," he was saying. "She swears it was overdone. Mention it to Gunther, will you? And Bill Radford says he's bored with our salad dressings, wants us to try something lemony. I suppose we should humor him. And—oh." He frowned briefly when he noticed us. "Miss Woodhouse. I'm surprised to see you here, I must say. This is my restaurant manager, Nancy Bracken." He tilted his head, ever so slightly, in my direction. "And this, I take it, is the incompetent young person who was supposed to keep my daughter out of trouble yesterday."

I felt like hiding behind Miss Woodhouse's skirt, but I stood my ground. The corners of her mouth tightened. "It wasn't her fault, Mr. Sinclair. I take full responsibility for what happened."

"Yes, I rather think you should," he said mildly, taking the clipboard and initialing something. "As you'll recall, I told you that Jennifer must be on drugs. As I recall, you told me that my fears were groundless. I paid you to get me some reliable information, and all you ever gave me was platitudes about learning to trust in and communicate with my daughter. Well, trust in Jennifer would have been a trifle misplaced, wouldn't it?" He put the clipboard down and looked at Miss Woodhouse directly. "As to communicating with her, at your urging, I tried that, yesterday morning. The results were not quite as heartwarming as you had predicted. She went into hysterics, ran from the house, and, before the end of the day, committed murder. Now, how much do I owe you for your professional services and advice?"

You could see how much she hated that, but she took it without so much as a scowl. "I'd like to help, Mr. Sinclair. I'd like to try to find Jennifer before she gets into more trouble. Could you tell me about your conversation yesterday, about why she got so upset? Perhaps that would tell me where to start."

He gave her a sideways glance. "I certainly didn't say anything that could inspire a murder. I did just as you suggested—I complimented her on the more positive aspects of the changes she's made in the last month, and I offered her the opportunity to become more a part of my life. I said, 'Jennifer, since you are apparently no longer intent on looking like a sideshow freak, perhaps you'd like to work toward dressing in a genuinely presentable way. I spoke to Miss Bracken last night, and she has agreed to take you to a beauty salon and a clothing store tomorrow. If the results are tolerable, you may come to the club for a soft drink the following afternoon; and if you behave in a reasonably civilized manner, perhaps someday you may stay for dinner." Now, why should she be upset by a generous offer such as that?"

I imagined how I would have felt, and thought Jennifer had shown a lot of restraint by shooting only one person that day.

But Nancy Bracken put a hand on his arm, her icy blue eyes thawing a degree or two. "I'm so very sorry Jennifer didn't accept, Chris. I would have been delighted to help, and I was looking forward to meeting her."

He patted her hand but didn't bother to look at her. "Thank you, Nancy. Yes, I'd hoped you could be a positive influence on her, but clearly she was already beyond help. Only a fool could fail to perceive that." He looked at us. "However, Miss Woodhouse, I believe in giving people second chances. So far, my friends in the media have done their best for me, but the publicity is bound to become intolerable if Jennifer remains a fugitive much longer. If you can locate her and turn her over to the police, if you can end this awkward business quickly and quietly, I will pay you."

This time, she did scowl. "I will not accept payment. I will continue to work on this case, but only because I feel sorry for Jennifer and responsible for what happened to her."

She turned away from him sharply and stalked out, and I did my best to stalk after her with similar style. I was feeling pretty rotten, though, and I think maybe I shuffled. And then, once we got outside the club, we had to stop stalking and idle under the awning while the parking lot attendant ambled to get Miss Woodhouse's car. He had a Schwarzenegger build and curly blond hair and smoky blue eyes and dimples, and I thought he was awful cute. Miss Woodhouse, however, was not impressed.

"This is ludicrous," she fumed. "This is the very definition of decadence. People come here, supposedly, to golf and swim and play tennis, to reap the benefits of fresh air and exercise. But they can't walk the length of a medium-sized parking lot. Oh, no. That would exhaust them. So they must stand about uselessly while some uniformed Adonis parks and fetches their cars. Well, I suppose the society matrons can work up a sweat just fantasizing about the fact that he's caressed their keys."

"I guess," I said, and cleared my throat. "Miss Woodhouse, it was real nice of you to take the blame in there, but I hope you don't really feel responsible. It was all my fault. I should have—"

"No. You're new at this, and I told you it was a routine assignment. I was wrong about that, wrong about everything. I thought Sinclair's drug theory was idiotic, so I assumed that there was no real reason to worry about Jennifer, that she wasn't in trouble of any sort. A stupid, stupid mistake. All those changes in her appearance and behavior—maybe they weren't the warning signs of drug abuse, but they were sure as hell the warning signs of something, and I just shrugged them off."

Her car pulled up in front of us then, and the parking lot attendant eased himself out. I hadn't paid strict attention in my high school mythology class, but I remembered enough to know that Adonis was a pretty good name for him.

He walked over to us, real slow, and grinned, and pressed Miss Woodhouse's keys into her hand. Just before he released them, he gave her a long, slow, head-to-toe look, letting his gaze wrap itself all around her. Then he grinned again, like he'd just had his thrill for the week, and gave me the same treatment.

It was all an act, I knew, a hokey, obvious act he probably used on all the ladies, but it pretty nearly took my breath away. Miss Woodhouse glared and didn't tip him.

We got into the car. "Do you think Jennifer was stealing things," I asked, "since the man she shot was a fence? You think she was messed up in a gang, a robbery ring, something like that?"

"Possibly. The one thing I'm sure of—and I should have realized it long ago—is that she was scared. I should have seen it in the way she walked, the way she carried herself. And the most obvious explanation for the hair and the clothes is that she didn't want to be recognized. Hiding out at home fits in with that theory, too, and so does bringing a gun into a church. She must have been afraid that she might have to defend herself."

"Do you think she might have been scared of something connected to her father's club?" I suggested tentatively. "After all, she got hysterical when he invited her to go there."

Iphigenia Woodhouse lifted an eyebrow and nodded slowly. "A surprisingly sensible suggestion, Miss Russo. You may be correct. Now, we must try to move beyond guesswork, toward certainty. So I will make some telephone calls and consult some sources, and you will go to the library."

"The library?" I felt disappointed. I'd been hoping she'd let me watch her grill some suspects.

"That's right." She pulled up in front of a long, low concrete building. "Jennifer cut off her hair and started dressing like a professional frump on Saturday, March ninth. Whatever scared her into making those changes, chances are it was violent, chances are it was illegal, and chances are it made the newspapers. See if you can find some possibilities. Check for a few days before the ninth, a few days after. Check the Baltimore papers as well as the Annapolis one. Check for murders, robberies, assaults, anything lively. Make a list. Then take a nap—Mother's very concerned about that bump on your head—and come to the house for dinner. Understand?"

"Understood," I said, wondering if the second assignment meant that I had the job, or at least a chance to redeem myself. But I didn't ask. It would be better, I thought, to wait until I'd impressed her by putting together the longest, goriest list I could manage. And it would definitely be better to wait until her mother was around.

The Woodhouses' kitchen is small and old fashioned and efficient—the walls and cupboards and all the appliances white, crisp gingham curtains, utensils hanging in a symmetrical pattern on a pegboard, clear counters, no clutter. Next to the refrigerator, there's a large oil painting in a scrolled gilt frame. It's a portrait of Winnie-the-Pooh—the Disney character—just the face, a little smudged here and there, a little shaky, and you can tell it's paint-by-number. Still, it's very bright and colorful, and she had mostly stayed inside the lines. I glanced over at Professor Woodhouse, who was standing by the sink slicing onions. "What a nice painting," I said. "Is it your work, professor?"

She looked up and smiled. "Why, yes. How clever of you to guess. It *does* cheer the room up a bit, doesn't it? I like to have a smiling face around—and with Iphigenia so glum and gloomy, I'm not likely to see smiles unless I paint them. Iphigenia, I shall need two more onions for this salad."

From what I could see, the salad consisted almost entirely of onions, but Miss Woodhouse fetched two more without commenting. Then she took a roast and baked potatoes from the oven, her mother added croutons and green olives to the salad, and we all walked into the dining room. It's a cool, lovely room, vaguely nautical but not cutesy, all dark woods and blue fabrics. The centerpiece is a big green Styrofoam cube dotted with colored pipe cleaners twisted into flower shapes and studded with sequins. I didn't waste much time wondering who the artist was.

"Would you mind if we discuss business at dinner, Mother?" Miss Woodhouse asked as soon as we were seated. "Miss Russo and I have—"

"Call her Harriet," the professor cut in. "Why must you be so cold and formal, Iphigenia? It's no wonder you don't have any friends. And no, I don't mind if you discuss business—not that it would make any difference if I *did* mind, since in either case you'd do exactly as you please, just as you always do, you nasty girl. And if I so much as murmur in protest, it's off to the asylum with me, and you'll run to That Man. No, don't bother denying it. You don't fool me, and you don't fool Harriet." She turned to me, crinkling her nose and smiling sweetly. "Now, little Harriet. Mean old Iphigenia made you work this afternoon, didn't she? She sent you to the library, even though I *told* her you needed to nap. Well, I'm sure you discovered some very exciting things. Tell us all about them. And have some salad."

She filled my plate with onions and croutons and olives, and I smiled, reaching for my purse and taking out a thick stack of index cards. "Thank you. Yes, I went to the library—I was very happy to go—and I looked through all the Annapolis, Baltimore, and Washington, D.C., papers for the last six weeks. I think I caught all the significant crimes. The murders are in red ink, and assaults in blue, the robberies in black. And one burglary, in green. It's not violent, but I think it's interesting."

I handed Miss Woodhouse the cards, and I could see she was impressed—by the amount of work I'd done, if not by the color coding. I'd put the green burglary card on the top of the stack, and she skimmed it and frowned. " 'March 12: Mr. and Mrs. William Radford return from a trip to the Bahamas to find their Annapolis home stripped of jewelry, paintings, appliances.' Well, it's fine that you took notes on this, Miss

Russo—Harriet—but I don't see why you consider it interesting."

"Because the Radfords belong to the Bay Club," I said eagerly. "Remember? This morning Mr. Sinclair was telling his restaurant manager that Bill Radford had complained about the salad dressings. So I called the Bay Club, just to make sure, and it's the same William Radford. And I thought maybe, if Jennifer was messed up with that fence she killed, she could have been keeping track of when club members were out of town, and passing the names on to him, and then they'd rip off the houses, and he'd fence what they stole. This burglary wasn't discovered until March twelfth, but it could have happened earlier, and maybe something went wrong."

Miss Woodhouse nodded slowly. "And maybe Jennifer got scared, and maybe that's why she changed her appearance on March ninth. Very intriguing."

"Much better than intriguing," Professor Woodhouse said, beaming. "It's ingenious. I'd like to see *you* come up with something half so clever, Iphigenia. Little Harriet has done a fine job. She has earned more salad." She piled another helping onto my plate.

Miss Woodhouse's mouth twitched in a brief, tiny grin. "Harriet's earned all the salad she wants, and then some. Now, let's see the murders. Two in Annapolis, both domestic —probably not what we're looking for. Baltimore had thirteen—rather a slow six weeks for Baltimore. And forty-nine in D.C. Why did you check the D.C. papers?"

"I wanted to be thorough. And since it's barely an hour away, I thought Jennifer might have—well, I hope you don't mind."

"Not at all. You've shown commendable initiative." She set to work, skimming the cards and sorting them into piles. "Please excuse me while I glance through these. Enjoy your dinner."

The roast was so tender you hardly needed teeth to chew it, the potatoes were firm and rich, and the salad was interesting. Professor Woodhouse chattered steadily as I ate, telling me long, confusing stories about her family, mostly about how her Uncle Ed had killed his father and married his mother, and later, I think, his daughter got buried alive. It was pretty gruesome stuff, but I'd read a little Sophocles in my mythology class, and I figured maybe Professor Woodhouse had just mixed up some stuff she'd lived and some stuff she used to teach. So I didn't let it bother me too much. I just ate, and smiled, and nodded, and out of the corner of my eye, I watched Miss Woodhouse. She was concentrating on the murders—I could see the red ink flash by every time she flipped a card—and she was making a big stack, a small stack, and a tiny stack.

Finally, she stopped sorting. She picked up the top card from the tiny stack and snapped it in the air. "This murder interests me most. The victim was Clayton Davis, age seventeen, black, high-school senior, resident of Fairfax, Virginia. Shot twice in the back, body found in a dumpster in D.C. at seven A.M. on Saturday, March ninth."

"Exactly one month ago yesterday," Professor Woodhouse observed, spreading mustard on her potato.

"That's right, Mother—you're exactly right, of course." She flashed me an I-told-you-so glance, as if I'd doubted her mother's intelligence and now they'd proved me wrong. "It exactly coincides with the change in Jennifer's appearance, too. And the one thing I've been able to discover about the night before she changed is that she went to a party with some friends and left, about midnight, with a black boy nobody had seen before." She ran a squared, unpolished fingernail under the bright red lines of my notes. "Now, the police assumed the shooting was drug-related—what else would they assume?—but apparently there's no evidence that he was ever involved with drugs. The dumpster interests me, too. Presumably, he wasn't shot there; presumably, the body was moved. He could have been shot anywhere."

"Like at the Radford house?" I suggested. "Maybe he helped her burglarize it, and then there was a quarrel, and the fence shot him, and then they dumped the body in a place that nobody would associate with the burglary, a place where the police would assume it was just another drug-related shooting."

"Possibly." Miss Woodhouse frowned. "It doesn't quite fit

the facts, but we're getting closer. I'll call some friends on the D.C. police force and see if they've learned anything more about the shooting."

Professor Woodhouse sighed impatiently as she served me more salad. "That's all well and good, but hadn't you better find that girl? She must be scared to death. Every time I turn on the radio, some policeman or prosecutor is talking about how much trouble she's in, and how much worse it will be if she doesn't give herself up. Dismal old things! As if threats would make that poor, frightened girl give herself up."

"That's true, Mother. But really, what else can they say?"

"They can promise her something nice," Professor Woodhouse shot back. "That's what you should do, Iphigenia. Go on the radio yourself, and say you'll give her something nice if she calls you. A pony, for example—that would be splendid. All girls like ponies. And I don't think she can be such a *very* bad girl, even if she *did* smoke in the girls' room. She went to church yesterday, after all."

"She probably went there to meet the fence," Miss Woodhouse pointed out, reaching for the butter.

Her mother slapped her hand. "Did it ever occur to you that perhaps she went there to pray? Why must you always think the worst of people, you nasty girl? Now, you send that poor thing a message. Promise to give her something nice if she calls you. Do as I say, Iphigenia, and do it now."

Miss Woodhouse froze, looking sort of stunned and dismayed, like she wanted to obey her mother but didn't know how she could manage it this time. Then she nodded slowly, and got up, and walked into the den. Ten minutes later, she came back, carrying a legal pad.

"I've written a message for her, Mother," she said, all soft and meek. "I'd like to put it in the newspaper, if that's all right, rather than on the radio. If Jennifer's still in Annapolis—and she probably doesn't have either the money or the courage to run—she may be reading the paper for news about her case. And if she's desperately searching for a way out of town, she might check the classifieds, and—well." She grimaced. "It's a long shot, but if she *does* see the ad, I think it would appeal to her."

She handed me the pad. "This ad should appeal to her, all right," I said, reading through it quickly. "But it should also appeal to every other teenager in the county. You'll get thousands of calls."

"That's why I'd like to put your telephone number in the ad," she said evenly. "I'd like you to screen all the calls and get in touch with me if you hear from any possible Jennifers. Can you manage that?"

"Of course she can!" Professor Woodhouse cried. She absolutely shimmered with delight. "That's the first good idea you've had in months. Dear little Harriet will find poor little Jennifer, and clear this whole unpleasant business up. And then, if you're very good, Iphigenia, you may invite them both over for a lovely slumber party. I will make you hot chocolate, and pop you some popcorn. Won't that be nice?"

"Very nice," Miss Woodhouse said. "Thank you so much, Mother." She turned to me, and I swear her eyes were all teary. "Will you take the calls?"

How could I say no?

Miss Woodhouse pulled some strings, and our ad made the next day's newspaper. By late afternoon, my phone number had to be the most popular seven digit sequence in history: the moment I set the receiver down, the phone shrilled again, and I had to go back into my act. After three solid hours of this, I'd gotten pretty good at eliminating callers quickly, but I still hadn't found any possible Jennifers. And I was exhausted. I left the phone off the hook, went into the bathroom to splash cold water on my face, did thirty situps, poured myself a stiff Diet Coke, sighed, and put the receiver back in place.

Of course the phone rang instantly. I shoved two fresh sticks of gum into my mouth. "Rockbuster Productions," I drawled. "The bands we book really cook. Whaddaya want?"

"I—um, well, hi." Female voice, definitely young, definitely nervous, maybe scared. "I'm, um, well, I'm calling about your ad. In the *Capital,* you know? About the job. Could you, um, well, tell me more about the job?"

So far, very promising. I snapped my gum. "It's just like the ad says, kid. The Hot Rivets are leaving for a Midwest tour, and they're looking for a roadie. A roadie, not a groupie. So if it's sex, drugs, and rock and roll you want, forget it."

"No sex," she said anxiously. "No drugs. Just rock and roll. That is, all I want is a job. But I love rock and roll, and even though I've never heard of the Hot Rivets, I—"

"Never heard of them?" I demanded incredulously. I was wearing jeans and my Paul Simon T-shirt, and I purposely hadn't washed my hair that morning, so it was easy for me to get into the part. "Don't you read *Rolling Stone?* The boys got a fabulous review, totally fabulous—said they bring new meaning to the term heavy metal techno-funk. And they just cut their second album, and we've got first-class gigs set every five inches, solid, from Columbus to Sioux Falls to Tucson. And you never heard of them?"

"Well, I missed the last issue of *Rolling Stone,"* she said apologetically. "But they sound great. I was wondering—well, um, the ad said it's an immediate opening. How soon is the band leaving?"

"Day after tomorrow, kid. Could you swing that?"

"Yes, I could," she said. "The sooner, the better. Does the —um, well, the band travels on its own bus, doesn't it? Not on a public bus? Is it leaving from the depot?"

Sort of a strange question—except from someone who figured the cops must be staking the depot out, watching for her. I sat up straighter. "Nah, they're leaving from the bass player's house, out on Riva Road. Now, there's no experience required, like the ad says, but you oughta know it's heavy work. Setting equipment up, lugging instruments around, like that. It ain't no job for Miss Junior Petite. So if you're some Skinny Minnie—"

"I'm not," she said eagerly. "I'm not skinny at all. I'm sort of heavy. And I'm very strong, and I'll work very, very hard."

"That's what it takes, kid—that, and a realistic attitude. This tour ain't going to make you rich and famous, you know."

"Fine with me," she said, a little bleakly. "I've been rich, and it stinks. And famous is the last thing I need. The ad said room and board and modest wages, and that's plenty for me."

"Yeah, well, the wages are pretty damn modest," I said, and cringed. I really don't like saying that word. "One more thing. We don't provide transportation back. The tour ends in Tucson, and that's where we leave you. You gotta find your own way home."

"I won't want to come home." The voice was utterly flat now. "Tucson sounds fine. It sounds great."

You sound great, I thought. I yawned to conceal my excitement. "Okay, then. Maybe you'll do. I'll check with the road manager, and if he's interested, I'll call you back to set up an interview. You can bring your parents along—they'll probably want to check us out, make sure we're legit."

There was a pause. "No, thank you. I mean, that isn't necessary. I'm on my own. I'm twenty-one—I don't look it, but I am. And my mother's dead, and my father—well, he's in prison. Sex crimes, you know? Can I just come to the interview alone?"

"Fine with me." It was hard not to bounce in my chair. This had to be Jennifer. Every other caller had been at least a little wary, had wanted to bring half a dozen relatives to the interview. "Give me your name and number, kid. Maybe I'll get back to you."

She hesitated for just an instant. "My name is Joan," she said. "Joan Mellencamp. My number is 555-9236, and I really hope you'll call."

"If you're lucky," I said and slapped the receiver down and immediately dialed Miss Woodhouse's number.

At eleven thirty the next morning, I was back at the Bay Club. The parking lot Adonis took my keys, gave me one of his slow, head-to-toe leers, and eased himself into my car with fluid grace. He grinned at me again as he pulled away. Miss Woodhouse was right. It's ludicrous and decadent to have valet parking at a country club. The man did have style, though.

I sighed away his spell and headed straight for the restaurant. Nancy Bracken was tiptoeing about the room, aiming sly peeks and smiles at the scattered early lunchers, occasionally hovering by a table long enough to drop a murmur or two. She stiffened up considerably when she saw me.

"It's Miss Russo, isn't it?" she said. "Are you looking for Mr. Sinclair? I'm so sorry. He's downtown, at the Rotary Club luncheon. Could I help you?"

"Lord, I sure hope so." Fretfully, I pushed my hair back from my forehead. "I'm in a real jam, Miss Bracken. It's just my first week on the job—I'm not even sure I *have* the job yet—and I just don't know what to do. Miss Woodhouse is in D.C. working on a real important case, and she told me to meet her there by noon, and already I'm not going to make it, but I don't see how I can leave town." I glanced nervously around the room and lowered my voice. "I found Jennifer."

She did a sharp doubletake, then recovered quickly and led me to an empty corner of the room. "That's wonderful. What did she say?"

"Nothing that makes any sense. She's a mess—hysterical, paranoid, incoherent." I lifted my hands helplessly. "She'd been hiding out in the basement of a friend's house. I won't go into all the details of how I found her, but when she saw me, she freaked. She wouldn't tell me anything—just went on and on about how people are after her, people want to kill her, that kind of garbage. I managed to get her in my car and take her to Miss Woodhouse's place, and then I slipped her a few sedatives. She's out cold now—I don't think she's slept in days, so she'll be all right for a while. But what should I do? I can't reach Miss Woodhouse, and I don't want to call the cops until Jennifer sees her father and talks to a lawyer."

"That's very wise." Her eyes got all squinty, and you could tell she was thinking it over. "So she's at Miss Woodhouse's. Alone?"

I shrugged. "Well, Professor Woodhouse is there—that's Miss Woodhouse's mother. But to tell you the truth, Professor Woodhouse is—well, I don't want to say she's senile, but she's very confused, you know? Thank goodness Miss Woodhouse gave me a complete set of keys to her house. There's a little attic bedroom, with a door that locks from the outside, so I put Jennifer there and locked her in. Maybe that sounds awful, but it seemed safest."

"I think you did exactly the right thing." She paused, and you could see the gears churning again. "Mr. Sinclair should know about this. I'll try to phone him. No, you wait here. I'll be right back."

She was gone maybe three minutes, and she looked all brisk and confident when she returned. "I couldn't reach him, but I'll keep trying. I don't see any reason why you can't leave for D.C. now."

She had some questions about Jennifer's state of mind and all, and kept me talking for another ten minutes. Then she seemed satisfied, and we shook hands, and I left. Adonis brought me my car, practically singeing me with his sultriest leer as he handed me my keys.

One forty-five in the afternoon. I lay on my side in the narrow bed, my face to the wall, the quilt pulled up snugly around my shoulders and neck. It was very quiet. I couldn't see her, of course, but in my mind I had a clear image of the ancient, hunched figure dozing in the rocking chair next to the bed, the thick glasses sliding down her nose, the afghan nearly enveloping her, the fat braid descending down her back.

I heard the door pushed open cautiously, a male voice, very soft. "Not locked," it said. Then a pause. "Damn. The old broad's in there."

The female voice was also soft, but unhesitating, ice-firm. "So we do them both. Old ladies fall all the time—this one can break her neck on the stairs. But first the kid gets her accidental overdose. Now, Frank. Nice and quiet and quick."

I lay absolutely still. Another second, two seconds, three, four. Then the quick rush of cold air as the quilt was pulled back from my shoulders.

One more second, and suddenly the room filled with noise and motion—a scream, a thud, a startled obscenity, grunts, a shouted order, feet pounding up the stairs, a soft crash as the bed collided with the wall. I flipped onto my other side in time to see Adonis hit the floor. Already Miss Woodhouse was on top of him, her afghan thrown aside, her braid swinging wildly as she struggled to pin down his arm, to dislodge the thing grasped in his fist. I looked toward the door and saw Nancy Bracken, shrieking, kicking wildly at the police detective who was holding her. Two other policemen crowded into the room, trying to help, making futile grabs at her.

Miss Woodhouse was still on the floor, wrestling with Adonis. She knocked the hypodermic needle from his grip, but he got a hand free and punched her, hard, in the face.

"I'll help you, Miss Woodhouse!" I cried and started to leap up and got tangled in the quilt and landed on the floor, face down and useless.

It didn't really matter. There was a tremendous bellow of rage, and suddenly the police detective had shoved Nancy Bracken aside and bounded across the room. He grabbed Adonis by the shoulders, yanked him to his feet, and threw him across the room. It's a pretty sturdy house, but I swear it shook when Adonis hit the wall. He just sort of melted then, oozing slowly to the floor and grinning foolishly. Even semiconscious, he looked good.

By now the other two policemen had succeeded in handcuffing the still-kicking, still-cursing Nancy Bracken. Miss Woodhouse was sitting crosslegged on the floor, rubbing her chin in an absentminded way, looking quite contented. She cast a reproachful, vaguely affectionate look at the police detective, who was easing the wobbly Adonis to his feet.

"You didn't have to do that," she said. "I could have handled him."

The police detective grinned at her. "I believe you could have, Jeannie," he said.

Instantly, I knew that he must be That Man, the long ago abandoned detective fiancé. Before I could recover from that jolt, there was another one—a clear, strong voice from downstairs, so loud it seemed to slice through the floor.

"Let go of me, young ruffian!" Professor Woodhouse shouted. "This is my house, and I'll go where I'll please! No, don't tell me it's not safe yet—*I'll* decide when it's safe. Don't you understand? My dear little Iphigenia's up there, and she may need me. Out of my way, you nasty boy!"

We heard a thud and a startled moan as some unfortunate

young policeman was knocked aside, and then the house shuddered again as Professor Woodhouse thundered up the stairs.

"Don't be afraid, little Iphigenia!" she cried. "Mummy's coming!"

Miss Woodhouse jumped to her feet. "I'm fine, Mother," she called. "I'll be right with you." She looked at the police detective one more time, and I thought I saw a shadow of regret in her smile, but when she turned to me, her eyes blazed with triumph. "You see?" she demanded.

Nobody felt much like cooking that night, and I've got to say I was relieved. We ordered a large pizza, with onions and olives and extra cheese, and ate in the living room so that Professor Woodhouse could watch *Lassie* and *Love Connection.*

"Don't think you're fooling me, Iphigenia," she said severely. "This whole silly business with Jennifer was an excuse. You just wanted to see That Man again, to get him into the house so that you could sneak into corners with him when my back was turned, and do nasty things."

Tonight there was nothing strained about Miss Woodhouse's smile. She had a bruise as big as Cleveland on her chin but seemed utterly at peace. "We didn't do any nasty things, Mother. All that ended years ago. But there was no one else I could turn to in this situation. Not many policemen would be willing to bend the rules that much to get evidence against those two. And without evidence, no jury would have believed Jennifer's story."

"*I* believed it," I said, a little tentatively. I still didn't know whether or not I'd gotten the job, so I wasn't sure I had the right to an opinion. "Oh, sure, it sounded crazy at first, when she realized the interview was a trap and got all hysterical. But I thought her story made sense. She goes to that party last month, meets Clayton Davis, likes him, wants to impress him. So she tells him that her father runs a country club and that she knows a way to sneak onto the grounds after hours, and they decide to grab a sixpack and take a midnight stroll on the golf course. That's not hard to believe. Lots of kids do crazy things like that."

"Yes," Miss Woodhouse agreed, "but the next part strains credibility a bit, doesn't it? That they just happened to be walking past the storage shed while Nancy Bracken and Adonis and the fence were inside, dividing the profits from the Bradford burglary. That Jennifer and Clayton could hear them quarreling about how long to wait before the next burglary. And poor Clayton just happening to step on a twig, at just exactly the wrong moment—that sounds like something from a cheap, melodramatic thriller."

I nodded. But it had never sounded like a thriller to me. It had sounded just plain sickening. I could still see Jennifer shaking as she told us about it—how she and Clayton had raced desperately across the golf course, how she had heard the two shots explode behind them, how Clayton had groaned and fallen, how she had looked back in terror, just once, and seen Nancy Bracken, her face grim and ugly in the glare of Adonis's flashlight, a gun in her hand. And then, somehow, Jennifer had made it to the woods bordering the fourth hole, had tumbled into a shallow gulley and huddled there, sweating and shivering and trying not to sob, until the footsteps and the curses had faded. Just before dawn, she had gone home and cut off her hair.

Miss Woodhouse reached for another slice of pizza, one with only a few traces of olive on it. While her mother was absorbed in watching a Tylenol commercial, she furtively plucked the olive bits off, rolling them up in a paper napkin. "Ironic, isn't it?" she said. "If Christopher Sinclair had been anything vaguely approximating a decent father, Jennifer would have been doomed. But he had never let her come to his club, didn't even have her picture on his desk, had barely mentioned her to Nancy Bracken. So Bracken had no reason to suspect that the orange-haired punkster running across the golf course might be her employer's daughter."

"Not until you urged him to be friendlier to Jennifer," Professor Woodhouse put in, and I almost choked on my pizza. I hadn't realized she was still listening. "That wasn't terribly bright of you, was it, Iphigenia?"

"Oh, but you can't blame her," I said, alarmed. True, Miss Woodhouse's attempt to help had set off a chain of nearly disastrous events—Christopher Sinclair's telling Nancy Bracken about the abrupt change in Jennifer, Nancy Bracken's figuring out the connection and calling the fence, who followed Jennifer to the church and tried to kill her. But it didn't seem fair to hold Miss Woodhouse responsible for all that. "How could she possibly have known what would happen?" I asked.

"She fancies herself a great detective," Professor Woodhouse countered. "Great detectives ought to be able to deduce things—things far more unlikely than the pitifully obvious scheme those nasties were operating. I declare, I'm ashamed of you, Iphigenia. It was right under your nose the entire time, but you never took the trouble to glance down."

I thought she was being awfully harsh, but Miss Woodhouse just nodded meekly. "You're quite right, Mother. It *was* obvious—Nancy Bracken chatting with club members to see when they'd be out of town, the parking lot attendant making impressions of their keys, the fence helping them pull the burglaries and dispose of their valuables. And the sudden change in Jennifer's appearance—I should have considered the possibility that she had witnessed a crime and was afraid of being recognized by the criminals. I was culpably unimaginative."

"If you ask me, Mr. Sinclair's the one who's culpable," I said. "Didn't it just rip your heart out when Jennifer said she was afraid to go to the police because they might not believe her, and she was afraid to go to her father because he *might* believe her, and might hand her over to Nancy Bracken, just to spare the club bad publicity. What a forty-carat creep! That was good advice you gave her, Miss Woodhouse, about keeping her grades up so she can go away to college next year. I hope she picks a school in California."

"Or, better yet, Alaska," Miss Woodhouse said. She looked at her mother with a shy, tentative smile. "There are so many horrible parents in the world. That's one reason why we must always cherish the good ones."

The professor stared at her coldly. "Don't try to flatter me, you nasty girl. You handled this case very clumsily, and no amount of sentiment can disguise that fact. You'll notice, by the way, that I was right about poor little Jennifer's reasons for going to that church. She went there to pray, of course. It was the anniversary of poor little Clayton's death, and she was feeling guilty and frightened and in need of guidance and forgiveness. And she nearly got killed. All thanks to you, Iphigenia."

Miss Woodhouse nodded again, looking low and miserable. Maybe it was stupid to step between mother and daughter just then, but I couldn't stop myself. "But she saved Jennifer, Professor Woodhouse," I protested. "The trap that we set this afternoon—telling Nancy Bracken that Jennifer was in the house, so that she'd tell Adonis to make copies of my keys and they'd come here to murder the witness—all that was Miss Woodhouse's idea. Jennifer's safe now, and the police believe every word of her story, and those two are on their way to prison. Doesn't your daughter deserve credit for that?"

The professor scowled at me. With great dignity, she took a last bite of pizza, then set her plate down on the coffee table and reached for a tangled mess of knitting. "That will be quite enough out of *you,*" she said, and thrust a knitting needle squarely into the middle of an immense knot of lilac and orange. "Why must you always take her side, you nasty girl?"

Miss Woodhouse sputtered loudly, just once, and clapped her hands over her mouth, and turned her face aside, her body shaking with suppressed laughter.

Suddenly, I somehow felt sure I had the job.